10-1-18
ad

"I wasn't trying to get away from you."

It took Boone a second. It wasn't until he let that slightly emphasized *you* sink in that he got the message. And even then, he didn't want to believe it.

Kate shifted on the sofa, digging into her pocket. "Jamie's sleeping longer than I thought," she said, pulling out her phone. "Why don't you peek on him. I'll see if Allie can come..."

Her voice trailed off.

He reached for her phone and plucked it from her fingers. She made a sound of protest, but her grip didn't tighten.

"Boone," she whispered. "This isn't a good idea."

She was right. Totally and completely right.

But that didn't stop him from sliding off the footstool and onto the sofa. Once he was at her side, hip bumping against hip, he wondered why the hell he had resisted before. Because nothing felt as right as being close to Kate.

Except, maybe, being closer.

Dear Reader,

Building a family is always a challenge. Imagine, though, trying to build one when the baby was a surprise...and Daddy isn't sure he can be the kind of parent his child deserves...and by the way, Mommy and Daddy live on separate continents. That's the situation Kate and Boone find themselves facing in this story. Believe me, it was a challenge and then, ultimately, the greatest treat to be able to face this dilemma with them!

By the way, if you missed the story of Kate's younger sister Allie, *Best Man Takes a Bride*, you can find it on Harlequin.com. I do hope you'll have the chance to check it out.

It's been a privilege to spend the last five years visiting Comeback Cove with you. Whenever I visit the real-world town of Morrisburg, Ontario, which was the inspiration for Comeback Cove, I half expect to turn the corner and find myself at the Flip Flop Fudge Shop, or to walk into a store and buy ice cream made by the Northstar Dairy. If you should ever find yourself there—perhaps to visit Upper Canada Village—I hope that you will feel the same way.

Yours,

Kris

KRIS FLETCHER

First Came Baby

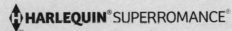

Recycling programs
for this product may
not exist in your area.

ISBN-13: 978-1-335-44916-0

First Came Baby

Printed in U.S.A.

Kris Fletcher would like you to believe that her children's science-fair volcanoes were all perfectly sculpted from papier-mâché, but the truth is that the mashed-potato episode of this book just might have a basis in fact. Ahem.

Kris grew up in Southern Ontario, went to school in Nova Scotia, married a man from Maine and now lives in central New York. She shares her very messy home with her husband, some of their many kids, two Facebook-fodder cats and a growing population of dust bunnies.

Books by Kris Fletcher

HARLEQUIN SUPERROMANCE

Comeback Cove, Canada

A Better Father
Now You See Me
Dating a Single Dad
A Family Come True
Picket Fence Surprise

Other titles by this author available in ebook format.

For Piya Campana. For five years, you soothed my nerves, calmed my fears and guided my thoughts and words to the place where I became proud to share them with the world. Most of all, you made me laugh, always in the very best of ways. I was truly blessed to begin my career with such a gifted and compassionate editor, and will forever raise my Iced Capp in your honor.

CHAPTER ONE

KATE HEBERT HAD always prided herself on being able to multitask. But even she was amazed when she realized she was painting a wall with her right hand while cradling her five-month-old in her left arm—and that she was doing both while breast-feeding.

"Check it out," she said to her sister, Allie. She raised the paint roller and wiggled little Jamie. "Call me vain, but I'm feeling seriously badass at this moment."

Allie started laughing. "Wonder Woman has nothing on you."

"We should write our own comic book. Super Mom. Instead of bracelets that can deflect bullets, she would have a nursing bra that bounces insults back at rude people."

Allie snickered. "Didn't Wonder Woman have a fancy lasso for making bad guys tell the truth? Maybe instead of that, Super Mom could shoot guilt trips with her eyes." She pitched her voice slightly lower in an imitation of their mother. "You want to tell me exactly what you're doing? And don't bother saying it's nothing, because I can see by the look in your eyes that it's definitely something."

Kate laughed hard enough that she had to put the paint roller into the tray or risk ending up with a polka-dot floor. Probably the wisest course, since the purpose of this work was to make the place marketable, not marked up.

"Good idea." Allie nodded toward the dormant roller. "In fact, you should sit down for a few minutes."

"I'm fine."

"I know you are. Now. But in about two or three minutes you're going to realize that you haven't had anything to drink in a couple of hours, and you're going to get suddenly and horribly overcome with thirst and exhaustion. Then I'm going to remember that I promised Mom I wouldn't let you overdo it, and I'm going to feel guilty and run off to get you some water. And when I come back you're going to be half-asleep in the chair. So then I'll have to burp Jamie, which means I have to get him off your boob, which kind of grosses me out. And *then*, he'll probably spit up on the clothes I have to wear until this room is done. I don't know about you, but I'd rather bypass the drama. So. Sit." She pointed at the ancient wingback Kate had dragged into the room. "I'll be back in a minute."

Kate had a fleeting notion to argue, then decided it would be easier to go along. Because though she hated to admit it, she did feel a little thirsty. "Okay." She lowered herself into the chair slowly, so as not to interrupt mealtime—though these days Jamie was more likely to be distracted by new sights and sounds than by movement—and settled in.

Oh. That felt good.

"Bring me a cheese stick, too, will you?" she called in the direction of the footsteps echoing down the stairs. Allie's answer came not in words but in a snort of laughter that Kate easily recognized as code for *told you so*.

As alone as it was possible to be with someone doing the vacuum cleaner thing at her breast, Kate closed her eyes and breathed out tension. Not that she had been working too hard. Far from it. She was still new-mama tired, but she hadn't made it to the ripe old age of thirty without learning how to pace herself. Nor did the tightness in her shoulders have anything to do with painting. She'd been doing plenty of that over the past months as she brought Nana's house back to life. Well, as much as she could do on her own.

No, it wasn't exhaustion or painting that had her wound so tight. It was the reason behind them.

Jamie was slowing down a little, the space between his swallows growing longer. Time for a burp. She broke the suction, raised him to her shoulder and patted his back while rocking in the chair and talking over his wails.

"I know, I know. You don't like to stop. But we do this every time, buddy. You might want to learn that pattern."

His little head smashed against her shoulder. Hard.

"Ow! Don't get violent, okay? You'll get more in a minute. But then you have to give me time to really paint, because the room has to be done this afternoon. We need to get it ready for—" she lowered her voice "—for your daddy."

So much for relaxation.

She patted some more, focusing on the April-fresh air coming through the window she'd cracked open, trying to soothe the anxiety that gripped her every time she thought of Boone coming home. Not that he had ever lived here, in either this house or Comeback Cove. Not that he even thought of Canada as home anymore.

But in two days, he would be here, whether she was ready or not. And painting was the least of her worries.

Allie bounded up the stairs, her footsteps eliciting the usual symphony of creaks and protests from the aging stairs. Jamie's loud burp was just one more note in the song. By the time Allie sailed in, Kate had Jamie settled on the other side, leav-

ing her free to cross her legs, sit back and gratefully accept her sister's offerings.

"Ooh. That's not a cheese stick." Kate drank
deeply before tucking the bottle of water at her
side and diving into the plate of cheddar, crackers and apple slices with gusto.

"Yeah, well, I figure I'm allowed to pamper you
once in a while. Though seriously, when are you
going to learn to set an alarm on your phone to
remind you to drink?" Allie mock scowled before
grinning and gesturing toward the wall in front of
her, where hints of faded wallpaper still peeked
out from the first coat of robin's-egg-blue paint.
"I still don't know if it was a good idea to paint
right over this."

"In a perfect world, I would have scraped off
all seven layers and made a fresh start. But there's
a limit. Besides, this place is so old that the wallpaper might be the only thing holding it up."

"You love it and you know it."

"Well, yeah. But love doesn't always make
you blind to faults." She grinned. "If it did, Mom
would have run out of things to say to us years
ago."

"True that." Allie grabbed her roller and attacked the wall once more. "So, Katydid, not that
I don't adore spending a gorgeous Sunday helping you paint instead of hanging out with Cash
the Wonder Boyfriend, but how about you tell me

the real reason this needed to be done so quickly? I mean, it was one thing when we had to get the first floor ready in record time. Things had to be perfect for Prince Jameson." She curtsied to the baby. "But you said you weren't going to put this place up for sale until he was a year old or so, and honestly, there's lots of other work that's more pressing than making this room look decent. So, what's the rush?"

Kate let her head fall back against the chair. She had known this talk was coming. She simply hadn't thought of the right way to handle it yet.

"Boone is coming."

Oops. She should have waited until Allie had finished reloading her roller. That might have helped prevent the blue streak now decorating the floor.

"Son of a…" Allie grabbed a rag from the bucket of water and swiped at the wayward paint. "He's finally making an appearance?"

"Don't say it like that."

"And why not? I mean, I know you guys only got married so Nana wouldn't freak when she found out you were pregnant, but still. He's been gone a year."

"Ten months."

Allie waved the words away. "Details. The point is, he has a beautiful baby who is five months old, growing every minute practically, and Boone hasn't bothered to even meet him? Excuse me if I'm not feeling incredibly gracious." She frowned at the half-painted wall. "Or if I suddenly don't feel like busting my butt on this."

"Allie, come on. You know he wanted to come back sooner, but it's not like you can easily do a long weekend run from Peru to here. And with his partners gone, it's been up to him to keep Project Sonqo running."

"I know. I know." Water splashed as Allie tossed the rag back into the bucket. "Look, I have lots of respect for what he's doing there. The way he and the MacPhersons started Project Sonqo, the way they're connecting the crafters with new markets and teaching the women how to see themselves as small businesses... It's all good. Great, really. And I know that Boone had to step up when— what's his name—Mr. MacPherson—"

"Craig. Craig and Jill." Jamie was falling asleep, his swallows slacking off and his eyes closing in the classic milk-drunk pose. Kate gave him a gentle jiggle. She had no problem with him nursing himself to sleep, but she wanted to be sure he'd had enough. She didn't want to lay him in his crib and get herself put back together only to have him wake up in fifteen minutes because he decided he needed more.

"Right. I understand that Boone had to take over when Craig got sick. I mean, look, cancer is bad enough when you're dealing with it here. I can't imagine what it must be like in that part of Peru, living so far from hospitals and everything. So, total sympathy, okay? But..." Allie scowled. "There must have been somebody Boone could have brought in to run things. Some way he could have been here when his own son was born."

Kate held her tongue. Allie was well aware that Jamie's arrival a couple of weeks ahead of schedule had complicated everyone's plans. If he had been born on time, or even late—as everyone had assured her was usually the case with first babies— Boone could well have been on hand for the big event.

At least, that was what she told herself.

"Allie, I know you're not happy about the way things turned out. But—"

"Don't tell me to let it go. Because you know that if the positions were reversed, you wouldn't."

There was some truth to that. Anyone who hurt Allie had to be prepared to face the wrath of Kate, and if that happened, they ended up counting their blessings, because it meant that Kate got to them before her mother did.

But this was different. Boone had been nothing but honest from the start. Ten minutes after meeting him at a fan convention in Ottawa, she had known that he was going to be around for only a few months, that even though he was still

Canadian he considered Peru his home, that there was no chance of anything long-term or forever between them. He wasn't a family man. Kate, on the rebound from a bad breakup, had been fine with that. She'd definitely wanted permanence and a family someday, but at that moment, short-term and fun and intense had been just what she'd needed.

That was, until a perfect storm of chances and failures had led to the perfect baby sleeping in her arms.

"The point is," she said, easing Jamie upright, "Craig and Jill are running things again, and as soon as they were caught up, Boone booked a flight. He'll be here Tuesday. Call me sentimental, but I didn't want to put him in a room that had faded flamingo wallpaper on one wall and giant chrysanthemums on the others. So we're painting."

Allie's grunt was all the proof Kate needed that her sister didn't approve of any of this. No surprise there. What was surprising was that Allie hadn't yet mentioned that they were prepping a second-story room for Boone, when Kate and Jamie were already established in Nana's old room on the first floor.

Any minute now…

"Hang on."

Kate lifted her chin. She could wait for Allie

to say it, or she could get the hardest part out of the way.

"That's right," she said as evenly as possible. "He's sleeping up here."

"You're putting your husband—the man you haven't seen in ten months, the guy who almost made you commit an act of public indecency on the beach that day—in a separate room?"

"That's right. And no, before you ask, I'm not moving my stuff up here." Kate rose from the chair with all the grace of a lame giraffe. "He's not coming just to meet Jamie, Allie. Or to help me get the place fixed up so I can sell it. He's also coming home so we can get a divorce."

JACKSON BOONE'S FEET slowed as he approached the door leading from the secure area of the Ottawa airport to the public space. Once he stepped through that door, everything was going to change.

God, he hoped he was ready.

His head knew that the real change had happened months ago, when Jamie was born. Or when he and Kate had decided to get married so her grandmother—set in her ways until the end, as Kate had said—could die in peace, knowing her first great-grandchild wouldn't be born out of wedlock.

Though really, everything had changed when he'd opted to leave his work in Peru for a few months to do some advanced study in nonprofit leadership in Ottawa. Or, more accurately, when he'd let a classmate drag him to a *Star Wars* fan gathering and he'd spied Kate across the crowded convention hall. One look at the purple streaks in her Princess Leia hair and his entire world had shifted.

Still, that had all been fun and games and some of the best times he had ever known. This, though. This was his kid. His son.

Boone had been a lot of things in his life. Student. Builder. Foster kid. The relative that had to be taken in. But in all his life, he had never really felt like a son. And he had no idea how he was supposed to be a father.

Think about Kate, he ordered himself yet again. *You're here to make things easier for her. That's what matters.*

Right. As long as he came out of this having helped Kate in whatever way he could, the rest would fall into line.

With that in mind, he hitched his backpack higher on his shoulder, braced himself and walked through the doors.

It took him a moment to find her in the crowd. He scanned the faces in front of him, looking for the thick brown hair and the glowing smile that had first drawn him to her. Winding his way through the reunions taking place on either side, he peered, ducked and—

There. She was over by the window, sitting on a bench tucked into an alcove.

Heat raced through him. They had talked regularly these past months, Skyping at least once a week, so it wasn't like he hadn't seen her since he left. He knew that she had cut her hair, and that the purple streaks were long gone. He had watched her jiggle little Jamie and pat his back and rock back and forth—probably without even knowing what she was doing, because if they gave out extra years for instinctive nurturing, Kate would have a lifespan stretching into the triple digits.

But it was one thing to watch all that happen from thousands of miles away and the safety of a computer screen. It was another to know that she was in front of him, to drink in the sight of her while voices bounced off the high ceilings and people laughed and cried on either side and folks brushed past him as they headed for the baggage area.

She hadn't spied him yet. She was curled over— well, he assumed it was Jamie. From this angle, all he could see was a gray lump, a pack of some sort, from which dangled a miniature leg and an impossibly tiny foot, wiggling back and forth like it was waving hello to him.

I helped make that foot.

His mother, during the rare times he had spent with her, had assured him regularly that he wasn't the type to have any success at making things. But as Boone stared at that tiny foot holding his attention as securely as if it were a hypnotist's watch, he knew that in this, at least, his mother had been dead wrong.

Kate finished fussing with the pack, gave a little pat to the front of it, and kissed the top of Jamie's head. The foot swung faster.

A loud wail pierced the roar of voices. Boone flinched and hurried forward. He'd heard Jamie cry over the phone many times. Intellectually, he understood when Kate laughed it off and assured him that cries were simply the way babies communicated, and that while there was always a reason, the reason was rarely the end of the world.

But this sounded different. More demanding. Maybe it was simply because it wasn't coming to him via satellite or whatever, but this cry went straight to Boone's gut.

Mierda.

Kate stood, her arms below the pack, swaying and jiggling. She raised her head and scanned the area, her hazel eyes squinting, then widening as she spotted him.

He wasn't sure what kind of welcome he had expected. A hug? Maybe. A kiss? No. Kate had made things very clear when they'd last talked. Their marriage was over, exactly as they'd planned. No hard feelings. They were both adults. They both knew this had been only temporary, and now that her grandmother was dead, well... But since they weren't planning a future together, she felt it was best if they kept things platonic while he was in town. Easier on everybody, she had said. And since the one thing Boone wanted most in this visit was to give Kate what she needed, he had agreed. He understood.

That didn't mean he liked it.

Whatever reunion he might have hoped for, it was washed away by Jamie's cries, which were becoming both stronger and more panicked. Kate hurried toward him and stopped a few inches away.

"Hey." Her smile was tired and strained, but he caught a hint of the glow that had first washed over him all those months ago. She raised a hand, and for a second he let himself think it was the prelude to an awkward hug, a quick brush of her lips to his cheek or mouth, but no. She simply cupped his cheek and patted it. The way she would one of the kids in the day care she would return to directing once her maternity leave ended.

He hadn't realized how much he'd been hoping she didn't mean the whole platonic thing until that moment.

"Hi." His voice sounded rough and strained to

his own ears. Probably because he hadn't said anything more than, "Coffee, please," to anyone since leaving Ollanta yesterday. His hand hovered near the kicking, squirming pile of frantic that was Jamie. Would it make things worse if Boone touched him? All the books he'd read about babies assured him that they needed and were soothed by touch, but there was a hell of a difference between theory and practice.

"Sorry about the warm greeting." Kate rolled her eyes. "We had a bad night. I think he's cutting his first tooth."

A memory surfaced from when he'd lived with… Was it his aunt Carol? No, it might have been one of his foster mothers. Gayle? She had been one of the younger ones. There had been a baby. There had been teething. There had been cold canned spaghetti and meatballs for dinner and lunch.

He had thought he couldn't admire Kate more than he already did. He'd been wrong.

"Let's get your bags before he breaks everyone's eardrums," she said, and headed for the escalator. Boone hurried behind her, glad to be upright and stretching his legs again. Once they reached the main floor, he aimed for the baggage carousel but stopped when he felt a tug on his sleeve.

"You get your things," she said over the baby's cries. "I'll take him outside. The change of scenery might calm him down a bit. I'll meet you right by the door."

Before he could answer, she zipped away. The usual airport cacophony sounded almost peaceful once the doors slid closed behind her.

He'd spent much of his travel time assuring himself that he was ready for this. He felt like every moment of the last few months that hadn't been devoted to work had been spent teaching himself how to be a father. He'd read everything about childcare that he could get his hands on. He'd played with the kids who came to the Project Sonqo office with their parents, perfecting his peekaboo skills. He'd even worked up the nerve to visit some websites for people who had grown up the way he had but who wanted to break that cycle with their own kids.

It had all seemed so possible when he was in Peru. So manageable. Now, with the echo of Jamie's cries rattling inside him, he had to work hard to convince himself this was a good idea.

Ten minutes later, his ancient suitcase rolling crookedly behind him, Boone exited the terminal into the welcome coolness of early spring. Not that Ollanta had been hot. In the mountains, it rarely grew more than pleasantly warm. But after four flights' worth of stale air, it felt good to breathe deep and not get a lungful of other people.

Kate waited by a bench. She was doing that

bouncing jiggly thing again. Jamie had stopped crying, at least loudly, but as Boone approached he could see that the wriggling hadn't slowed.

"Is he really chewing on his hand?" he asked.

"Yep. He's hungry." She set off across the parking lot at such a brisk speed that he was glad his legs were long enough to keep up. No cramped-plane stiffness for her. They hustled in silence—well, silent other than the snuffling noises coming from the baby—until they reached the little red Mazda he recognized.

Kate hit the button to unlock the doors and pop the trunk, then handed the keys to Boone. "Go ahead and stow your stuff. Then maybe you could start the car so it can warm up a bit? I need to hang out in the back seat with little Mr. Piggy for a few minutes."

"Sure." Good God. People always talked about culture shock when traveling from one country to another. No one had ever warned him that parenthood was the biggest culture shock he would ever know, but so far that was the case.

And he'd been here only fifteen minutes.

Once he'd deposited his things and got the car started, he screwed up his courage and twisted in the driver's seat to take in the scene behind him. Kate had tossed her coat across the car seat. He had a great view of her pink sweater and the snorting, squirming baby in her arms.

"Doesn't he ever stop moving?" Even as Boone spoke, that hypnotic foot started thrusting rhythmically once more.

"Sure. When he's asleep."

Jamie made a strange sound, like a cry mixed with a snort, then seemed to attack. Kate winced.

"Whoa. Are you okay?" Boone hadn't expected that. Kate had nursed the baby many times when they were Skyping, but again, yeah. Different continent, whole different experience.

"Like I said, he's cutting a tooth. His mouth hurts. When he nurses, that increases the pressure, so it hurts him more. So he stops earlier, but then he's still hungry, so he has to eat again sooner than he usually would." She brushed Jamie's cheek with her finger. "Plus he's kind of stuffed up, which often happens when they're teething, so it's hard for him to breathe and eat at the same time."

How the hell did anyone ever make it past infancy?

"So." She smiled, though with a little more force than he had ever seen before. "How were your flights?"

"I survived."

"I see that." The corners of her mouth twitched. Some of the stiffness seemed to be fading. "What do you need most? Shower, food or sleep?"

You.

He pushed the thought away before it could show in his face. Platonic. Separate bedrooms. All for the best.

He got it. He really did. But it had been a lot easier to agree when she wasn't sitting a few inches away from him with Jamie weaving tiny fingers through her hair and her sweater hiked up so that everything essential was hidden from his eyes but most definitely not from his memory.

He stared down at his fingers, pretending he was inspecting them for grime. "A shower would probably be a good idea. It would help me stay awake, too." He smiled and risked a glance her way. "But after that, yeah. Something other than airline food would be great."

"Good. We can take care of all of that once Little Mister here decides he's done." As she spoke, she did a complicated maneuver with her hand and the baby's face that looked as smooth and practiced as a magician's performance. He wasn't sure precisely what was happening. One minute everyone was happy. The next, Jamie was crying and she was tugging her sweater down, and he was pretty sure he'd glimpsed something he shouldn't be glimpsing if he wanted to get through these next weeks with any semblance of sanity.

"Burp time," she sang out, undoubtedly for his benefit. She glanced from Jamie to him. "You want to try?"

He froze. "That… I mean, uh…"

"Don't freak, Boone." Another hint of the laughing woman he remembered peeked around the fatigue. "I'm just messing with you. No one's first time holding their baby should involve gas and spit-up."

Part of him tried to absorb her words, but he was distracted by the bright, trusting eyes of his son soaking in the world around him. It was a good thing he was going to be around for only a few weeks. Because while Kate made this all look so possible, he knew it was anything but. Knew, too, that no matter how much he read or practiced, the odds were high that he could never be the kind of father he wanted to be.

CHAPTER TWO

BOONE HOPPED OUT OF the car as soon as it came to a halt, eager to be vertical once again. The drive from the airport to Kate's little hometown on the Saint Lawrence River might have been the most comfortable hour of his journey, but it had been the one that most sent him out of whack. He needed to enjoy some sunshine and refresh himself and then get busy. Once his hands and his brain were occupied, he would be more grounded. More confident.

More able to stop thinking about all the ways he wasn't anywhere near as ready to be a father as he'd convinced himself he was.

The trunk was already popped. He grabbed his bags, slung his backpack over his shoulder, and, while Kate was freeing Jamie from his restraints, let himself take in the house.

Boone had never been here. Kate had been living and working in Ottawa when they met. In their few months together last year, he had made only one trip to Comeback Cove with her, and that had been when they'd driven down to get married in her mother's living room. That was as far as her grandmother had been able to travel by that point. They had offered to hold the ceremony by her bedside, but she'd been a tough old bugger who'd insisted that she was not going to sit in bed wearing her nightgown as she watched her oldest granddaughter get married. She had made it to the ceremony in full wedding regalia—flowered dress, floppy hat and all. She had been the happiest person in the room.

Not difficult, since he and Kate had both still been in shock, and her mother and sister had spent the whole ceremony giving him the evil eye.

Nana had died a month after he'd left. He was glad he'd had the chance to meet her and quietly satisfied that he'd been able to contribute to an easy passing for her.

But as he took in the house, he couldn't help but think that Kate inheriting it might not have been the blessing she'd deemed it.

Kate, Jamie on her shoulder, came to stand beside him.

"It used to be amazing," she said softly.

He could see that. The wraparound porch, deep enough to shade rocking chairs; the strong Queen Anne lines; the turret on the right all gave the house character. Charm. Potential.

It also needed a new roof and new windows in the turret and a new railing on the porch. And that was just the work he could spy with a casual glance.

Well, the good news was that fixing this place would leave him so wiped there'd be no question of insomnia.

"Nana couldn't keep up with it. She tried, but it was too much. We told her she should sell and move in with Mom, but she always said this was the house that welcomed her as a bride and gave her the happiest years of her life, and she had no intention of leaving until she had to be carried out. Which is exactly what happened."

Boone, who had never lived more than six months in the same place until the end of high school, couldn't begin to comprehend what it must have been like to spend almost an entire life in one house.

"Come on." She headed for the steps. "Careful on the porch. The chairs are strategically placed to cover the spots where the boards need to be replaced."

He did as instructed, trying not to wince at the number of chairs to be skirted, then followed her into the house, braced for water marks and sagging floors and God only knew what else. So it was a pleasant surprise to walk through the ornately carved front door, through the tiny, sunlight-filled vestibule, and into a cheery yellow room filled with the cushy furniture he recognized from her old place. Sun catchers in the bay window sent prisms dancing over every surface, adding to the feelings of warmth and welcome.

"This is better than I expected." He kicked off his sneakers and flexed his toes. "Oh, man, that feels good. I've been wearing those shoes for about thirty-six hours."

She wrinkled her nose. "Yeah, I can tell."

Her grin told him she was teasing. Which shouldn't have been as much of a relief as it was.

She nodded toward the doorway into the next room. "Come on. I'm going to see if I can get Jamie into his crib. Then I'll give you the grand tour."

He kept his eyes firmly glued on the walls and the ceiling as he followed her. For one thing, it gave him a chance to assess the structure. For another, it was safer than watching the sway of her hips as she padded in stocking feet across the plank floors. Or the brush of her hair against her neck. Or the curve of her shoulder where he used to bury his face and inhale her and…

The floors. Right. Think about the floors. They would need to be sanded and refinished before the place went on the market.

"You lived here for a while when you were a kid, right?"

"Right. Just long enough to make it the first home I can remember."

As soon as they passed into the kitchen, his heart sank. Someone had obviously painted in here—the walls were a great shade of green, not too minty, just fresh and vibrant—but the cupboards needed a total face-lift, if not a complete gutting. The linoleum on the floor was cracked and peeling. And the window above the sink bore a long strip of...

"Duct tape?" He glanced from the glass to Kate.

She seemed embarrassed. "That just cracked last week," she said. "We had a windstorm. A nasty one. We lost power overnight and had to stay with my mom. When I came back, I found that. I called the glass guys, but as you can imagine, they've been pretty busy. I'm on the list for next week."

"Cancel them. I can have that fixed in a day or two." He measured the window with his eyes. "Okay, maybe a little longer, depending on whether the glass is a standard size. But I can definitely do that."

"Okay." She lifted the lid on a slow cooker, releasing a rich aroma he hadn't smelled in too long.

"Chili?" he asked.

"Mmm-hmm. I figured that would be a good one for tonight. If your flight was delayed, it would only get better." She replaced the lid and kept moving.

Boone was getting a good hint about which one

of them had given Jamie the gene that kept that foot swinging all the time.

He shook his head and followed her into the next room. It held only a rocking chair—strategically placed in front of a truly massive stone fireplace, complete with rock mantel—a computer desk, a bookshelf, and something that he was pretty sure was a changing table. At least, it looked like the pictures that had come up on the Google searches he'd conducted before Jamie's birth, when Kate would talk to him about baby equipment. Changing tables and bassinets, bottle brushes and onesies, diaper pails and breast pumps.

He shuddered. Yeah. He'd probably spent a good ten minutes staring at the pump thing, trying to figure out how it worked and why it wasn't prohibited as an instrument of torture.

"When I was little, Nana and Poppy used this as a dining room," Kate said as she sailed through. "But I don't have a big table, and it's kind of silly to have a separate place to eat when it's just me. So I turned it into a home office. I was going to move Jamie's crib in here, but then he started cutting this tooth and waking up at night again, and it's just easier to have him in with me."

"Where's that?"

She swayed ever so slightly, as if she'd thought about stopping and decided against it at the last second. Too late, he realized how his question could have come off.

Okay, maybe he shouldn't have asked right away. But he would be here for six weeks. If he was going to spend time with his son, he needed to know where to find the crib. It was only logical.

Yeah, you can talk circles around anybody you want, whispered his mother's voice in the back of his head. *But since when did that do anybody any good?*

Kate smiled brightly. "This way," she said, and led him through a small hallway that held a dresser against one wall, past a door that she said led to the basement, and into a tiny room that was almost completely filled with the bed he remembered so well.

Now he was the one swaying.

"It's small, I know," she said, gently laying Jamie on the bed and working the zippers on his coat while he made noises that had Boone suspecting the nap was over. "I had to take the doors off the closet to make enough room for the crib. That's another reason I have to move it. If I wait much longer, he's going to figure out he's sleeping in a closet and then he's going to develop claustrophobia or something."

She spoke so casually that Boone would have thought she wasn't remotely affected by the fact that he was in her room and they were standing mere breaths apart in front of the bed where they had most likely made Jamie.

Then he caught the pinkness in her cheeks and the way she kept her focus firmly on the zippers. On their squirming, protesting son.

Probably an excellent strategy.

KATE GAVE THANKS that Jamie seemed happier when he woke up. She doubted the tooth had come through yet, but it seemed things had subsided, at least for the moment. And this way she didn't have to sit down and nurse him again right away.

It wasn't that she was shy about feeding the baby in front of Boone. She'd had plenty of practice during their Skype calls, though that had mostly been in the early days, when Jamie's schedule could best be described as All Chaos, All The Time. Now things were far more settled, which was just the way she liked it. Easier to predict. Easier to work around.

But it had felt different when they were in the car. The confined space had made her far too aware of Boone's presence, his blue eyes darting everywhere, his shoulders filling her little front seat, his breath apparently stealing all the oxygen.

It hadn't been the breath itself that got to her, though. More like the way it had hitched a little when she'd adjusted her clothing. And, undoubtedly, flashed him the tiniest bit.

With Jamie on her hip, she led the way to the stairs. Boone had been very understanding when she'd said there would be separate bedrooms on this visit, but even though she didn't know him as well as a so-called wife should know her husband, there were some areas in which they were oh-so-intimately acquainted. Boone was no monk. And before he returned to Peru, he had told her that even though their marriage wasn't what anyone would call typical, he planned to honor his vows while they were separated. There would be no other women while he was gone.

Since one of the other things she knew about him was that he was a man of his word, she'd had no cause to doubt him. Which meant that she would spend the next six weeks with a very deprived man who was probably feeling the memories as much as she was.

"Grab your things," she said when they reached the front door again. "I'll show you where to drop them."

Because yeah. Boone wasn't the only one who had been deprived. Somehow, when she'd told him to stay here, she had assumed that fatigue and common sense would be enough to guard herself against wayward thoughts and urges.

Wrong.

"This banister needs work." Boone gave it a wiggle.

"I know. It's on the list."

He made a sound that could have been a groan or a snort. "I'm starting to wonder if six weeks is going to be enough."

"Whatever we can't get done, I'll hire someone to finish. Or if we even get to the point of the cosmetic stuff, painting and such, I'll be good. Allie can help me." She reached the landing and brushed her fingers across the chunk of driftwood nestled on the deep windowsill. "Cash is pretty handy, too. He might be able to tackle some odds and ends."

"Cash? Who... Oh. Right. Allie's new boyfriend." Boone gave the upper banister a shake. "Guess those flights took more out of me than I thought. I forgot his name for a minute there."

"Not to worry. Everything was such a whirlwind, with Allie getting engaged and then almost married..."

"Did the Mounties really storm the wedding and haul the groom away in handcuffs?"

Kate shuddered as she remembered how close her baby sister had come to marrying a man who had a thing for identity fraud. "Yep. Good thing, too. Otherwise, she might have gone through with it, and then she would be stuck with the wrong guy. Anyway, the fiancé is history. She realized that it was really Cash she wanted, and they are wandering around town like the two most dazed lovebirds you ever saw. So if you blanked on his name, don't feel bad. There are times when I still have to stop and remind myself who's in and who's out." She gestured to the open door. "Here you go."

Boone brushed past her, suitcase hefted, into the room that had seemed so airy until he entered. What was it about him? No matter where he went, he seemed to fill the space. Not in a bad way. More like once he was there, the emptiness was gone. Like he wasn't sucking up the space but was filling a hole.

She shook her head. *Filling a hole?* Good Lord, a teenager couldn't have been more snigger worthy. Time to move on. Fast.

"There's extra blankets in that closet." She pointed from the doorway. No way was she going into the room with Boone. "And the bathroom is right down here."

"Is that a water stain?" Boone's voice pulled her around to where he stared up at the ceiling.

"I think so. It's old, though. It was there before I moved in, and it hasn't gotten any bigger." She squinted. "At least, I don't think it has. I, um, don't come up here very much."

The look he shot her was carefully blank.

"I'll add it to the list."

She pulled Jamie's hand from the neckline of her sweater, which he seemed determined to yank down. "I'd better warn you that this entire bathroom is on the list, too."

She opened the door to the room in question and braced herself. Boone's long, low whistle only confirmed her fears.

"What color is that?" he asked.

She didn't need to look over his shoulder to remember the hideous greenish-brown shade that covered the walls. "I think it's something Nana got on sale. Or maybe she had a couple of half cans that she combined."

Boone shook his head. "Did you ever see *American Graffiti*? There's a part when Harrison Ford's character says the other guy's car is a cross between piss yellow and puke green." He tapped the wall. "I think this might come under that banner."

"Nana was more into frugality than style. At least everything still works." She knocked on the door frame for luck. "Though you do have to jiggle the handle on the toilet sometimes." She thought for a moment. "And the pipes bang when you first get in the shower, but that passes quickly. Other than that, you're golden. If the fixtures looked as good as they work, it'd be great, but…"

He walked into the room, hands on hips, taking it all in. "I've seen worse."

Oh, that was reassuring, considering he spent

a good chunk of his time in villages without indoor plumbing.

"This will be the rainy-day project, I think." He pointed from one element to the next. "New toilet. New vanity and sink. The tub..." He pulled back the shower curtain. "Oh, yeah. This is one of those old-fashioned ones. People love those. It can probably stay." He moved in a slow circle. "It's a nice room. Plenty of space. We'll take down those god-awful shutters, put up some curtains, new fixtures, a coat of paint, and it'll be—"

He came to a standstill, his gaze frozen on Jamie and his mouth gaping slightly.

She glanced down. At Jamie's hand, curled around the neckline of her sweater. Which he had dragged halfway down her chest, revealing a whole lot of skin and a whole lot of bra. And even though no one in their right mind would ever describe a nursing bra as seductive, from the way Boone seemed to have been turned to stone, she was pretty sure he thought it was the best bit of satin he'd seen in ages.

Almost a year, to be exact.

"Oops." She disengaged Jamie's fingers and tugged, but the fabric was bunched beneath his wriggling little body. "Here." And without thinking, she pulled the baby off her and held him out to Boone.

The expression on Boone's face shifted from naked lust to stark terror in the space of a heartbeat.

"I…" His gaze bounced from her face, to her chest, to Jamie, then back to her face. "How do I…?"

Whoa. He had told her he didn't have a lot of experience with babies, but given the tight lines in his face, she had a strong suspicion that he'd been underreporting.

"Have you never held a baby?"

His eyes closed. His lips thinned, like he was trying to hold in a grimace. "I have," he said slowly. "But it's been a long time."

Time alone couldn't account for the way his hands suddenly seemed plastered to his thighs.

Something inside Kate contracted in empathy.

Boone had never given her more than the basics about his childhood. She knew that the only thing his father had given him was twenty-three chromosomes and that it probably would have been better if his mother's role had stopped about there, as well. She knew that there had been indifferent relatives and foster care and periodic reunions with his mother that seemed to always stop just short of physical abuse. She knew that as far as Boone was concerned, his life hadn't really begun until he'd met up with the MacPhersons and gone to Peru.

None of that explained why the mention of holding a baby—holding *their* baby—left him looking like he'd been dropped into a pit of snakes.

Kate closed her eyes and concentrated on breathing for a second. Then she put Jamie on her hip, pulled her sweater into position—no point in adding another level of challenge to the situation—and marched over to Boone. "Stick out your arms."

"Here?" He looked around, his gaze lingering once more on the tub, the sink, the tile floor. "Everything is solid. Hard. What if I drop him?"

"You won't. I won't let you," she added when panic filled his eyes. She switched to teacher mode. "Come on. Arms out. That's right, bent at the elbows. Now, I'm going to put him up against your shoulder. You're going to put your left hand under his little bum. Your right hand goes across his back. Got it?"

He took a step back.

Oh, no. No way was she letting him run away from this.

"Boone. Whatever has you worried, you can forget about it. I'm right here. Don't you want to hold your son?"

His nod was slow in coming, but at least he was affirming.

"He moves a lot, so you'll need to keep your grip secure. But not too tight."

"Are you sure this is a good—"

She pushed the baby toward him before he could get any more freaked out. As she'd expected, his arms closed around Jamie—tentatively at first, then tight enough that she felt good about letting go and stepping back.

"There," she said softly. "Jameson Boone, meet Jackson Boone. But he thinks *Jackson* is a preppy name, so don't call him that. Which you won't anyway, because he's your father."

Jamie leaned back and stared at Boone. Boone stared rigidly back.

Too late, she wished she had her phone or a camera nearby. But since she didn't—and there was no way she was going to ruin the moment by running off—she focused instead on soaking up every possible detail so she could carry them in her memory.

Two cleft chins. Two sets of wide-spaced blue eyes. Two slightly upturned noses and two heads of light brown hair and two matching expressions of misgiving.

Her throat tightened, swiftly and unexpectedly. *Daddy. I should have said, "He's your daddy."*

At last, Boone cracked a smile. "Hey, buddy."

Jamie's response was to open his mouth and let out a wail that could have punched a hole in the ceiling.

Oh, no. "It's okay," she said to Boone, to Jamie, to herself as she reached and grabbed. "He just doesn't know you, that's all. Give him a couple of days to warm up and he'll be fine."

"Sure," Boone said in a hollow sort of voice. "Totally understandable."

"I'll take him downstairs. Change his diaper while you have a shower." A joke might help. "Don't worry, we won't have the diaper lesson until tomorrow."

"Probably a good plan," Boone said, and grabbed a towel from the closet.

Kate backed out of the bathroom and hurried down the stairs. She shouldn't have pushed it. Damn it, she was an early childhood educator. She was well aware that even a father who had been present from a kid's first breath could sometimes be rejected in favor of the mom, and vice versa. She should never have forced this, especially when it was so obvious that Boone had been on the edge about it.

"But I want him to love you," she whispered to Jamie as she placed him on the changing table. "I want him to know that you are the most miraculous little thing on the whole planet. I want him to hate every minute he has to be away from you. I want him to be in your life. Not because he has to be, but because he wants to be."

It didn't feel like too much to ask. And it wasn't. Not from anyone else.

She just didn't know if Boone could do it.

CHAPTER THREE

BOONE WOKE THE next morning to the smell of coffee and the sound of music.

He fumbled for his phone, squinted at the time and fell back against the pillow. It was barely five thirty. How the hell could Kate be doing the Julie Andrews thing at this hour?

But even as he lay there, he admitted that even though it was early, it wasn't all bad. He'd almost fallen asleep over dinner last night. Thirty-six hours of travel with no more than a nap did tend to take a toll.

It wasn't until just now, waking up a lot more refreshed and a lot less cramped, that he realized Kate had probably pulled off a similar marathon of wakefulness more than once since Jamie's birth.

God, Boone, could you be any more clueless?

As soon as the words crossed his mind he stopped himself from piling on any more guilt. Not because it wasn't true. He was clueless sometimes. But the words in his head had been a straight echo of his mother's voice. He'd learned a long time ago that anything that sounded like her wasn't something that should be indulged.

"Go downstairs," he ordered himself. "Ask how you can help. And for the love of God, don't freak if Jamie doesn't want anything to do with you. You read the books. It's just gonna take time."

Time, and a whole lot of guts he wasn't sure he had. Which Kate had probably figured out the moment he froze at the mention of holding Jamie.

He'd thought he was ready. After all the time he'd spent giving himself pep talks, he'd thought he'd convinced himself the mistakes he'd made as a kid were simply that, and not a guarantee history would be repeated. But when Kate had pushed Jamie toward him, all he could see was the unrelenting surfaces of porcelain and tile. All he could feel was little limbs slipping from his grasp. All he could hear was cries of pain.

He wanted to be a good father. He might not be an always-around one, but he still could be a dad who tickled his kid and changed diapers with ease and even tossed him in the air. But it was obviously going to take a lot more determination than he'd expected.

Remembering that one second when Jamie had first settled in his arms and looked up at him told him that it would be worth it.

Remembering the confusion on Kate's face told

him that he needed to let her know why this was gonna take work.

With his marching orders clear, he pulled on sweatpants and followed his nose to the kitchen.

Kate sat at the kitchen table with Jamie on her lap. He squealed and bobbed and dove like a prize fighter. The spoon in her hand hovered just out of Jamie's grasp, like she was waiting for the perfect moment to swoop in and shove food in his mouth. Or maybe she was waiting for the right moment in the song she was singing—something about wheels and a bus and *beep, beep, beep*. Boone was torn between fear that Jamie would slide right off the slippery little robe Kate wore, and admiration at how easy she made it look.

She glanced his way with a faint smile. "Good morning, Sleeping Beauty."

He could say the same. Except for her, even with her hair askew and glasses instead of contacts, it would be true.

"Hope we didn't wake you," she continued. "Somebody decided that five was the new eight."

"I guarantee you, he didn't inherit that from me."

She waved toward the counter. "Coffee's ready. Help yourself."

A couple of minutes later, coffee appropriately doctored and that first life-altering sip working its way down his throat, he pulled out a chair on the other side of Jamie. "Safe to sit here?"

"Should be. We haven't started finger food yet, so he doesn't have anything to throw."

Boone peered into the bowl that sat on the table just out of Jamie's reach, assessing the contents while wondering how to start the conversation he knew was needed. "Do I want to know what that is?"

"Rice cereal. This is his first solid food, so we're still figuring it out." As she spoke, she slipped the minuscule spoon between Jamie's lips.

"It looks like there's more coming out of him than staying in."

"That's okay. He's getting the hang of it, aren't you, Jamiekins?" She buried a yawn in her up-raised arm. "Sorry. Rough night."

The guilt devil shoved a pitchfork in Boone's conscience. "Did you get any sleep?"

"Some. I've had worse."

Jab, jab.

She spooned up more slop and took aim, but stopped before the spoon made it to Jamie's mouth. She sat a little straighter, took a deep breath, then turned to Boone with the spoon extended.

"Here you go, Daddy. Your turn."

It was so obvious she was forcing herself to do this that his gut twisted.

Mierda.

He took the spoon and set it gently on the table, then leaned forward in his chair, arms braced along his thighs, hands clasped. "Kate, I need to explain something."

She tipped her head but stayed silent.

"Last night, when I was so…weird…about holding Jamie, it wasn't anything to do with him, okay? It's because…" Damn. This was harder than he'd expected. "When I was twelve, I was in a foster home with a bunch of other kids. There was a baby. Tristan. He was…maybe a year old? I can't remember exactly, though I know he was older than Jamie."

Actually, what he remembered the most was the weight of Tristan in his arms, more solid and bulky than Jamie. Though since Boone had still been just a preadolescent himself at the time, it was hard to compare.

"Anyway, one night Tristan was sick. I don't know what was wrong exactly. I just remember I was the only other kid home, and the mom was out of medicine and Tristan was asleep, so she asked me to keep an eye on him while she ran to the store. Ten minutes, tops."

Which had been true. What had turned out to be false was the assurance that Tristan would sleep through her entire absence.

"As soon as she was out of the driveway and around the corner, he woke up. And I could tell something was wrong. He was shaking. Hard. His arms and legs were jerking and he kept tossing his head back and forth while he made this weird sound."

Kate lowered her free hand, which she had cupped over her mouth as soon as he launched into the description. "A febrile seizure?" she whispered.

He wasn't at all surprised that she knew what had happened even without seeing it. "Yeah. That's what it was. The thing is, I had no idea what the hell was happening. For a minute there I thought...well... You can imagine all the things I figured might be happening."

"Boone, you were twelve. Nobody would expect you to—"

"I know. The thing was, I also didn't know what to do about it. And so instead of leaving him in his crib and calling for help, I picked him up and tried to hold him."

Kate's quick inhalation told him that she'd figured out what had happened faster even than it had played out in real life.

"It was so fast. One minute I was putting him up on my shoulder, and then he twisted and threw himself backward." Boone glanced up at the ceiling to steady himself. Even now, twenty years later, he could still feel his hands trying to grip

Tristan as he arched and flew back. "He, um, hit the floor. Hard."

Kate probably had no idea that she was clutching Jamie tight to her chest. "Oh, God. Boone. You... He... What..."

"Broken leg. Concussion. Hairline fracture of the collarbone."

Kate's death grip on Jamie eased slightly. "Oh, that poor sweet bunny. But at least... I mean, those are all things that can be fixed."

"Yeah." Not that that had been much consolation at the time. Boone would never forget the cold rush of panic that had raced through him when Tristan's moans had become high-pitched howls of pain.

"I guess that explains why you were a little freaked at the thought of holding Jamie."

Kate's soft words pulled Boone back from the past trap. He focused on Jamie's wary eyes, the hideous cupboards, the hum of the refrigerator. Here. Now. This was what mattered. History was just that. He couldn't change it but he could learn from it.

And he could damned well make sure it didn't ruin the moment.

"So. I guess we kept Jamie waiting long enough." He made himself smile as he reached for the spoon. "Shall I?"

It was ridiculous to be so warmed by the pride in Kate's eyes, but there it was.

"Absolutely." She pushed the bowl in his direction. "Just put a little on there, and slip it in gently."

He could do this. He *would* do this.

Jamie's eyes followed his movements as Boone scooped up a hummingbird-sized portion of slop and aimed for the target. But his son was no dummy. At the last second, he turned his face so the food ended up smeared across his cheek.

"Crap." Boone caught Kate's eye. "Wait. Am I allowed to say that in front of him?"

She tapped her finger against the end of her nose. "Well," she said after a moment, "the other day, I dropped a hammer on my foot and let loose with some words that I'm pretty sure were never spoken in Nana's house before. So trust me. He's heard far worse."

That was a relief.

"And by the way," she added softly, "the first time I gave him cereal, I made it too thick and gave him too much and he choked on it. For a few seconds I thought I was going to have to do the baby Heimlich on him."

Boone was pretty sure she'd told him about that for his benefit far more than from any need to confess.

Did that make him any less appreciative? Oh, hell, no.

"Go on," she urged softly. "Try again."

Boone loaded his spoon once more and leveled his gaze on Jamie, now rocking back and forth on Kate's lap. His little arms windmilled at his sides.

"Is he trying to take off?"

"Hope not," she said. "He doesn't have a passport yet."

Babies needed passports?

"That's something I thought maybe we could take care of while you're here," she said. "Not that I'm planning any major adventures for the next while. I'm probably going to stick close to home for the near future."

The satisfaction in her voice told him she didn't have any problem with that.

"But my great-aunt Donna is in the States, in Vermont, and I know Mom would like us to visit before I go back to work in November."

"Oh. Sure, whatever you need." Boone squinted at Jamie. "Okay, kid. We're going to do this. My job is to get the spoon to your mouth. Your job is to open up. Got it?"

Jamie stopped baby break-dancing and stared at Boone. It was almost possible to see him making the mental leap. *Big guy...not Mom...doesn't know how to hold me...*

His mouth opened. Probably to cry, but one

thing Boone knew was how to take advantage of an opportunity. Praying he wouldn't hit something, he popped the spoon into the opening and deposited the food.

"There you go!" Kate all but applauded. It was ridiculous. Though not as ridiculous as how pleased he felt about it himself.

Jamie, of course, chose that moment to let loose with the wail that had been brewing. Kate picked him up and put him on her shoulder.

"Don't be so fussy," she said. "This is your daddy. And you are very, very lucky to have him."

AN HOUR LATER, Kate zipped Jamie into his front pack, grabbed a clipboard, and headed outside to survey the property with Boone.

He was already out on the porch, walking slowly from one end to the other, carefully putting his weight on each board as he stepped.

"How's it look?" She handed him the clipboard.

"Other than those spots you already know about, the floor is solid. A half a dozen new boards, a fresh coat of stain or paint, and it should be good. We'll need to replace some of the railings, too." He scribbled something on the paper. "You said you got estimates on these repairs already?"

"Right. I thought the best strategy would be to figure out what needs to be done, then balance what you and I can do ourselves against the cost of everything, and go from there."

"Prioritize. Right." He nodded, started to write something, then stopped and looked down at Jamie. "Sorry, buddy. I forgot to get your input."

Jamie shoved his hand in his mouth and gnawed, but he didn't start crying.

It was a good sign, but Kate opted against saying anything. She didn't want Boone to feel that she was watching his every move, or judging his interactions with Jamie, especially after the mealtime revelation.

She shivered. Dear Lord, what else was Boone keeping bottled up inside him?

No, it was definitely best to let things unfold naturally. All Boone and Jamie needed was some time and togetherness.

She refused to dwell on the thought that time and togetherness were the most limited factors in this relationship.

Instead, she laughed. "You want proof that you can take a guy out of Canada but you can't take the Canadian out of the guy? You just apologized to a *baby*. For something he can't even understand yet."

Boone's grin was slow to appear, but when it did—in full surprised delight—it was well worth the wait. "I guess some things are too ingrained to forget."

Kate was inclined to agree. Especially when Boone gave his jacket a tug and a pat, and she remembered the way he always did that when he got dressed. A final tug. A final pat. And then, usually, a final kiss before he headed out the door.

How many times had that last kiss turned into something more?

And how many times would she be fool enough to torture herself with memories such as that before she—

Boone looked past her to the road. "Looks like you have company."

Kate turned. One glance at the little white hatchback turning into her driveway and her heart sank.

"Oh, God," she said bleakly. "It's my mother."

Boone flinched. "She still pissed at me?"

"Yes." There was no point in sugarcoating the truth, especially when Boone was well aware that he was high on Maggie Hebert's hit list. "I meant to warn you, but I thought she'd give us at least a full day."

"And lose the element of surprise?"

At least he didn't sound too worried.

"There's one thing in your favor. Allie's former fiancé moved into the Number One Scum spot when the Mounties showed up. You, at least, tried to do the right thing." Kate waved at her mother, now walking toward them. "If we can get her talking about that, it'll remind her that you're a prince in comparison."

"I'm not holding my breath," he said, then waved as cheerfully as if Kate hadn't just given him the equivalent of a battle plan. "Hello, Maggie!"

Kate winced. "It's Mrs. Hebert to you," she reminded him, but it was too late. Maggie was already scowling as she climbed the steps.

"Good morning, Katie. Good morning, sweet little Jamie." She looked past them. "Boone."

Kate closed her eyes against the whirlwind generated by being dragged abruptly back into adolescent embarrassment over her mother.

"Mom. Be nice."

"I'm always nice."

Right. According to Maggie, the fact that Boone still had testicles was proof of her magnanimity.

"What can we do for you, Mom?"

Maggie sent a cold look in Boone's direction before turning to focus on Jamie. "Well," she said in a much milder tone as she grabbed the tiny foot, "I came by to invite you to dinner on Sunday." She sighed and glanced up at Boone. "All of you."

Oh, joy.

"You could have called," Kate said.

"I'm well aware of that, Katherine. But I was out running errands already, and I saw you outside, and this way I got to have a minute with the sweetest little guy in the whole wide world. Right, Jamiekins?"

Kate was never quite sure how her mother managed to adore everything about Jamie while claiming to be plotting revenge against the man who had fathered him. But then, there were many things about Maggie Hebert that had never made sense.

"I don't know," she began, only to be interrupted.

"Allie and Cash are coming, too, and there's no one booked for the bed and breakfast that night. I thought we could have a real *family* meal."

Dear Lord. If the sarcasm were any thicker, they could spread it on toast in place of peanut butter.

Something warm landed on Kate's shoulder. Boone's hand. He squeezed, gentle but heartening, and she got the message. They were going to have to do this eventually, and if Allie and Cash were present, there might be a buffer zone.

"Okay. We'll be there."

Maggie grabbed Jamie's hands and pulled them together in an imitation of applause. "Yay! Can you say *yay*, sweetie? You'll be talking soon, you smart boy."

"Mom. He's not going to say anything like that for a while."

"She is such an unbeliever, isn't she?" Maggie

made a sourpuss face, drawing a giggle from Jamie. "That's right. You know it's the truth, don't you, sweetheart?"

"Very kind of you to invite us," Boone said, and Kate marveled at the evenness of his voice. "What time should we get there?"

"Oh, the usual. Kate knows."

Yes, Kate knew. She knew many things. Like how her mother had the ability to convey about twelve different messages with two tiny words.

They were going to have to talk. Soon.

"So, not to be rude, Mom, but we have a lot to get through today, and since we're going to see you soon anyway…"

Maggie straightened and gave the house a brisk once-over. "You told him about the roof, right?"

Kate opened her mouth to answer but Boone beat her to it. "I'm going up there after we look around from the ground, but my suspicion is that it will need to be completely reshingled."

"It will. The porch needs to be fixed first, though, before Katie goes through it."

"Hello?" Kate waved her hand in front of Maggie's face. "Standing right here in front of you?"

"It's on the list." Boone gave her shoulder another squeeze. Purely to help her stay calm, Kate knew, but at the same time, oh, it felt so good. All that heat and strength. All that promise.

All that heartache, Kate.

"Make sure you check out the basement. Katie says it's good, but I think there's some water seeping in at the back wall. The upstairs bathroom needs to be completely gutted. The kitchen could use an overhaul, too, but—"

"Mom." Kate had to put an end to this. "We've got this, okay?"

Maggie looked between them, searching, though for what, Kate wasn't sure. The only certainty was that when she spied Boone's hand, she snapped to rigid uprightness so fast that it was like someone had replaced her spine with a titanium rod.

Boone left his palm exactly where it was. Which was a good thing. It kept Kate from turning and walking away in disgust.

"That's right," Maggie said. "You've got this." And she tickled Jamie's stomach.

God, Kate thought, *please help me remember this when someone breaks Jamie's heart someday.*

"Well, it's good to know that the place will get the makeover it needs." Maggie shielded her eyes as she looked over the house again, this time with her face softening. "It's a good, sturdy home. It's a shame to think that it will finally get the attention it deserves only to be let go, but—" she shot daggers at Boone "—I guess these things happen."

"Mom. We've talked about this. I love this place, too, but it's too big and too expensive. The heating bills alone would put me in the poorhouse. Add in the village taxes and the furnace on its last legs and—"

"I know. You're right, of course. I just hate to see how easily people let go of things these days. Like they don't matter. Home, family. *Whish*. Thrown to the wind."

Okay, that did it. "I think Jamie needs a diaper change. We'd better take care of that. Don't want him to get a rash, right, Mom?" She leaned forward and dropped a fast, totally unauthentic kiss on Maggie's cheek. "See you Sunday. Come on, Boone."

She turned quickly, and then, just to piss off her mother, reached back and grabbed Boone's hand. Probably a mistake, given the rush of memories that flooded her at the small bit of contact—not to mention the sea of hormones that threatened to swamp her—but hey. Maggie needed to know she and Boone were a team. An unconventional one, to be sure, but a team nonetheless.

Of course, that was assuming her mother hadn't terrified Boone to the point of bumping up his return flight by, oh, five weeks and change.

BOONE KNEW THAT Kate had taken his hand only to annoy her mother, and maybe to ensure that he followed her into the house. Not that he had needed any assistance on that score. Kate's mom took the whole mother bear image to new heights.

But no matter the reason, he was grateful. He and Kate had been all about the physical in their months together. Being with her without that set him off-center, left him uncertain how to act and what to say.

Not that they had been in it only for the sex. He had liked hanging out with her. He still did. They had been able to laugh and understand each other in a way that had surprised him, given how little they had in common. There had been a lot more between them than just fun in the sack, and if circumstances had been different and he didn't have the history he did, he could have easily seen them building something long-term.

But he *was* who he was, and life was what it was. And if he had to be an idiot over something, well, there were far worse things than the feel of Kate's hand in his.

Like the almost-visible clouds of steam coming off her head.

"I can't believe that she...argh!" Kate shook her hand loose, much to his dismay, and jerked at the zippers on the front of Jamie's pack. "There are times when I could cheerfully toss my mother in the river."

"I don't have a lot of experience, but I think your mom was just doing what good mothers are supposed to do. You know." He grinned at her and thought of every TV mom he'd ever seen. "Defend her kid."

"I know. I get that. And honestly, truthfully, I know it's because she loves me and wants the best for me and Allie and Jamie, and that she wants me to have an easier life than she had. But still." She tugged at the second zipper. "She refuses to believe that there's a world of difference between her situation and mine, and... Damn, why isn't this thing unfastening?"

Boone squinted at the offending zipper, then bent for a closer look. "I think there's a piece of cloth caught in it. Let me..." He reached forward gingerly. Jamie was such a squirmer that Boone wasn't sure he could fix this without making it worse.

Which was kind of the story of his life, but right now he needed focus, not a trip down memory lane.

He held his breath and pulled at the fabric. "Yeah, that's the problem. The pant leg got caught. Give me a second..." He worked the zipper while pulling gently on the gray corduroy. "Here we go...almost got it..."

The zipper gave way. The hand holding the fabric jerked up. And for one moment, his fingers slid off the pack and onto a part of Kate's anatomy where they had no business going anymore.

He wasn't sure which one of them stepped back

first. Maybe they did it together. All he knew was that her cheeks were red and her eyes were wide and his hand was a lot happier than it had been in almost a year.

"Well. Thank you." She sounded more than a little flustered, which made two of them. "So. Right. I'm sorry about Mom." She lifted Jamie out of the pack and headed through the kitchen into the office.

Kate continued speaking as she set Jamie on the changing table. "I would tell you that you don't have to join us, but she would probably drive over here and drag you there by the ear."

"So you're saying I should just resign myself to a night of misery?"

"Unfortunately, yes."

"What did you mean when you said that your situation is different from hers?"

"Oh. Well." Kate reached for a fresh diaper and flipped open the box of wipes, all while keeping one hand on a squirming tummy. Once again, Boone marveled at the way she handled everything so easily. So…gracefully. "I told you that my biological father was never in the picture, right?"

"Right."

"Well, I didn't tell you the whole story. All Mom ever said when I was growing up was that my bio father was a summer guy, and that she didn't know how to get hold of him when she found out she was pregnant. It was one of those things you just accept, right? Because why wouldn't your mother tell you the truth about something as basic as your father?"

Having grown up knowing that anything his mother said was more likely a lie than the truth, Boone stayed silent.

"But after Neil—my stepfather—after he died, I started to think more about it. I was almost thirteen then, and I knew things weren't adding up. So I started bugging her." She shot him a quick grin that had him remembering a whole lot of mischief. "Let me tell you, Mom had cause to regret all those lectures about standing my ground and never letting up when I wanted something."

Oh, to have been a fly on that wall.

"She finally caved and told me a little bit about him. Not much. Just his name, and that his parents had absolutely not approved of her. It was the classic story—rich boy getting ready to go to university, not-rich girl who spent her summers cleaning rooms at her parents' motel, a hot and heavy summer romance. She didn't find out she was pregnant until he was gone." Kate's voice faltered. "And then, she said, she spent a couple of months in denial, hoping that…that something would happen so she wouldn't have to make any decisions."

Boone spared a moment of sympathy for the scared kid Maggie must have been.

"Anyway, the whole romance had been such a secret that Nana and Poppy didn't know about it. Well, she said they had suspicions, but nothing definite. And by the time she knew she had to tell them, Mom had made up her mind that she wasn't going to let anyone know the truth. My father's family lived near Windsor. He was going to school in London."

"Which London?"

"The Ontario one." Kate dropped wipes into the trash. "Mom said she knew that if she named him, she could get child support, but she would also have to share me. And, her being the stubborn type—"

Boone coughed.

"Quiet. She said she didn't want me spending extended periods of time with any of them. She thought he was the only decent one in the whole family." She lifted Jamie and nuzzled his stomach, then nodded toward the rocking chair in front of the fireplace. "Sit. You're going to hold him again."

He noticed she didn't bother asking.

He also noticed that she had chosen a well-padded place for him to try again. Definitely a woman who knew how to adapt to her audience.

He lowered himself into the chair and waited. Kate came close and burst out laughing.

"You look like you're waiting for me to draw blood or something!"

"That good, eh?" Maybe if he distracted himself, kept her talking, it would get him through this. Not so distracted that he wouldn't be able to keep his focus on what he was doing. Just enough to take the edge off his nerves.

He breathed in, held out his hands and waited. "So, what happened?"

"What happened when?" She lowered Jamie onto his lap. Boone held his breath and slowly closed his hands around his son's warmth. For a second he couldn't think of anything but the placement of his hands and the distance to the floor and the odds of Kate staying precisely where she was, crouching in front of him.

Purely because he wanted her there to catch Jamie if anything happened, of course.

Talk, Boone. You can do this.

"What, uh, happened with your father?" Boone risked a fast glance toward Kate. Her face could have been carved from stone. Because of him holding Jamie? Or because...

"Nothing."

The part of Boone that wasn't actively trying to slow his heart rate and relax into the feel of

Jamie on his lap was pretty sure Kate was hiding something.

"What do you mean, nothing?"

"That's it." She shrugged. "Mom gave me his name. I tracked him down."

"And?" Jamie's eyes were getting big. Boone was pretty sure that wasn't a good sign.

"And, he had his lawyer send my mother a check."

Boone's hands tightened around Jamie. "That was it?"

"Not quite." She took a small step back, straightened, clasped her hands in front of her. "There were also instructions. If Mom and I refrained from any further contact with him, there would be another check on my eighteenth birthday, for double the child support he should have been paying all these years. If we didn't stay quiet, the lawyers would make sure Mom would have to jump through a boatload of legal hoops to get more. They promised it would end up costing far more than she could ever get out of him."

"They thought she was just—"

"After his money. Right." Her mouth twisted. "It seemed he was getting ready to run for office and he didn't want an illegitimate child upending all his plans."

Boone stared down at the whorls of Jamie's

hair. It was so fine. So perfect. Had Kate's been like that?

"So he wanted nothing to do with you."

"Not a thing." Again she shrugged, not that he believed her casual air. "Apparently he'd grown up to be just as awful as his parents after all."

Home, family. *Whish.* Thrown to the wind.

Much as he hated to admit it, Boone was starting to understand Maggie's antipathy toward him.

Jamie whimpered. Boone looked to Kate.

"I think he needs you again."

"He's okay," she replied, but there was no denying the relief that rushed through Boone when she took Jamie back. Relief, but also an undeniable feeling of loss.

According to Boone's mother, his father had no idea he existed. That was bad enough. But for Kate's father to have made it clear she wasn't worth anything more than a check?

"No wonder your mother thinks I'm the scum of the earth."

"She doesn't think that." Kate bit her lip. "At least, not precisely."

"I'll have to knock myself out to prove that I'm one of the good guys."

"Oh, please. Change my mother's mind? We're talking Jedi master level accomplishment."

He laughed along with her, because she was right. But he had to try. Not that he cared what

Maggie thought of him, but he could see it bothered Kate. She shouldn't have to spend her days defending him to her mother.

He needed to find a way to prove to Maggie that he was nothing like Kate's father. That even though he might not be a traditional kind of dad, he did love his son. And Kate had not made the worst mistake of her life when she hooked up with him.

As he remembered Maggie's comments about wanting to keep the house in the family…and the longing in Kate's voice when she said it wasn't practical…he got a pretty good idea about how he could pull it off.

CHAPTER FOUR

AFTER A LONG and exhausting day planning repairs, guiding Jamie toward Boone and revealing way too much about her past, Kate was more than ready for bed once Jamie was down for the night. She grabbed a book about restoring older homes, climbed under the covers, and fell asleep reading about crown molding. At least, she thought that was the part where she passed out, given that she had a wild dream in which Boone was really Prince Harry, but she was the only one who saw it.

She woke up to the sound of snuffles right before she was going to meet the Queen.

"Damn it," she grumbled as she hauled Jamie's sleep-warm body close and crawled back into bed. "All that practice curtseying for nothing."

With the morning well and truly begun, she made her plan. Feed Jamie. Get him changed and dressed. Hop into the shower and... Ooh. Did she dare leave Boone in charge of the baby while she had a shower?

"I think you could handle it," she said to the

tiny head working so studiously. "But your dad might pass out."

As if he agreed, Jamie ceased gulping to gaze up at her, swat her chin with his palm, and gurgle something that sounded like *uh-huh*. Kate burst out laughing and cuddled him closer, tickling his tummy with her hair until he giggled.

Boone should be here.

The thought hit her fast and hard, making her hands shake as she went through the pat, burp, re-settle routine. What would it be like to have Boone in the bed right now? To lean against his bare chest and laugh softly together over their son's antics...to look up and back for a quick kiss... to have him reach around her so they were all wrapped together in one embrace...

No. She couldn't let herself think that way. Not when she knew it was nothing but an exercise in self-torture.

"I know he had a crappy childhood," she whispered to Jamie. "But you would think that would make him want all the family he could get, not the other way around."

Though she knew that wasn't always true. Boone didn't like to talk about his childhood, but the parts he did let slip set a whole armada of red flags flying in her educator's brain. She knew the kinds of lingering effects a childhood such as his could have on future relationships. Given his insistence right from the start that he wasn't a family guy, she had a pretty strong hunch that those long-ago traumas still had their claws sunk into him.

"I want him in your life, Jamiekins. I want you to know that you have an awesome and amazing dad who is making the world a better place for a lot of people." Her voice dropped. "But I want you to have brothers and sisters, too. And I don't want to be alone all my life."

She'd hidden behind house repairs and getting reacquainted for two days. It was time to talk about the divorce.

BOONE HAD SET his alarm for five thirty, hoping that would give him enough lead time to jump in the shower and have the coffee going for Kate when she got up. But he woke on his own a few minutes after four, jerked out of sleep by the need to escape a bad dream. He couldn't remember the details. There had been slamming doors and a child crying and a sense of deep loss that still clung to him. And cold. So, so cold.

He pulled the quilt higher, paying careful attention to the soft rub of the flannel sheets against his skin, the slightly floral scent of the fabric softener, the comforting weight of the blankets over his body. Tiny details. All those things that tied him to the moment.

What's done is done. What's ahead is unknown. But right now, you're fine.

He distracted himself by carefully examining the decision he'd made the previous day, the one he didn't dare reveal to Kate until he was certain he could pull it off. Logic said it was impossible. But if there was one thing he'd learned after years of writing grants for a cash-strapped nonprofit, it was that when it came to finances, logic didn't always have the last word.

Kate wanted to stay in this house. She was putting a good face on the need to repair and sell, but he knew her. She was all about history and tradition and family.

Family.

He sent a mental scowl toward the bastard who had fathered her. To be rejected like that, sight unseen, would have been a killer for any kid. For Kate, who had just lost the only father she'd known, who had grown up steeped in family history, it must have been devastating.

He couldn't make up for that. But he could damned well find a way to keep her in this house where her grandmother had lived and died, to get it fixed up to the point that she wouldn't have to worry about falling through the frickin' floor every time she crossed the porch.

He was going to need a second job. Or a loan. Or, probably, both.

He had no idea how to make that happen. But if nothing else, mentally calculating interest rates and updating his résumé made it possible for him to fall asleep again.

Which was good—except he slept through the alarm.

Which was also good—until he woke up and heard Kate singing.

"Que huevon," he said as he threw back the covers. Yeah. He definitely wasn't acclimated if he was still relying on Peruvian slang to call himself a lazy ass.

Half an hour later, showered and dressed, he made it downstairs only to find Kate eating toast at the computer. Jamie lay tummy-down on a blanket by her side, staring at the stuffed alpaca Boone had brought for him. Jamie made a sound, and Kate stretched out one enticingly bare foot and tapped his back with her toes.

"Coffee's ready," she sang out without looking up.

"All this and coffee, too?" Boone let out a low whistle. "God, you're amazing."

He knew he shouldn't have said it as soon as the words slipped out. It was the kind of thing he would have said last year.

Did he still mean it? More than ever. But now he couldn't think of a single way it could sound anything but wrong.

Kate stopped chewing for a second, stopped tapping on the keyboard.

Then, with a deep breath, she turned to him with a smile.

"Yep, that's me. Kate Hebert, semisingle mom, day care director, able to push those buttons and start that coffee like nobody's business."

Retreat seemed the best option.

He took his time doctoring his cup, giving them both a few minutes to find their equilibrium before he tried again, sitting in the rocking chair and focusing on Jamie.

"Morning, squirt."

Jaime squealed and waved his arms in a swimming motion. Boone risked a glance at Kate.

"Is this how Michael Phelps started?"

"That, I can't answer. But it's good that he's doing that. It helps with his bilateral coordination. Also, God help me, it's a precursor to crawling."

"Of course. I knew that." He bent down and mock whispered in Jamie's direction. "Here's a hint, kid. Don't give your mother an opening before you're really awake."

Kate huffed and hit the keyboard a bit harder.

"Do you need the car this morning? I should run to the hardware store." And the bank, but he wasn't going to mention that.

"Be my guest." She leaned closer to the computer monitor, peering so intently that Boone wondered if the prime minister had been photographed shirtless in public again. "I need some things, too. You can be my lackey."

He mock bowed in his chair. "Your wish is my command."

Too late, he remembered another time he had said that. In a very different location. With a lot fewer clothes.

Would he ever learn?

"Here." She grabbed a paper from the printer, made a couple of marks on it with a pen, then handed the printout to him. "You're going to need this. Not today, but, soon. Ish."

He read over the list of names and addresses, first in confusion, then with the sense of inevitability he hadn't felt since he was a kid.

"Divorce lawyers?" It shouldn't have been so hard to ask. He'd known this was coming. Hell, he had been the one who'd followed "You know, we could get married" with an almost-immediate "Temporarily, of course."

With a start he realized his hand had gone to his throat, searching for the fake rabbit's foot he used to wear when he was a kid. Good God. He hadn't thought about that in years.

She cleared her throat. "Yes. Right."

Sure. That was why he was here.

"I... Look, of course you'll want to choose your own lawyer, but I thought it might be easier if I pulled together some names for you. A starting point, since I know who is most convenient."

He ran a finger down the list, lingering over the names she'd starred, buying time. "It's not like either of us is fighting this." At least, not legally. "I don't see why we need to pay two lawyers when we're in agreement already."

"Conflict of interest. Legal ethics."

"Lawyers have ethics?"

Her head snapped up. For the first time since he walked in, she smiled.

"Crazy as it might seem, it's true."

She had what appeared to be a death grip on her pen. If it had been a pencil, he would have expected it to snap in half by now. He wanted to walk across the room, place his hand over hers and give it a squeeze. Remind her that they were in this together, the way they had been all along.

Well, as much as possible.

But the rules were clear. No physical contact. Maybe someday they could reach the point when a squeeze of a hand or a tap on the shoulder would be seen as no more than a gesture of support, but right now, there was too much else floating between them to risk it.

"We've done the hardest part already," she said softly. "Figuring out support and custody. I mean, we'll each need the legal eagles to give it their pricey approval, but as long as we're in agreement, it should be smooth sailing." She hesitated. "Unless, of course, you want to make any changes."

"No. I'm good. Kate, we both know that there won't be any every-other-weekend thing with us. Jamie's life will be here, with you."

She pulled the pen in close to her chest. It was almost like she was guarding it. Or cradling it?

Her actions perplexed him. Shouldn't she be happy about this? He knew all too well how it felt to be traded from home to home. That wasn't what he wanted for Jamie. He had no intention of swooping in like the Big Bad Wolf and disrupting their lives.

And yet Kate maintained her death grip on the pen.

"Is that a problem?"

She said nothing. Which worried him more than anything she could have said, because he had never known Kate to be at a loss for words.

"Hmm? Oh, no. No. I just thought… I mean, I want him here with me. Obviously. But I don't want him to miss out." She took a deep breath. "It's fine."

Boone might not be a family man, but that didn't mean he was clueless when it came to family dynamics. On the contrary. He had learned fast and early how to read a situation and know when someone was telling the truth and when they were lying through their teeth—or through a smile. He didn't always know what to do about it, but he could tell when there was a problem.

And right now, every instinct he had was telling him Kate was most certainly not fine.

I don't want him to miss out.

"Kate." Again, he stopped himself from reaching for her hand. "If we want any chance of making this work, we have to be honest. Even when we think the other person won't like what we have to say." He spread his palms wide open. "Cards on the table, okay?"

She stared at his hands. Silently. Like she was weighing her options. Which surprised him, because it all seemed pretty straightforward to him.

Then she said in a rush, "I want him to know that you want him."

Her words sent him rocking back in his chair. Or was it the way she'd said it—low and desperate, like she wasn't sure she had the right to ask but needed to anyway?

Did she think he didn't love his son?

"Kate." The hell with restrictions. He left the chair to kneel in front of her, tipping her chin up with one finger, steeling himself against the flood of remembered pleasure at the brief brush of skin on skin. "Kate, I know that what I feel for Jamie doesn't come close to what you have with him, and it never will. I'm okay with that. But don't ever doubt for a minute… I mean, it's truc I don't know a lot about babies, and I'm still terrified I'll do something wrong and hurt him."

Some of the worry in her face was pushed aside by a slight smile. "I hate to burst your bubble, but I already figured that out."

Ah. There was the Kate he knew.

He let his hand drop back down to his side. "We got caught by surprise. Things are more complicated than either of us expected. But complicated can still be amazing."

"And wanted?"

"Wanted. And very much loved."

This time, when she ducked her head, he was pretty sure it was to hold back the flash of moisture he saw in her eyes.

"I want to know Jamie." If he had to spell it out, he would. "I want to talk to him as much as he would like, and come here to hang out with him every year, and maybe, soon, start having him spend some time in Peru. With you, of course," he said when her head snapped up. "But I'm okay with leaving the details of when we take each step kind of fluid."

"Fluid." She said the word slowly, as if trying it on for size. After a moment, she nodded. "Okay. I see what you mean. As long as we both agree on what the next step should be, I'm good with leaving the timing loose."

Down on the floor, Jamie grabbed a squeaky toy and smashed it on the blanket.

"Rock on, dude." Boone cocked his head toward the baby but spoke to Kate. "Maybe he'll be a drummer."

"Oh, no. No wishing drums on him when you'll be on another continent." She reached behind her, grabbed a paper and squinted at it. "Okay, since His Highness is still happy down there, let's talk about some things we haven't covered yet. Like guardians." She frowned before looking at him. "Right now, I have Allie listed. It made the most sense, since she's here and he knows her. But do you want to leave it that way? Or if something were to happen to me…"

Boone's mind went blank. He couldn't help it. The thought of Kate not being alive drove all capacity for thought from his mind.

"Would you want to…" She carried on, totally oblivious that parts of him had frozen at the thought of her dying. "I mean, I think it would be easier on Jamie if he were to stay with people and places he knows, but you're his father. It would be up to you."

Oh, God. She expected him to answer.

The floor was hard against his knee as he pushed back upright. The chair was solid beneath him as he sat down once more, the wood of the armrests smooth and slightly warm against his palms as he gripped them.

He could handle this. If she had the guts to sit there and calmly talk about what would happen if she were to die, then surely he could manage something coherent.

"I…uh…I haven't thought about that." Start with the facts. Buy himself time. "I, uh, need to think about it, but my feeling is, yeah. Having Allie take over would undoubtedly be easiest on Jamie. As long as she's okay with me still being in the picture."

Kate smirked. "There's a reason I asked her and not my mother, and let me give you a hint—it had nothing to do with age."

Damn, it felt good to laugh. The tightness in his chest eased and lightness filled him.

"But while we're on the subject," she said, "we probably should think about what we would like to do when and if either of us remarries."

"That's not going to happen." The words were out of his mouth before he processed them. He wasn't even sure who he was talking about. Him, definitely. But her?

Though judging from the way she was watching him, as if he had suddenly sprouted alien antennae, he had a feeling that maybe he should have waited to speak.

"Kate, come on. We both know I'm not going to…that is, if not for Jamie…"

Oh, God. She was clutching the pen.

When she looked up again, her face was set in a resolve he'd seen only a couple of times before. When she'd told him that no matter what, she was keeping their baby. When she told Maggie that no matter what, they were getting married.

When she had taken him to the airport for his flight back to Peru. And why hadn't he put that together until just now?

"I know that you don't see yourself as a family man, Boone, and that's…well, it is what it is. It's part of you. But as we both know, things happen."

She had a point. Maybe he should look into getting a vasectomy while he was here.

"But I'm not you. I want to have more kids. I would like to have them with someone I can build a life with."

She wants to be with someone else.

Once, when he was helping build the expansion on the project's office, the guy carrying the other end of a board had slipped and Boone had taken a solid chunk of wood to the torso. Kate's words made him feel like he was doubled over in the yard once again, struggling to breathe through a chest that had forgotten how to move.

"I…guess that's another thing I hadn't thought about."

Maybe because it was impossible for him to think about her being with someone else and still see straight.

And then he had to know. "Is there someone?"

"What, do you mean, like, am I taking applications?" She started at him blankly before bursting into laughter.

"No. No, Kate, I'm not…"

Her laughter faded into a bemused smile. "I've been kind of busy, you know?"

Yeah. He knew.

"Sorry." He attempted a smile. "You caught me by surprise."

"Obviously." Her gaze slid sideways, though he doubted she was really seeing Jamie chewing on the alpaca. "I mean, it would be one thing if you thought that maybe, someday…"

His breath caught in his throat. She shook her head.

"But you're there, and I'm here. And if it turns out this is the only life Jamie ever knows, then that'll be his normal and it will be wonderful." She stretched her foot out again to straighten the corner of the blanket. "I only remember a little from the years when it was just me and Mom, living here with Nana and Poppy, but I know it was good. Then she married Neil, and then Allie came along, and things just felt so different. Like we'd found something we never knew was missing." Her voice dropped. "Someday, I would like to have that for Jamie."

"And for you?"

He shouldn't have asked. He had no right. Yes, she was his wife, but that was only a matter of time. She would always be the mother of his son, but that didn't give him any say over who was in her life, or her heart, or her bed.

Jamie. Keep it focused on Jamie.

"As long as this future potential…person…is good to Jamie, I don't see how I would have any input."

"Well, you wouldn't, really. But I want you to think about it. If someone else was in our lives, day in, day out, he would become the father figure. You would still be Daddy, but things would be…different."

Different. Yeah, that was one way to describe it.

He was pretty sure he was okay with things being different. Change was good. But he was also pretty sure that Kate would prefer the version she had laid out.

That, he wasn't so certain he could handle.

But he also knew that he had no choice.

CHAPTER FIVE

KATE HAD PLANNED to spend the morning prepping the bedroom beside Boone's. She sent him off with lists, directions and a hand-drawn map. Then she carried Jamie and her supplies up the stairs and down the hall, steadfastly resisting the temptation to peek in Boone's room. Nope. Not looking. Even though the door was wide-open and the ladder-back chair was right there and his jacket was tossed over it and...

Okay. So she peeked for a second. But she didn't stick her head into the room and inhale, no matter how much she wanted to.

Just as she finished getting Jamie settled and her equipment set up, Kate heard a car outside. Huh. She wasn't expecting anyone, and Boone hadn't been gone long enough to get through his list.

"Think Daddy forgot something?" she asked Jamie, but he was too busy trying to pull off his socks to answer. She peeked out the window and spied not her own little red Mazda but a sporty hatchback painted with the familiar logo of Allie's restaurant, Bits and Pizzas.

"Woo-hoo, Jamie! Aunt Allie is here!" Kate put her mouth to the window she'd cracked open just enough to let in a hint of spring warmth. "Come on in! We're upstairs!"

Soon enough, Allie was in the room, cuddling Jamie and offering explanations.

"I saw Boone walking around downtown while I was running errands. So I thought, well, this might be my only chance. You know." Allie winked. "To find out how well that whole separate bedrooms thing is working."

Heaven save her from her sister. "Very well, thank you. Now keep your nephew happy. I have wallpaper to scrape."

"I thought you were a fan of the paint-over-it school."

"Sometimes you have to. But this room has only two layers, and it's been coming off pretty easy so far."

"Plus it's great exercise. Especially if you have to, oh—" Allie batted her eyes rapidly. "—work off some frustration."

Kate leveled the scraper in Allie's direction. "Don't you give me the innocent puppy-dog look. You're not getting a rise out of me."

"Ah, but the question is, are you getting one out of Boone?"

Kate sagged against the wall, her energy spent. "Al..."

Thank goodness, the message seemed to sink in. "Sorry. None of my business. I'll shut up now."

"You don't have to shut up. Just—"

"Don't harass you about your love life. Got it. Cash wants me to move in with him."

Whoa.

"He wants what?" Kate shook her head, trying to clear the onslaught of questions. "Um, did he forget that you guys have only been *together* together for a couple of months?"

"No. He knows, and not just because it's the first thing I said when he came out with this." Allie's ponytail swung out behind her as she whirled Jamie in slow circles. "But my lease is up at the end of May, and my landlady is pushing me to sign up for another two years. She said if I do it, she won't raise the rent at all and she'll let me get a cat, even though I'm not supposed to have pets, because she hates hunting for new tenants and she wants me to stay, basically forever."

"Oh, that's not fair. I mean, it is, but—"

"I know." Allie giggled along with Jamie as they dipped and turned. "I love living there. It's a great apartment, walking distance to work, with parking, which doesn't matter most of the time but hello, when tourist season rolls around I start singing *glory hallelujah*. Also, all the stained glass?

"It's not allowed now. And yeah, if I needed to I could probably buy my way out of the lease, or whatever, but I'm still paying off the wedding that didn't happen."

And probably trying to save for one that would take place, Kate suspected. But there was no way she was going to say that at this point.

"What about selling the lot that Nana left you?"

Allie was shaking her head almost before the question was finished. "That would be the very last resort. I have plans for that space."

"Oh?" Kate pictured the wooded chunk of riverfront. "I don't suppose those plans include a house and a mini Cash or two."

"Log cabin. Complete with a front porch and matching rocking chairs. So cute it'll make you hurl."

The churning in Kate's stomach had nothing to do with anticipated cuteness.

"Well," she said briskly as she attacked the wall with her scraper. "How long do you have before you need to... Whoa, what's this?"

"What's what?" Allie scooted up beside Kate, who automatically reached as Jamie lunged forward.

"Check this out." Kate used her nonbaby hand to grab Allie's finger and run it down the ridge now evident beneath the mangled bits of wallpaper.

"It feels like a frame." Allie flattened her palms against the wall, patting and tracing the line

Kate had uncovered. "Or a…give me the thingy, that's… Look. It connects to another one down here. And then it goes…" She nudged Kate aside, drawing the scraper along the path she was following, outlining a rectangle that looked about Jamie-sized. "It's a panel of some kind."

"I think I read a Nancy Drew story like this once." Kate eyed the shape Allie had made so obvious.

"What, the mystery of the boarded-up panel?"

"No. *The Hidden Window Mystery.*"

Allie grinned. "You're kidding."

"I'm not." Kate knocked on the wall in the center of the shape, then off to the area outside the line. "Hear that? It sounds different. Like this area is—"

"Hollow." Allie thumped the areas Kate had tried. "Oh, wow. We have to get this scraped so we can see what's behind here."

"Maybe Nana had a secret stash," Kate said as she set Jamie back on his blanket and waved a toy in his face.

"Or maybe it's Great-grandpa Charlie's lost treasure."

Kate's stomach did a funny little flip at hearing Allie say the words that Kate didn't dare.

Everyone in Comeback Cove knew the story of Charlie Hebert and the treasure he supposedly found before his untimely death. Officially, everyone was in agreement that it was nothing more than a local legend.

Officially, Kate agreed.

As if to bring her back to reality, Jamie whimpered.

"*If* Charlie really found something, and *if* he stashed it here, I think that whoever papered over this cupboard would have found it."

Allie scowled. "Spoilsport."

"Just doing my job. Jamie, Jamie, stop fussing. Mommy and Auntie Allie have to solve a mystery. You're okay. You like tummy time, remember?"

"Do you have another scraper?"

"Down in the crypt."

Allie made a face. "It's bad enough that it's the world's worst basement. Calling it the crypt doesn't help."

Constant damp, old stone walls, frequent critters… "Yeah, but it's accurate." Kate thought for a moment. "Boone stashed some tools in the bathroom up here. I bet I could use a screwdriver on the edges. A few scratches shouldn't hurt, since we'll be painting over it anyway."

"That better have been the royal *we*," Allie called as Kate headed down the hall.

As soon as she stepped into the bathroom, she knew she'd made a mistake. The air still carried the faint scent of his body wash. His towel, neatly draped over the curtain rod, whispered a reminder that it had been wrapped around that torso she used to embrace. His toothbrush and toothpaste and comb were laid out on the counter in the same positions they used to occupy in his Ottawa bathroom. It was like she had stepped into a strange blend of the past and the present, into a place where satisfaction and frustration seemed to coexist, and for a moment she had to place her palm against the solid door frame to steady herself.

Deep breath, Kate.

It helped for a second. Then she realized she was filling herself with the smells of a freshly showered, eminently lickable Boone, and she closed her eyes to block the assault on her senses.

That was an epic failure, for obvious reasons.

"Screwdriver," she reminded herself. "Now."

Once she remembered why she had come into the room, she was able to block out the Boone mementos and zoom in on the toolbox under the sink. She grabbed the screwdriver and sprinted back down the hall, not sure if she was racing toward the mystery or away from temptation.

But as soon as she entered the room, she could tell that work time was over, at least for the moment. Jamie was snuffling and chewing on his hand.

"Crap," she said with a sigh. "I guess it's lunchtime."

"Already?" Allie pulled out her phone. "Shoot. I have to fly. And this was just getting fun."

"I know. Want me to attack it while he naps, or wait until you can come back?"

"Hey, if you have time, feel free. I'm dying to know what might be here." Allie grinned. "Even if it isn't the treasure."

"Okay. I'll keep you posted." Kate scooped Jamie up to her shoulder. "Shhh, shhh, just a minute, little piggy. And I'll try to come up with some brilliant suggestion about you and Cash."

"Thanks. Damn, I am seriously late." Allie bestowed flying kisses on Jamie, then Kate. "Later!"

Kate gave herself a moment to stare at the mystery wall, racking her brain for anything Nana might have said about a hidden cupboard.

"It's probably nothing, Jamiekins. If someone papered over a cupboard, they wouldn't leave anything important in it, right? That wouldn't make sense."

Jamie squirmed and let out a wail that made it very clear the only hidden containers he cared about were the ones nestled beneath her bra.

Kate shook off the lure of the wall and headed for the stairs.

It was probably nothing, true. But still, she couldn't wait to show it to Boone.

BOONE PULLED INTO the parking lot of the hardware store, stopped the car, and allowed himself a moment of pride. He'd made it here without any wrong turns or any guidance other than his own memory and Kate's hand-drawn map. And not that he would ever tell her, but if Canada's early explorers had been dependent on her cartography skills, they would never have gotten more than a day's journey from the coast.

He whistled as he climbed out of the Kate-sized car, stretched and ambled into the store. He was kind of surprised at how cheerful he felt. The visit to the bank had been intimidating, to say the least. He'd spent the last hour seated across from a scary guy who seemed to be wringing every ounce of power he could from his position of loan officer. Though to be fair, Boone had to admit that the situation wasn't exactly typical.

Hi. Yes, I'd like to borrow a ridiculous sum of money to fix up an old house that I'm listing as my permanent address even though I'll never really live there. Because I live in Peru, where I work for a nonprofit and make so little money that between these payments and child support, it'll take me a full year to save up the plane fare to come back and visit my son again. But I swear I'm a good credit risk. Because even though I won't be living in the house, my heart will.

Boone was pretty sure he was going to have better luck trying to pick up a part-time consulting gig or something else he could do from Peru. But for the moment it was on to round two: finding out where he could get everything he needed for the house repairs.

He spent a few minutes wandering the aisles of the store, acquainting himself with what could and couldn't be found within. He had a feeling he'd be spending a lot of time here over the next few weeks. He couldn't help but look at the neatly stocked shelves and overflowing bins and think of what he could do with all of this back at Project Sonqo. They had made great strides over the last ten years, and he and Craig had learned a lot from the villagers—masters at repurposing ruins into homes. But even so, the contents of this store alone would—

"Can I help you?"

Boone snapped back to reality and focused on a man who looked to be about his age, wearing a polo shirt with Village Hardware embroidered on the front.

"Sure. I'm in town for a few weeks, doing some work on an old house. How much of this do you carry, and where can I get hold of the things you don't?" Boone handed over his preliminary list. The other man's eyes widened.

"Looks like you have a project on your hands."

"That's one way to describe it."

"What house?"

Ah. Boone hadn't spent a lot of time in small towns, but from things Kate had said—usually accompanied by a rueful smile and a roll of her eyes—this was the kind of response he should have expected.

"The Queen Anne on Maple Street. Belongs to Kate Hebert."

The man frowned. "Katie's still living in her grandmother's house? I heard she was going to sell."

Boone shouldn't have been surprised. "You know her?"

"Sure. Kate and I were in high school together." He extended a hand. "Eric McCabe."

"Jackson Boone."

The shake was quick, but before it was over, Eric's eyes had widened.

"Say," he said, "are you the mysterious husband we've heard about?"

Mierda. Kate hadn't been lying.

"I am."

"Good to finally meet you. But…didn't you say you're only here for a few weeks?"

Boone might not be familiar with small-town politics, but he sure knew when his own line had been crossed. This was it.

"That's right. So I need to get to this as quickly as possible." He tapped the list. "What do we need to do?"

Eric tipped his head, then gestured for Boone to follow him to a cluttered workstation at the back of the store. He gestured to a chair that sat in front before pulling up to a computer that looked barely younger than the one Boone used back in Ollanta.

The thought was oddly cheering.

"So, how's Katie doing?" Eric jotted some figures on a pad of paper. "That little boy of hers—yours—must be keeping her busy."

"We're all fine, thanks."

"It's good that she's home again. I know she liked living in Ottawa all those years, but there's something special about Comeback Cove. Folks can't wait to leave once they're done with school, but then they can't wait to move back when it comes time to raise their own families."

"Is that what you did?"

Eric laughed. "Nah, I've been here all along, except for university. My dad owned this place. It's in my blood." His fingers moved slowly over the keyboard. "Seems more and more folks are drifting in, though. Not a week goes by that I don't have someone from school wandering in here. Always a surprise." He frowned at the screen in front of him. "Though you could have knocked me over with a feather when Katie came back."

It struck Boone that this Eric seemed awfully interested in Kate "I've never heard anyone else call her Katie. Other than her family, that is."

"Really? That's what everyone called her back

in school. It suited her, you know?" He shrugged.
"Though I guess we all change over time."

It took Boone a second to understand the emotion building low in his gut. The pit of his stomach churned like the time he accidentally put twice the required ají peppers in his *papas rellenas*. When he did put a name to what he was feeling, it was so unexpected that he had to give himself a second to be sure.

He was jealous.

Now who was the one who could have been knocked over with a feather?

Eric was rummaging through his desk drawer, muttering something about a calculator. Boone was grateful for the break. He needed a second.

I want to have more kids. I would like to have them with someone I can build a life with.

A new and entirely unwelcome thought hit Boone. Was he sitting across the desk from his replacement?

Oh, hell. He should not have thought that.

"Okay. Here's what we can do," Eric said, and Boone made himself focus on shingles and nails and floor tiles and toilets. Eric talked about what they had and what they could order, and Boone nodded and asked questions and tried to keep from thinking about this very helpful, very Comeback Cove guy being the one who might teach

Jamie how to tie his shoes. Or cheer for Jamie at soccer games.

Or help give Jamie that brother or sister Kate wanted.

Yeah, keep thinking like that, Boone. That'll really help with the burning in your gut.

At last they were done. Boone made arrangements to have the supplies delivered and hauled ass out of the store before good old Eric could ask anything else about Kate.

But once he was back in the car, Boone didn't return directly to the house. Instead, he drove slowly up and down the streets until he saw what he was looking for: a florist shop.

Ten minutes later, he was back in the driver's seat, a bouquet of mixed flowers at his side and new determination in his head.

He might not be Kate's forever husband, but he was going to do his damnedest to be the best one possible while he was here.

KATE SAT ON the porch swing with Jamie, trying to enjoy the unexpectedly mild afternoon, but she couldn't stop fretting. Why was Boone taking so long?

Yeah, the man could navigate airports and countries and alpaca trails in languages she had barely heard of, but she didn't trust that he could handle himself on the streets of Comeback Cove. Right.

She needed a plan. In a minute she would put Jamie in his crib for his nap. Then she should head upstairs and resume scraping. If she really worked, she might have the cupboard or whatever completely uncovered by the time she had to turn back into Mommy.

But even though she was dying to know what might be behind the ancient paper, part of her wanted to wait and have Boone help. Because the thing was, she *liked* Boone. She wanted to spend time with him while he was here. Yes, it was hell on her willpower, but who knew when she would have another adult in residence again?

She rose slowly from the swing, intending to get started on her plan, but at that moment the clouds parted and sunshine poured down, and it was so inviting, such an early summer preview, that instead of going inside she moved to the top step to better soak up the sun.

Oh, that felt good.

She should put on sunblock and her arms ached from scraping, but ten minutes wouldn't hurt and the ache was the good kind, or so she told herself. Of course, it would be a different story tonight when she tried to sleep. She would have to make sure she took something before bed.

Or you could keep those muscles warm and supple by using them in other ways…

"Not helpful, Kate," she murmured. Maybe instead of returning to work immediately once Jamie was down, she would come back out here for a while. She could bring her checklist. Or better yet, a book. Not one of the home repair manuals she'd been reading, but something captivating that would suck her in and make her laugh out loud and tempt her to give up precious hours of sleep to get to the end. When was the last time she'd sat down and read for pleasure?

When was the last time she'd done *anything* for pleasure?

"Again, not helpful," she ordered herself. But this rogue thought was a lot harder to dismiss.

She rocked slowly on the step, feeling Jamie grow heavier on her shoulder. When *was* the last time she'd done something just for fun?

She was happy. She knew that. She was healthy, Jamie was thriving, and they had a roof over their heads, plenty to eat and family in town. She was blessed beyond reason. Life was good.

But she couldn't remember the last time she'd done something just for her.

Well, no. She could. That day she had impulsively wrapped herself in a white bathrobe, gelled her hair beyond reason to hold the infamous cinnamon-bun shape, and marched into Ottawa's EY Centre with her head held regally high in her best Princess Leia imitation. *That* had been fun. Not just because she had met Boone there, though heck, that had morphed into the best time she'd had in ages. But even before she saw him, she'd been having a blast. Kicking back. Mingling with people she didn't know. Laughing.

"I need more fun in my life," she announced to the fat robin perched in the maple at the edge of the porch. "Any suggestions?"

The robin hopped out of the tree and down to the grass. Probably hunting for worms.

"Not my idea of a good time, but thanks anyway."

Because who needed cold worms when you could be heating up the sheets with—

Boone pulled into the driveway. She groaned. *Now*, he had to show up?

She let her eyes feast on him as he uncurled from the car. The muscled shoulders...the shaggy hair...the hint of stubble on his jawline. His T-shirt was the tiniest bit too small and his jeans were just right and the whole long length of him called to her, teased her, reminded her...

"Hey." He grinned, shielded his eyes against the midday sun and waved at her. She waved back and started to get up, but caught herself just in time. No standing. Standing led to walking to him, which led to getting close to him, which led to reaching up to smooth his hair, which led to the baby sleeping on her shoulder.

Right. She was staying firmly planted on this step where her Nana had trod.

Then Boone reached into the passenger seat and emerged with an armful of something pink and purple and floral, and even if she had truly wanted to stay put, it wouldn't have been possible. She was on her feet before she knew it.

"Boone?"

He bounded up the steps. "Hi," he said, and handed her an assortment of tulips and irises and baby's breath.

"They're beautiful," she whispered, the fingers of her free hand rubbing the velvety petals. "Thank you. But you didn't need to—"

"And you didn't need to put up with everything you have since you met me. But you did." He touched the flowers. "So I did."

She continued to trace the lines of purple and gold and white in the irises. Not because they were so very gorgeous, though they were. But because if she was focused on them, she wasn't looking at Boone.

Boone. Who was standing on the step below her. So close that they were just a dozen blooms and some paper apart. So level with her that she could look straight into his eyes above the bouquet. So near that if he were to lean the tiniest bit forward, she could catch his lips with hers and kiss him, kiss him the way she had wanted to

since before he'd stepped off that plane, kiss him
so close and so hard that Jamie would be a little pancake between them and they would laugh
and shift and rearrange themselves and reach for
each other again, filling themselves with each
other. And Mr. Oliphant across the street would
get the show of his life and call her mother and
Kate wouldn't care because she would be holding Boone and pressed against Boone and damn
it, she had missed him and—

His eyes darkened. His lips parted.

"Kate?"

It was barely more than a movement of his lips.
She heard, though. How could she not when she
was leaning and he was leaning and—

Jamie let out a sigh against her ear.

Holy craparoni, what was wrong with her?

"Thank you." Bright smile, step back, regain
sanity. "You really shouldn't have, but I'm not
going to turn them down." Back up, back away.
"I'll just go put them in water and—"

It happened so fast that her brain couldn't keep
up. One second she was chattering nervously,
moving backward and trying to put distance between her and Boone. The next, a chair scraped
and something cracked and the world kind of
tilted and Boone was racing toward her and the

flowers flew as she grabbed tight to Jamie and her foot plunged down—

And the irises hit the deck just as Boone yanked her against him.

CHAPTER SIX

BOONE WASN'T A medical professional, but living where he did meant that he'd had to pick up more than a few side skills over the years. So when he ran his hand gently over Kate's ankle and felt the telltale swelling but no extreme tenderness over the bone, he was confident that they were dealing with a sprain but not a fracture.

"I am such an idiot," Kate said for the umpteenth time. She lay where Boone had deposited her on the living room sofa, her ankle propped up on pillows and strategically covered by a bag of frozen peas. "How could I have forgotten about that board?"

Boone didn't answer, and not just because she had been babbling a variation on that theme since he tucked Jamie into his crib and then returned to look after her. He had a pretty good idea why practical, focused Kate would have been hustling backward so fast that she stepped in the wrong place. She was trying to get away from him.

Looked like that whole make-things-easier-for-Kate idea had backfired big time.

And you're surprised? Loser.

"I'm fixing it this afternoon." Like he should have done the day after he arrived.

"No you're not."

It wasn't a good idea to distress someone who was injured, so he proceeded cautiously. "You want to tell me why?"

"Because if I'm confined to the sofa, you are on Jamie duty."

Okay. Intellectually, a part of him had known that already. That didn't mean he'd been ready for the words.

She patted his arm as he adjusted the peas. "You can do this, Boone."

"I hate pep talks."

"Good, because I hate giving them to anyone over the age of four. So stop fussing over me and sit down."

She patted the few inches of sofa at her side. He hesitated. The last time they'd sat like that, her on her back and him at her side, was for the one and only sonogram appointment he'd attended with her. He'd walked around for months remembering that moment, sweaty hands clutched tight, both of them struck silent by the image of the tiny heart fluttering on the screen.

He reached back, grabbed the oversize footstool and pulled it up to the side of the sofa. "Don't want to bump you," he lied.

Her eye roll was meant to convey exasperation, he knew, but he found it ridiculously reassuring.

"Listen. When Jamie wakes up, you're going to have to change his diaper and bring him to me. It might be a good idea to bring the changing table in here so I can talk you through it. Then there's laundry that needs to go in the dryer, and the dishwasher has to be unloaded, and...well..." She paused and smiled, though it was a little strained. "I guess you really are my lackey."

"Oh, the hardship."

He kept the words flip. He had to. If he didn't, he was going to freak out at the thought of how much childcare was going to be required of him over the next couple of days.

God, if You can spare any guardian angels for a day or two, I'd be grateful.

"My mom has some crutches that I could... Wait. No. What am I thinking? If she finds out about this, she'll move in."

Boone couldn't repress the instinctive shudder.

"My feelings exactly." Kate grinned and pointed to her ankle. "Any guesses how long until I can be up and moving?"

He shook his head. "I can tell you it's sprained, but for more than that, you need to see someone who at least plays a doctor on TV."

"No can do. My mom's best friend works for

our family doc. If I so much as slow down going past the parking lot, Mom gets a call."

"This small-town gossip thing is real, isn't it?"

"I'll say. It's one of the big reasons I moved to Ottawa," she said ruefully. "But even though it's a pain sometimes, I really am glad to be back here. Most of the time, I like being in a place where I know so many people and have backup when I need it."

His guilt must have shown in his face, because the next thing he knew, she was shaking her head vehemently. "And that doesn't mean I want you to feel bad, okay? I made my choice and I'm glad that things worked out so it's as easy as possible. Besides, I'm totally being the selfish one."

"How's that?" he asked, expecting her to say something about having Jamie all the time.

"I think the work you're doing with the project is amazing. And I couldn't handle the guilt if you left there because you felt like you had to be here all the time."

He wasn't sure if he should be relieved or bothered. Not that he had much brain power left to figure it out. His thoughts were bopping between trying to remember everything he'd read about baby care and wondering if he could fix the porch without waking Jamie and sending little reminders to himself that all of this was his fault.

Of course it was your fault, said his mother's voice. *You want to tell me a time when it wasn't?*

"Kate. Listen. When we were out there…" Shit, this wasn't easy. What was he supposed to say? "Sorry I brought you flowers"? "Sorry I messed up letting you know that you're still important to me"? "I'm sorry I made you back up."

There. That he could say without any dishonesty. Plus it sounded a lot better than saying, "Sorry I'm not the man you and Jamie deserve," which was how he really felt at the moment.

She stared at her hands knotted in her lap. Pink rose in her cheeks.

"Stop." Her words were low and urgent. "It wasn't your fault."

"Yeah, it—"

"Boone." She straightened, grimaced, then said very slowly, like she was trying to convey some hidden meaning, "Do not beat yourself up. I wasn't trying to get away from you."

It took him a second. It wasn't until he let that slightly emphasized *you* sink in that he got the message. And even then, he didn't understand it.

Did she mean she'd been trying to get away from herself? But that made no sense.

Though come to think of it, hadn't she been the one leaning toward him?

Ah, hell. He'd been so intent on honoring Kate's

request that things stay platonic that he'd never really considered she might...

He stood abruptly and grabbed the bag of peas from her ankle. "I'd better get you some fresh ice."

WHILE BOONE SLAMMED things around in the kitchen, Kate called Allie. She told herself it was simply to see if Aunt Allie might be available to lend a hand. It had absolutely nothing to do with Kate needing to practice those deep cleansing breaths every time Boone placed his warm palm on her ankle. Or leaned over her while checking on her. Or said something that sent her flying back to that moment before she fell, before sanity reared its head, when the world had contracted to him and her and the *want, want, want* that had been pulsing through her.

But thirty seconds into the call, Kate knew there was no way Allie would be playing nurse. Bits and Pizzas was hosting a high school fundraiser that night. Allie was interrupted three times before Kate made it through her greatly abbreviated explanation.

"Of course I'll come if you really need me," Allie said when she finally made it back to the conversation. "But Boone is there, right?"

"Right. Don't worry about a thing. I'm fine."

"Are you sure? It's just that Nadine is off sick,

and the new girl hasn't handled a fund-raiser before, and I really need to—"

"Allie. I'm *fine*."

"Do you want me to call Mom?"

"Do you want me to hobble over there and drop-
kick you into the river with my one good foot?"

Allie snickered. "You really are okay. Tell you
what, I'll send over a house special. Feed you guys
and ease my guilt, all at the same time."

Kate said goodbye and hung up before she
could blurt out anything about pizza not easing
the real hunger she was battling.

But as it turned out, there was no time for seduction or discussion or anything remotely re-
sembling temptation, because when Jamie woke
up it was clear that he was one unhappy bunny.

"It's the tooth," she said as Boone brought her
the baby meds. "I can feel it right there below
his gum. It's probably going to break through tonight."

Boone sat on the ottoman at her side and placed
a cautious hand on Jamie's back. "He feels warm."

"Fevers happen with teething. It's normal."

Thank God Boone had told her about the episode with Tristan. It meant that when he pulled
back at the mention of a fever, she understood.

Understood, and ached for him.

"It's okay," she said softly. "Jamie is going to
be miserable for a while, but he's not sick. He's

not going to have a seizure." Seeing that Boone didn't seem reassured, she added, "And if he did, you're not twelve years old anymore. You would know what to do this time."

She wasn't sure if she'd helped or not until Boone blew out a long breath, then rested his palm on Jamie's forehead with a hesitant tenderness that had Kate smiling in pride. And relief. And gratefulness that for at least this milestone, they were together.

It seemed she could let go of those worries about Boone loving his son.

The medicine helped, bringing the fever down and making it possible for Jamie to stop howling so pitifully, but he still wasn't his usual sunny self. The slightest upset started him whimpering again. He wasn't interested in lying on the floor or sitting in his bouncy seat or attempting cereal. All he wanted was to be held, and nursed and cuddled.

"My mom always swore by brandy for a teething baby." Kate rocked back and forth as best she could while keeping her ankle elevated. Boone looked shocked.

"Isn't that bad for them?"

"It is. But as Mom said, the brandy was to give to the parent, not the baby."

Boone nodded. "I'll drink to that."

True to her word, Allie had a pizza delivered complete with salad, breadsticks and cheesecake, but Kate soon found that there was a world of difference between eating around a baby when she was at the table, and eating around a fussy, squirming baby while half reclining.

"Should I feed you?" Boone asked, and Kate was horrified when she realized he wasn't entirely joking. Her reaction must have been obvious because he stood in front of her for a moment, apparently engaging in some internal debate, then swooped in and plucked the baby from her chest.

Jamie wailed, of course. Kate scrambled to cover up.

"Are you sure—" she began, then stopped herself. Boone had voluntarily taken Jamie. She absolutely could not say anything to discourage this.

Besides, given the way Jamie was protesting full-tilt, it seemed he had decided to take that particular task on for his own.

"Hey, buddy." Boone walked in front of the sofa, back and forth, his voice a low monotone. "I read something that said that babies like the way a guy's voice rumbles in the chest. So I'm just gonna keep talking while we give her a chance to grab a bite. Because I worked my fingers to the bone to make this meal and it needs to be appreciated. And that's not true, but I don't know what the hell I'm supposed to say here."

Kate looked down to hide her grin. Not that it mattered. Jamie hadn't stopped crying, but he did seem slightly less frantic.

"Sing to him," she suggested.

"I don't know many songs, Jamie, but Mom thinks that it might help. What do you say? Should we give it a try? Because it's kind of weird to walk around here, talking to someone who doesn't understand me, even though I think maybe you're getting the feel of this."

"I think he is."

"The secret is to talk really low. Gotta be a bass to make that rumble, right, buddy? Someday, when you're all grown up, you're going to want to impress someone. And when that happens, you just find a fussy baby and walk back and forth while you say whatever pops into your head, and people will be amazed, but you can smile and say, "Shucks, it's nothing." And I can't think of anything else to say because Mommy is looking at me like I'm off my meds, so maybe I'll give singing a try. Do you like 'Oh! Susanna'?" And he switched to a low croon. "Oh, there, Jamie. Oh, don't you cry for me. I flew up here to see you son, so don't you cry for me."

Kate was going to applaud, but stopped herself in the nick of time. Because when Boone started singing, Jamie stopped crying.

His little head bobbed back. His gaze lingered on Boone. One tiny hand lifted to pat the rough stubble.

She held her breath.

A tiny, trying-so-hard smile crept across Jamie's mouth.

And Boone, frozen, whispered, "I love you, Jamie. Daddy loves you."

BOONE LOST COUNT of the minutes, and the laps around the living room, and the songs he sang. His arms ached and his voice was scratchy and he didn't care, because his son was asleep against his chest and Kate was dozing on the sofa, and if he had to walk through the night to give them both a break, he would do so. Happily. Gratefully.

If he walked enough—say, the equivalent of from Comeback Cove to Toronto—he might tire himself out enough that he would no longer be tempted by the memory of Kate leaning toward him over the flowers. Or staring at her hands when she insisted she hadn't been trying to get away from him.

Yeah, not gonna happen.

Jamie stirred and stretched. Boone patted his back and wandered into the office, where he could walk and talk without fear of disturbing Kate.

"So here's the plan, buddy," he said in a low voice. "I sell my soul to the bank, or someone who needs a remote assistant. They give me money to give to your mom, so she can get this place fixed up the way she wants. She says she's okay with moving, but I think she's just saying that to make me feel better. What do you think?"

The only answer was a yawn.

"Then you would get to stay here, too. We can put a swing in that tree out front. And maybe a sandbox in the back, huh? We can make things nice for you, and I can know that even though I'm not with you, I'm still all around you."

As soon as he said the words he recognized their truth. He wanted to have a presence with Jamie, to leave his mark on Jamie's world. He wanted to make this place solid and safe for Kate—no more rotted boards, not on his watch—but he also wanted to turn this into a magical place for Jamie, the kind of house that all the kids would envy.

"So when the other kids ask where your daddy is, you can tell them, well, he lives in Peru, but he made me this great tree house. And this... I don't know. What? Some kind of hiding place. Like Harry Potter's cupboard under the stairs, but fun."

Jamie had stopped fussing. Maybe because, if the pain in Boone's shoulder was any indication, Jamie was now chewing on it.

"Does that help, buddy? I hope so. It's not like I can do a lot else for you right now."

And wasn't that the truth?

"See, Jamie, it's like this. Daddy loves you. But guys like me—we don't always make the best parents. There's too much baggage. Too much history. Not the good kind, like what your mom has and this house has, but the bad kind. That's what I have to offer."

Jamie shifted and bit harder. Boone sucked in a breath.

"This parenting thing... It's so easy to mess up. Trust me on that, okay? My mother... I don't think she meant to do a number on me. But she was too young. Too alone." He nuzzled the wisps of his son's hair. "I think your mom thinks I'm staying in Peru because I don't love you. But she's got it wrong. Most of the time she's dead-on right, but not this time. 'Cause the truth is, Jamie, I love you so much it scares me. And that's why it's better for me to be Daddy from a distance. Because I know how easy it is to mess up. I know how easy it is to do a number on a kid, even when you don't mean to." He closed his eyes and filled himself with Jamie's sweet warmth. "And I'm scared to death that someday the past is gonna come roaring back, and I'll be the one doing the hurting."

KATE WOKE SLOWLY, her senses kicking in one by one. Boone's voice, rumbling, slightly hoarse, nearby. Dryness in her mouth, the kind that always followed up a meal that included pepperoni.

An unfamiliar ache in her hip, and the realization that she wasn't in her bed. She was on the sofa, and her ankle was cold, but the rest of her was warm from a fluffy comforter that draped over her. And right, the board, her ankle, Jamie—

Her eyes flew open. The room was shadowed, but she could still make out a sight she had never expected to see: Boone pacing in slow circles, crooning classic rock while Jamie rested against his chest.

The part of her that was trying very hard to resist him momentarily forgot to breathe.

You could build an awful lot of memories in five and a half weeks, whispered her inner temptress. *You always regret the chances you didn't take more than the ones you did. What do you have to lose?*

She had no good answer for the first two, but the third was clear. Her heart. She could lose her heart so easily to Boone. She had done it before, the loss of him hitting her faster and harder than she had expected when he returned to Peru, and she had no doubt that saying goodbye this time was going to be even worse. Because now she was seeing a new side to him. Now she knew how it felt to lie on a sofa and watch him walk endless circles around her while he sang "Carry On Wayward Son" in a voice that grew more strained by the moment. Now she knew what it was like to be his partner. Not in bed, but planning and parenting.

Now she had even more reasons to fall for him. And she was so, so close to doing just that.

Damn it. Ottawa was full of great guys, many of them government employees who were building a career and a life right there in the city. She could have chosen one of them for her rebound fling. Instead, she had picked up the gorgeous stranger with the Harrison Ford smile and the guaranteed easy exit strategy.

And here she was, a year and a half later, terrifyingly close to throwing herself once again at a man who lived on a different continent.

And she wasn't talking distance.

THE TROUBLE BEGAN when it came time for bed.

Boone kept busy during the evening by staying focused on Jamie, who still needed to be walked and sung to and bathed and diapered and delivered to Kate for nursing sessions that should have helped but that left each of them increasingly exhausted and frustrated. Jamie wailed and Kate muttered about increased pressure on his gums. Boone glued himself to his laptop, frantically searching for insights as to how to deal with teething, but it seemed they had tried everything. Well, except the brandy.

He had half a mind to run to the liquor store

while he could. True, he was going to need caffeine more than alcohol, but a hit of something in his coffee might not be a bad idea.

Jamie finally conked out around eleven, melting into Boone's shoulder like the most welcome of weights.

"I doubt it will last long," Kate whispered. "But we should try to sleep while we can."

Oh, yeah.

"If you can help me to my room, we can pull his crib right up beside the bed. That way we won't need to bother you in the night."

The temptation was strong.

The need to do his part while he could was even stronger.

"Nope." When her eyes widened, he added, "I'll get you settled, and then I'll take the sofa. That way I'll be close if either of you need anything."

"Boone, really. You've been beyond wonderful. I don't know how I would have made it through this day without you."

Well, for one thing, if he hadn't been here, she wouldn't be dealing with a bum ankle.

"But I'll be fine," she continued, and the corner of his mind that wasn't exhausted sat up and took notice.

I'll be fine. I'm fine. It's fine. She said it a lot.

But it seemed to him she said it most when she meant it least.

"No you won't," he said.

"Okay, maybe not. But I'm sure that I—"

"Could manage if you had to," he interrupted, pretty certain that she hadn't planned to say anything of the sort. "But I'm here."

He could see how torn she was. Time to play his trump card.

"Katie." Maybe if he used her mother's name for her, she'd be more inclined to listen. "Come on. I won't have many chances to lend a hand. Let me help this time. It's what a father should do."

He knew he'd won before she said a word. It was all there in her long, low sigh.

"Fine. But only because..." She stopped, smiled, shook her head. "Did you know I'm a bit of a control freak?"

"I didn't have a clue." He rubbed Jamie's back, soaking up the steady rhythm of his child's regular, deep breathing. "Let me get him settled and then I'll come back for you."

Much to his relief, Jamie handled the transfer to the crib with little more than a whimper, though even that was enough to make Boone's breath catch. When he was certain that they had at least a few minutes to operate, he returned to the living room, grabbing the monitor on the way.

"There," he said, setting it on the coffee table beside the sofa. "Now I'll be able to hear him."

Kate wanted to say something. He could see it.

But she inhaled, sharp and deep, and offered him her biggest smile.

"Now, your turn." He moved in front of her, crouching and reaching, his heart thudding as memories of other times he'd pulled her upright roared to the fore. But she shook her head and slipped her hands into his.

"It's feeling better. I really think this will be enough."

"Kate—"

"Really, I do."

"You doubt my strength?"

She half laughed. "Not at all. But at least let me try."

The truth finally seeped into his semifunctional brain. She was trying to avoid touching him any more than necessary.

I wasn't trying to get away from you.

His pulse rate kicked up about a dozen notches. Maybe from worry. Probably from the effort of reminding himself that *platonic* meant *hands off* and *distance is golden*.

"Fine. We'll give it a try. But if you feel the least bit wobbly, go ahead and fall against me, okay? I'm braced for whatever."

She bit her lip. "Sure. Fine. Thank you."

He spread his feet and bent his knees slightly, making himself as stable as possible, then counted to three. A tug, a tightness in his arms, and she was upright, cautiously standing on both feet, carefully positioned with space between them.

"How is it?" he asked.

"Not all better, but definitely nothing like it was."

"Good. Let's get you settled."

Arms around waists, they moved her to her room. Jamie's deep breaths filled the little bit of space not occupied by the bed, which had taken on mammoth proportions, at least when it came to the amount of Boone's head space that it suddenly occupied.

He pulled back the covers and she dropped onto the mattress, emitting a tiny, involuntary moan of relief that had him wincing. She reached for the blankets as if to lie back, but he grabbed her hand.

"Hang on. You're not sleeping in your clothes."

"Oh, yes, I am."

Her words were steady but the pink in her cheeks gave him all the insights into her reasons that he needed.

"Where are your pajamas?"

"I'll be—"

"No, you won't." Not that he hadn't slept in his clothes many times, but she was going to have a rough enough night as it was. She needed as much comfort and ease as possible. "Look, if it helps, I'm so wiped out that there's no way I could even think about doing anything, okay? So let me help you into your pajamas so I can go crash myself."

Did he feel a little scummy for going for the guilt factor? Slightly. But it wasn't like he was doing it for his benefit. That had to count for something.

"A nightgown will be easier." Her voice was tight and low. "Top right-hand drawer of my dresser."

"Got it." He walked briskly around the bed, giving himself orders all the way. *Grab the nightgown. Turn around while she pulls it on. No, wait outside the room. Or even go into the other room. You'll hear her over the monitor if she needs anything.*

He yanked the drawer open.

And for the love of God, don't look at anything in her...

Too late.

CHAPTER SEVEN

THE FIRST THING Boone saw was a flowing white gown that he recognized right away. How could he not? It had haunted his dreams the entire time he was away from her.

A month or so after they met, he had said something about the Princess Leia outfit she'd been wearing the first time he saw her. She had laughed it off and made some joke about it getting blown up along with the Death Star.

But the next night when he came over, she had met him at the door in this. Her hair had been twisted into side buns and she had handed him a Nerf gun and a vest that he was pretty sure was supposed to turn him into Han Solo, and the next thing he knew, his princess was leading him through a recreation of the movie that she had set up throughout her apartment.

There was a stripped-down sofa against the wall, screened off to resemble a prisoner's cell and bed. A cardboard dashboard taped up against the kitchen table, reminiscent of the *Millennium Falcon*. And the already-narrow hall had been lined with an inflated air mattress to simulate the infamous trash compactor. In each location, she had spouted lines from the movie, but with a twist that turned them into lines of seduction.

It had been a night to remember even before they figured out that it was probably the night when they had made Jamie.

Get out of here, Boone.

He grabbed blindly, searching until his fingers closed over serviceable cotton. He gave the drawer a wicked shove and hurried back to Kate, who was still perched on the side of the bed.

Watching him.

With silent understanding and apology all over her face.

"Here you go." He tossed the gown on her lap. "You can manage from here, right?"

"I… Yes. Absolutely."

It was the momentary hesitation that made him stop and take a good look at what she was wearing.

Jeans. Of course it would be jeans. The most difficult item of clothing to remove, even without an injured ankle.

"Can you manage your sweater?" It came out rough and raw, but since he wasn't sure he could speak at all, given the task ahead of him, he was glad to be able to say anything.

"Yes."

"Okay. You do that and then I'll help you with—" he gestured toward the devil denim "—those."

Slowly and deliberately, he turned his back to her. Not that it made a difference. He still had ears, still had memories. Every inch of what was being revealed with every rustle of fabric was thoroughly, exquisitely branded into his very being.

"Ready," she whispered.

He breathed in deep, closed his eyes as much as he could without needing to resort to groping and slid his hands under the nightgown.

Her breath hitched.

Lucky her. He had stopped breathing completely with the first touch.

"I'm going to unsnap them," he said. "And then I'm going to hold your legs and lift your butt off the bed. Your job is to push them past your hips. I'll take it from there."

"This is a really bad idea."

"Agreed." He popped the snap, the sound echoing in the shadowed silence. "You want me to stop?"

She made a sound. It sure as hell didn't sound like a yes to him.

His fingers closed over the tab of the zipper. He tugged.

"I can do that."

"I know you can."

Shivers ran through him, a new ripple with every sound of a zipper tooth releasing. By the time he had the jeans totally undone, the trembling had spread down his thighs and into his knees, making it almost impossible for him to stay upright.

Of course, if he fell, he would land on her. He couldn't think of a sweeter landing pad.

He pulled his hands back and slid his arms beneath her thighs, lifting them and her hips off the bed. "Go ahead." There was no hiding the raw edge to his voice.

She shifted. Pushed. Wiggled.

"Done."

It seemed he wasn't the only one having a hard time getting the words out.

He gently lowered her hips back onto the mattress before grabbing hold of the waistband. He eased the jeans down, doing his best to not touch her, dying a little each time it happened anyway.

"I can manage from here." She lunged forward, shoved his hands away, easing the pants over her shins and ankles, reaching and grabbing them and tossing them toward the laundry hamper in the corner.

"Basket," she said in a strangled kind of whisper.

He wanted to come back with a witty reply, something that would get them both through the moment—and him out the door—but someone or something had glued his feet where he stood. Flight was impossible. He hovered at her side, his hand suspended above the bare skin of her shin while he relived moments when his foot had slid up and down that leg, when his fingers had sunk into her thighs, when he had collapsed on top of her and her knees had come up around him and her arms had tightened across his back and for a moment, every part of her had clung to him, holding him against her and within her.

And now she sat upright in her bed, tugging the sheet back over her legs.

He couldn't stop himself. He gripped her knee through the sheet, one fast squeeze, one reassurance and reminder. One moment of the most exquisite torture he had ever known.

Then he turned as fast as he could and returned to his lonely sofa.

BOONE KNEW THAT IT WAS TOO much to expect that Maggie wouldn't go all Mama Bear when she heard about Kate's ankle.

The tooth had indeed come through in the night, and Jamie had woken up as sunny and gurgling as always. Kate surrendered to the inevitable and said she would call Maggie to cancel dinner. Boone put Jamie in the stroller—an education in itself—and the two of them walked down to the corner to get some fresh air.

Boone wasn't going to congratulate himself too much, but when they made it back to the house without either of them breaking into tears, it did feel like a major success. Then Maggie pulled into the driveway and all bets were off.

Boone fumbled with the buckle holding Jamie in place. "Come on, buddy. Make this open. If I'm holding you, your grandmother won't beat me up."

The gods must have been on his side, because the fastenings gave way just as Maggie slammed out of the car and stalked toward him, her finger targeting him like Harry Potter using his wand to fight off the Death Eaters.

"I *told* you to fix that porch before she went through it."

"Hello, Maggie. Good to see you, too." He raised Jamie's hand in an imitation of a wave. "Hi, Granny."

Her scowl deepened. "He calls me Grandma."

Actually, since Jamie couldn't speak yet, Boone was pretty sure he didn't call her anything. But he didn't think this was the time to mention that.

"Where's Kate?"

"Sleeping." Probably not true. When they were leaving, she had said something about research-ing new bathroom fixtures. But if Maggie thought there was a nap taking place, she wouldn't go inside, meaning Kate could catch some peace.

It meant that he was stuck talking to his mother-in-law by himself, too, but hey. Every once in a while a guy had to take one for the team.

"I won't go in, then."

Yes!

She gave him the evil eye and he got the strong suspicion that she had come over mostly to put the fear of God into him.

"Why wasn't that board fixed already?"

"Kate and I made the repair list together. We agreed it was a simple job that wasn't as badly needed as others."

"Which turned out to be a mistake."

"It did." That he would give her. "But since neither of us is able to see the future, I—"

"Spare me." Maggie reached as if to take Jamie from him.

Boone tightened his grip.

She stepped back, eyes narrowed but still spitting fire. "Since she's asleep and I have you alone, let me make one thing perfectly clear. If you break her heart, you had better hope you're already on a plane when I find out about it."

Since a broken heart usually required love, Boone felt pretty safe. Not that he couldn't see himself falling big-time for Kate under different circumstances. He had certainly tumbled hard and fast in the short months they'd been together, which still kind of blew him away.

None of this was Maggie's business. But he could appreciate where she was coming from.

"I know you want to protect your daughter," he said, patting Jamie's back with each syllable. "I understand and respect that, and whether you choose to believe it or not, I want her happiness almost as much as you do."

Maggie could say more with one fast sniff than many people could with whole paragraphs.

"But, Maggie, Jamie is my son. Whether you like it or not, I intend to be part of his life. Not the way most fathers are, that's for sure, but I'm not just walking away from him. I'll thank you to not speak ill of me to him or in front of him, and since habits can take a while to change, I suggest we start practicing right now, before he's old enough to figure out that you would like nothing more than to throw me into the river."

Maggie reared back.

Boone barely resisted the urge to do the same.

Instead, he did the one thing he knew Maggie couldn't refuse.

"Now." He pulled Jamie off his shoulder and maneuvered him in Maggie's direction, praying with everything he had that he was holding the kid properly. "I'll be honest. I don't know much about babies. *Yet*. I've seen Kate hold him so he's facing out but I don't feel comfortable trying that on my own yet. I'd appreciate it if you could show me what to do."

As he'd expected, Maggie practically snatched the baby away from him. She snuggled him against her chest, no thought, no deliberation, just more of that automatic ease that Boone kept reminding himself came only with time and practice.

Her mouth turned down. Her eyes spoke volumes, none of them in a language he wanted to learn. But after glaring at him long enough that he was pretty sure he hadn't done a thing to change her mind—that, in fact, he had probably totally and completely blown his chances of ever getting her to accept him—she shifted Jamie so he was facing Boone.

"One arm in front around his belly. The other under his little bum and legs." Her words were jerky, but at least they were civil. "You have to hold him tight, but give him room to wiggle a bit. Might be good to practice with a bag of flour for a while if you feel like you don't know what you're doing."

It wasn't much, but he would take what he could get.

"Thank you." Then, because he knew that he needed to give her something, he bent to look his son in the eye. "You're very lucky to have a grandmother who loves you," he said. "Make sure you don't take her for granted."

"And you make sure you don't let Kate overdo things."

"I won't," he said, but she shook her head.

"She won't tell you what she needs. She likes to put on a show, that one, pretend she's fine even when she isn't. She's done it since we lost Allie's father. It's like she has to convince everyone she's okay so no one will worry about her." Maggie jiggled Jamie as she talked. "Don't let her tell you she doesn't need anything. Make sure she has food and water close by all the time. Books, too. I have some in my car for her. And a lasagna. It's her favorite." She jerked her head toward the car. "It's in the back seat. I'll hold Jamie while you take it inside."

Glad for the momentary reprieve, Boone hurried to do as instructed. When he returned, Maggie gave Jamie a kiss on the top of his head and handed him over.

"Mind what I said. Get that porch fixed. If anything else happens to her, you'll answer to me."

Considering he'd been braced for much worse, he thought he'd gotten off rather easy.

Maggie marched back to the car. Boone made Jamie's hand wave again, then made him pretend to blow kisses, the way Kate did during their Skype calls. "Well, that was interesting," he said to Jamie. "If anything happens to me and the police say it was an accident, tell them to talk to your granny, okay?"

And then it hit him that he had juggled a baby in his arms while carrying on a conversation. Two things at once. It was almost like something Kate would do, yet here he was, just a few days in, making it happen.

Like a boss.

Like he knew what he was doing.

KATE HAD NEVER really grasped how much work was involved in being a solo parent until she was forced to sit back and watch Boone take on chores that would usually have been hers. It was one thing to live a whirlwind of laundry, feeding, cleaning, organizing and home repair; it was quite another to watch someone else juggle it. And, as Boone pointed out more than once, he didn't have to stop and nurse someone in the middle of all the activity.

No wonder she always felt like she was just one bad cold away from disaster.

The true danger of being a little less busy, of course, was that it left her with too much time to think. To imagine. To remember. For two long days she filled her hours with writing overdue thank-you notes, overhauling the day care's staff handbook and updating Jamie's baby book. None of it was enough to keep her from watching Boone as he moved through the house, ever more confident, ever more appealing.

None of it was enough to make her forget that it didn't take two good ankles to rock someone's world.

BOONE FINALLY GOT a chance to attack the broken board three days after Kate's plunge.

Attack was definitely the right word.

He put Jamie down for his nap, warned Kate that things might get noisy, and closed every first floor door to help muffle the sounds. He knew exactly how to make the repair pry up the remaining bits of broken board, toss them in the Dumpster, cut a new one and put it in place. Once they painted or stained the porch floor, whichever Kate decided would work best, no one would ever know that it wasn't original.

But when he made it to the porch, the vivid memory of the moment she fell through had him lifting the crowbar over his head, taking careful aim, and smashing it into the jagged edges around the hole.

"There you go, you son of a…" He grunted the words between his teeth, seeing again the way Kate had shifted, then plunged, the shock in her fear-widened eyes. He heard again the panicked cry that had slipped out of her.

Most of all, he remembered the way her grip had tightened around Jamie. How, even though she was pitching and falling and twisting, she had never once let him slip out of her arms. How, when Boone grabbed her arm and pulled her up, her first question had been for the baby.

That was what a good parent did. Protected. Put the child first.

Wham!

A good parent would never do anything as shortsighted as bringing flowers, which could be interpreted as a prelude to seduction. Or as stupid as offering them up when the other party was holding a baby and standing on a porch he knew damned well was riddled with weak spots.

Smash!

Maybe he was being an idiot to try to keep the place for her. God knew the house had problems to spare. What if he helped her stay here, only to have something come down on her head? What if he patched up the floors only to have Jamie break through the banister?

What if he ended up making things worse?

Maybe he should just back away. Withdraw the loan application, do what he could to rescue the place, then let her sell it as planned so she could move someplace newer. Safer. The last thing she needed was to be saddled with something so damaged. Even if she did love it, it could only lead to trouble down the—

He stopped in midswing, his actions halted by the glint of light reflecting off something beneath the porch.

He grunted and scowled. Probably trash. Something an animal had dragged in at some point over the last century.

Still…

Given how long the house had been in her family, he should probably have a look.

He set down the crowbar, hit the flashlight app on his phone and shone the light into the hole.

Even with the beam from the phone, it took him a few seconds to understand what he was seeing. Lots of glass…curves and corners…

"Bottles?"

Huh. He could imagine the scenario now. Dear old Nana had been such a teetotaler she hadn't even tasted the mock champagne he and Kate had used to toast their marriage. Boone would bet good money he'd stumbled across Kate's Poppy's secret stash.

Though it wasn't in what anyone would call a convenient location. And…he leaned down, shone the light again, peered around and whistled. That seemed like an awful lot of bottles for a stash.

He pushed to his feet and went in search of

Kate, finding her in the kitchen, in front of the open fridge.

"Hey." He frowned, temporarily distracted. "You're not supposed to be on that ankle for longer than it takes to get to the bathroom."

She rolled her eyes. "I was in the office. The kitchen is closer to my desk than the bathroom is. I used my walking stick." She pointed to the stick Boone had brought in for her that morning, now resting against the counter. "I'm grabbing an apple, and I'll be back at the desk in about thirty seconds. Less than that if I don't have to waste time arguing with you."

It seemed she was feeling better. "Fine." He reached past her, grabbed two apples from the bin and nodded toward the door. "Get yourself back in there. I'll be the delivery boy."

She muttered something under her breath and hobbled away. He grinned behind her back, washed the apples and snagged a box of crackers for good measure.

"Here you go, m'lady." He bowed as he entered with his offerings.

"I don't need that much."

"The crackers are for future snacking. The other apple is for me." He set the plate on the desk, grabbed his apple, and glanced toward the bedroom. "Any sounds from Jamie?"

"Nothing."

"And you swear—"

"Yes, I cross my heart and promise I won't try to go in there and get him myself. You can stop hovering anytime now, Boone."

Well, no. He couldn't. Especially since he was the one who—

Enough already, Boone.

He bit into the apple, forcing himself to stop the cycle of blame. He was channeling the past again. It wasn't healthy and it wasn't helpful, and he knew from experience that it wouldn't do a bit of good. Someday he would remember that before he let himself get sucked in the way he had out on the porch.

On the other hand, if he hadn't been so busy destroying the board, he might not have seen the bottles.

"So, I have a question," he said. "By any chance did your grandfather have a drinking problem?"

Oops. Her sudden choking cough made him realize, too late, that he probably should have eased into that.

"What the hell?" She punctuated the question with one last cough.

"Sorry. But when I was working on the porch, I found a bunch of bottles under there. Too many to be random trash."

"Bottles?" Her brow furrowed, and then her eyes opened wide. "No way."

She reached for her walking stick. He grabbed for her wrist, but she was moving fast and his hand slid higher up her arm in something terrifyingly like a caress. In a flash he remembered lying in bed with her, grabbing her wrists and raising them over her head while she laughed up at him, his palms flattening against the soft skin of her arms as he slid them lower and he hovered above her and she arched up to meet him and...

The bottles.

"You're not going out there."

"Boone, I promise to be careful, okay? This could be important."

"There's a giant hole in the floor."

"Yeah, I know. But I also know how to go slow and use my stick and let you lead the way." She breathed in slowly, then gave him a smile that was so obviously fake he almost burst out laughing. "I can even resist the temptation to push you through the hole if you don't stop acting like I lost what little sense you think I have when I fell."

He remembered when Craig and Jill had returned to the office after Craig's illness, when Jill had offered up what seemed like a mild reminder to take things easy and Craig had practically snapped her head off before storming out of the room. Jill had waited until he was well out of hearing distance before letting out a quiet but enthusiastic, "Yes!" Perplexed, Boone couldn't help but ask why she was so happy to be snarled at.

"Because," Jill had said, "grumpiness is a sign that he's getting better."

In truth, Kate was standing straighter. And as far as he could recall, she hadn't winced once all day.

"Okay." He rolled his shoulders to ease the need to reach for her. "You're right. Sorry. But at least tell me why you're so eager to see them. I mean, it's probably just the spot where the guys who were building the place tossed their empties, but—"

"But that's just the thing." Kate had already grabbed her stick and was clomping through the house with far more speed than he thought safe. Not that he was going to mention it. He was pretty sure the stick would really hurt if she decided to whack him with it. "My great-uncle was the first owner of this house. My great-grandfather helped build it." She stopped and looked back at him, eyes glowing. "You know. The one who was a rumrunner during Prohibition."

CHAPTER EIGHT

KATE FORCED HERSELF to sit obediently in the swing while Boone tied a slipknot in a length of rope and used it to try to lasso one of the bottles that lay just beyond his reach. To be honest, she wasn't sure which part was more frustrating—needing to wait for him to do the work, or watching him stretch out on the boards, reaching and straining and practically begging her to admire the long, muscled length of him.

She swallowed hard and concentrated on telling him the story of her great-grandparents.

"So he was a rumrunner, and she was the daughter of rich Americans who summered in one of the big houses on the Thousand Islands. Classic *Romeo and Juliet* story."

"Your family specializes in those, don't they?"

"What do you… Oh, right. Mom." Funny, she had never put that together. "Anyway, they tried to sneak away one night—"

"Trying to elope before summer was over?"

"Trying to get away from her family before she started showing."

He raised up on one elbow to peer at her. "You mean your great-grandmother, your mother and you all got pregnant without being married?" He shook his head. "And to think I was always jealous when the other kids talked about their family traditions."

"Shut up, you. So Daisy and Charlie were making a run for it. They thought they would be safe because Charlie had made a deal with the American authorities. He said if they gave him and Daisy safe passage, he would tell them where to find the treasure."

Over at the hole, Boone ceased swearing at the rope and the bottles and rolled over to stare at her. "Hang on. What treasure?"

"I never told you about that?"

"I can't swear on a stack of Bibles that you didn't. But I'm pretty sure I would have remembered that."

"Well, that's good. It's proof that you didn't marry me for my money."

The look he gave her before rolling back onto his stomach and returning to the rope made it all too clear that her so-called joke had fallen flat. Better give him the whole story.

"As you can imagine, one of the requirements for being a successful rumrunner was a detailed knowledge of the Saint Lawrence. The riverbanks, the islands, the whole shebang. So when Charlie wasn't busy building houses or hiding from the Feds, he was out scouting the water. The story goes that on one of those outings, he stumbled across some kind of treasure."

"Come here you son of a—what was it?"

"Well, that's the thing. Nobody knows. He didn't even tell Daisy. All he told her was that he had given a piece to the Americans."

"Why would he do that?"

She used her good foot to push against the floor, setting the swing gliding slowly. "No idea. There's a ton of shipwrecks out there on the river. My best guess is he found something from the Revolutionary War. Or maybe the War of 1812. There were a few fights out on the river, not to mention the Battle of Crysler's Farm. That was just down the road, near Morrisburg."

"Wait." He leaned back for a moment, head tipped in apparent surprise. "The War of 1812 happened here, too? I thought it was mostly in New York, and down around Lake Ontario." He lowered himself into position once more. "And the whole bit about burning down the White House, of course."

"Boone, Boone, Boone. You make it sound so barbaric. First the British sat down and ate the meal that was already set out on the tables. *Then* they torched the place." Seriously, did he have to make those low breathy noises when he stretched?

It sounded way too much like the sounds he used to make against her ear when—

"Of course, that's assuming he was telling the truth," she said.

"You suspect your own great-grandfather of lying?"

"The man was a rumrunner, Boone. A smuggler. I highly doubt he would have been bothered by telling a lie."

"I don't know about that."

"Honor among thieves?"

He pushed up and grinned. "Han Solo was a smuggler."

Want curled low and hot in her belly. Did he have any idea how he looked—slightly sweaty, more than a little rumpled, all hot smile and inside jokes? And did he have to mention Han Solo?

Boone must have figured out he'd crossed into forbidden territory because he dropped back down and resumed his quest. Kate breathed in deep and decided she had better do the same.

"Well whatever it was, even if he only found one thing, it was enough to do the trick. The Americans agreed to Charlie's terms. He and Daisy picked a night and everything was set."

"Except?"

"Except, something went wrong. Either the Feds changed their mind or someone from Daisy's family found out what was up. That part was never clear. All we know is that it was night, and there was a shootout on the water, and Charlie died protecting Daisy."

"Not exactly the fairy-tale ending I was rooting for."

"Since when did you start believing in fairy tales?"

"I like 'em. I never said I believe in them." He sat up, a smile of triumph on his face and something clutched in his hands. "Though right now, I might make an exception."

Kate sat up straighter, cursing both her stupid ankle and the fact that if she stood up, Boone would probably punish her by refusing to hand over his finding. "What is it?"

"A bottle, just like I suspected." The swing dipped as he sat beside her. He handed it to her and swiped his forehead with the back of his arm.

It was indeed a bottle, rectangular and heavy, the glass thick and clouded by time. It bore no marks to indicate where it might have come from or how it had landed beneath her porch.

"Oh, wow." She ran her fingers over the sides, brushing away the dirt that clung to it. "Charlie, was this yours?"

"Nice to think it might have been." Boone leaned in closer, peering at the bottle. "So you say he built this place?"

"He helped. His father was the official builder, from what I heard. Charlie was just one of the crew. But still…" She used the corner of her T-shirt to rub at the glass. "Daisy managed to get the boat here, to Comeback Cove. Charlie's family took her in. Charles Junior was my Poppy."

"But Daisy never lived here?"

"Hmm? Oh, no. She lived in the house my mom has now. The bed-and-breakfast."

An easy quiet settled around them, broken only by the creak of the swing and the cheery song of a robin. Kate was exquisitely aware of Boone's nearness—his knee brushing hers, his arm stretched along the swing behind her—but for once, surprisingly, it wasn't torture. Maybe it was because they were talking about her family. Maybe it was because they were doing something so everyday and homey, sitting together, rocking and looking at the same thing. But for that moment, she didn't feel aroused as much as she felt relaxed. Comfortable. Like they had sat this way hundreds of times before.

Like they expected to sit this way hundreds of times again.

"I think about Daisy a lot," she said quietly. "How it must have been for her without Charlie. She was so young. She didn't know anyone here. And you can bet there would have been talk about her, even though she told everyone she was a widow and called herself Daisy Hebert."

"Did you know her?"

"Sort of. She died when I was, oh, maybe five. Before Mom married Neil, I know that. All I remember is her sitting in a chair with blankets over her legs." She wrinkled her nose. "And knitting. I definitely remember her knitting."

"Mittens for her great-grandchild?"

"Maybe." Kate thought some more. "Her big thing was quilting. Mom still has a couple of Daisy's quilts on display. I'll have to show you when we finally make it there for dinner."

"Don't hurry on my part," he said with such horror that Kate couldn't hold back the laughter.

"I'll tell you a secret. There's a secret passage in Mom's house. If she gets to be too bad, I promise I'll show you where—"

She stopped abruptly.

"We have to go upstairs."

"Stairs? Are you out of your—"

"Boone. The other day, right before I hurt my ankle, Allie and I found something. In the room beside yours." She grabbed her walking stick. "We thought it might be a cupboard that someone painted over, but now I wonder if—"

"A secret passage?"

"Smugglers do love their hidey holes," she said.

TWENTY MINUTES, ONE set of scraped knuckles, and a whole lot of swear words later, Boone had the cupboard ready to open.

"I can't believe you forgot about this," he said as he wedged a utility knife into the crack and gave it an experimental wiggle.

"What can I say? I was busy making sure you didn't smother me with kindness."

He glanced over at the spot where he had ordered her to sit. She was, of course, standing.

"You sure you weren't busy thinking of ways to get around my orders?"

"Maybe." Her expression was all innocence. "Is it opening up?"

He slid the knife higher, then lower, loosening the door enough that it wouldn't take effort to pull it open. When he was satisfied that it would cooperate without needing to be yanked, he stepped back and crooked his finger at Kate to have her move closer.

"Come on," he said. "Let's see what's in there."

"You want me to open it?"

"Your house, your family, your history. It only seems right."

Her expression softened. Huh. He hadn't put a lot of thought into his statement, but it seemed he'd said the right thing. Bonus.

"I would be honorable and tell you that you

did the work and have just as much right as I do."
She clomped over. "But I'm too excited to waste
time arguing."

He wanted to tell her that was one of the things
he liked best about her—that refusal to delay when
she knew she really wanted something. But there
was no way he could say it without it sounding
like a come-on, and since that was probably closer
to the truth than it should be, he opted for silence.

There was no handle, of course. There was a
hole in the center of the right edge that looked like
it might once have held a knob, but whoever had
decided to paper over the space had undoubtedly
removed it. He watched as Kate slipped her fingers into the opening he'd created, gave a small
tug...

And stopped.

"Problem?"

"I'm nervous." She shook her head, laughing,
like she couldn't believe her own words. "Though
that's not exactly right. It's like...remember when
I said I didn't want to find out if Jamie was a boy
or a girl, because I wanted to keep both options
open as long as possible?"

He did. It had struck him as a surprisingly
whimsical response from a woman who was usually so practical. Whimsical, and endearing.

"It's kind of the same way now," she said quietly. "As long as I don't open this, anything could be behind it. Old photos. Trash. A time capsule."

And then he got it.

"Or your grandfather's treasure?"

This time, her laugh was accompanied by the faintest blush.

"I know it seems silly. I mean, probably the only thing I'm going to find behind there is a mouse skeleton." Her nose wrinkled. "But yeah. It's like Schrödinger's cat. As long as I don't open it, there's no limit."

"You don't have to look."

"Oh, hell yes I do. You seriously think I have the strength to resist this?"

Since she was doing way too good a job resisting *him*, he wasn't sure how he was supposed to answer that.

She curled her fingers a little deeper, opened the door a tiny bit wider. "Logic tells me that Charlie didn't really find anything, or at least nothing more than what he used to cut his deal with the Americans. Those islands have all been mapped and explored countless times in the last hundred years. Not to mention that the entire shoreline changed when they created the Seaway. The shipping channels were dug up and deepened, they widened the river so much that a whole whack of villages were lost... I mean, the odds are that if the stories were true, the treasure would have turned up by now."

"But you still want to believe it."

"It makes about as much sense as a kid wanting to believe in Santa even after they know he's not real, but yeah. A part of me wants to believe that there's something. And while I don't think it would be in here, I guess I'm hoping for a map. A clue." She laughed again. "GPS coordinates."

"That would certainly simplify things."

"Yeah." She pulled a little more. "Have you ever felt like that? Like there was something you knew was totally make-believe, but you wanted it anyway?"

A family.

He blinked, barely keeping himself from blurting out the words. To tell the truth, he wasn't exactly sure where they had come from. If anyone else had asked, he would have said, "Nah, I'm fine. There's enough in the real world not to waste time or energy wondering about things that never will be." Especially since he knew that he was absolutely okay on his own.

But this was Kate. And they were a sort-of family. And even though their marriage was going to end, he still felt closer to her than anyone else he'd ever known.

She was looking for someone to share her life,

but that didn't mean he couldn't share his secrets with her right now.

"Yeah," he said quietly. "That kind of describes my whole childhood."

"Oh, Boone." One hand to her mouth, she twisted to face him, compassion filling her face. "Oh, crap. I totally… God, I'm such a clueless…"

Before he could figure out what she was doing, she leaned forward and kissed him.

It was light. Fleeting. Not an invitation, he knew, but a comfort, an apology. It was so quick that he scarcely had time to register what was happening before she was gone, hand to her mouth again. But this time her eyes were squeezed closed.

"I am so sorry," she whispered. "I shouldn't have… That wasn't fair."

"It's okay."

She shook her head but said nothing.

"Kate. Really. I know you were just trying to make things better."

"Hell of a stupid way to do it."

Hang on. That was his line.

He searched his memory for the things she used to say to him.

"How many times have you told me that everyone messes up sometimes?"

She scowled. "It's a lot easier to believe that when I'm not the one who blew it."

"Tell me something I don't know."

Well, at least that got a grin out of her.

"Tell you what. I'll forgive myself for that if you'll stop blaming yourself for this." She pointed to her ankle. "Deal?"

"That was different."

She waved a finger in his face. "Deal or no deal."

Could he do it? He wasn't sure. His brain knew that beating himself up didn't help anyone, but to actually forgive himself?

On the other hand, would he want Kate to do that to herself?

"Deal," he said. "But on one condition."

"What?"

"That you open up that damn cupboard before I turn into Schrödinger's worst critic."

This time, her grin was almost normal. "Sir, yes sir."

With a deep breath, she wedged her fingers under the door and pulled. He sent up a silent prayer that there not be anything dead within.

"Oh." She reached forward and pulled out the sole contents of the cupboard. "It's a…a painting?" She breathed in deep, coughed, then blew dust from the surface. "It is. A painting of this house."

"Seriously?"

She nodded and held it up so he could see. It

was about the size of a sheet of printer paper, maybe smaller. "At least, I think it is," she said. "The shape is the same."

"There's no turret."

"That was added later. I remember Poppy talking about it being built." She frowned. "The colors are different, too."

"People probably painted the outside over the last century."

"True, but do you think the porch was ever really silver? And it's more than that. It's like… look…there's nothing around it. No trees or anything. Like it's unfinished."

"You mean someone painted a picture of it before it was done?"

She held the painting toward him. He took one side and studied it while she gripped the other.

She was right.

"You know how people take before and after pictures of projects?" he asked. "Maybe this is the equivalent."

"It's a lot more work to paint a picture than to snap a photograph."

"True. But if pocket cameras hadn't been invented yet, it's not like that would be an option."

She mock scowled at him. "That's entirely too logical."

"I try."

They studied it in silence for a few moments.

There was no signature, nothing to indicate why it had been hidden away. It had probably been forgotten. Overlooked in the rush of getting wallpaper up.

On the other hand, whoever removed the handle from the cupboard door would have seen the painting. Assuming the handle was removed when the room was papered, of course, and not simply broken off years earlier.

"Well, it's not what I expected," Kate said. "But it's pretty. And it will be a nice memento after I sell this place."

He was pretty sure she was trying to hide the longing in her voice. It wasn't working.

He might not have found her great-grandfather's treasure. But damn it to hell, he was going to find a way to help her keep the house.

FOUR DAYS AFTER going through the porch floor, Kate buckled Jamie into his Jolly Jumper, joined Boone at the lunch table, and pulled a digital recorder from her pocket.

Boone did the one-eyebrow thing.

"I have a project that needs your help."

"You mean something other than this whole house?"

"Cute. I spent a lot of time updating Jamie's baby book while I was resting my ankle, and it got me thinking. I know we can call you anytime, but I want to have lots of stories about you to share with Jamie. You know. 'When Daddy was your age, he lived here and went to school there, and his favorite thing to do was watch TV.' That kind of stuff." She pushed the recorder toward him, choosing to ignore his expression of disbelief. "Keep this in your pocket. While you're working, you can tell stories. Then we can transfer them to my laptop for Jamie to listen to whenever he wants."

"Are you sure you didn't hit your head when you went through the porch?"

She hadn't expected him to be ecstatic over the idea, but she'd thought he might be a bit more open to it. "Boone, I know you didn't have a great childhood, but—"

"Let's see. Eight or nine foster families, a handful of relatives who made it clear I was complicating their lives, and a mother who never missed the chance to let me know that I was the cause of everything that ever went wrong in her life. Yeah. That's really something I want to share with my son."

Holy—she had known it was rough. She hadn't realized the extent of what he'd lived through.

For a few never-ending moments, the only sounds were the squeaks and squeals coming from the doorway, where Jamie kicked and bounced like an Irish dancer on steroids.

At last, Boone rubbed his hand over his face. He sighed. And then he picked up the recorder.

"I can't talk about when I was little, okay? But I know what you're trying to do. I get it. So I'll talk about other stuff. Like Peru."

"That works." She scrabbled for a way to save this. "You, um, never told me the whole story of how you ended up there. I know you went with Craig and Jill, but not the details. Why don't you start with that?"

"You mean right now?"

It wasn't like either of them seemed hungry anymore. "Why not?"

He eyed first her, then the recorder, as if determining which was more dangerous. Then, decision seemingly made, he hit the power button.

CHAPTER NINE

KATE WAITED. FINALLY Boone spoke.

"I went to Peru when I was twenty-one, after I finished university."

"And?"

He shrugged. "What else do you want me to say?"

She knew this ploy: pretend to cooperate, but do the task so incompetently that the other party gives up in disgust. It was a favorite of children everywhere.

Since she made her living wrangling kiddos, he might as well have saved himself the effort.

"And how did you meet them?"

He sighed and bit into his sandwich. Stalling, no doubt. "You already know."

Her answer was to point one finger toward Jamie dancing in the doorway.

"Fine." He added a little more drama to his sigh. "They were my teachers in high school. Jill taught me math in grades nine and twelve. Craig was... well, they called it tech back then, but I think it has some other name now. Jill did her best to drill algebra into my head, but Craig really pushed me."

"Like how?"

"Like, I'd be building something—say, a clock—and I'd run into a problem I didn't know how to handle. And even though he would usually just tell the other kids how to fix things, with me, it was a cross-examination. What had I tried already? What happened? Why did I think nothing had worked yet? Could I come at it from another angle?" Boone leaned back with a half smile. "At first I thought he was a giant pain in the ass. Then it got to be like a game. How many questions would it take before I figured out what he was really asking?"

"Did you ever get it in less than ten?"

"Don't remember. But years later, when we were in Ollanta, and we had a leaky roof in the office, he started in again. And it hit me that all those times, he wasn't trying to get me to the right answer. He was trying to get me to think outside the box. To rely on myself, not on the standard answers."

"What did he say when you figured that one out?"

The grin widened. "He said if I were any slower on the uptake, a dead man could have beaten me to it."

Somehow, Kate didn't think Boone had taken it as an insult.

"So how did you end up living with them? Were they ever your official foster parents?"

"No. And thank God for that."

Jamie let out a laugh and kicked like he was auditioning for *Riverdance*.

"I agree," Kate said, nodding to her son. "Why thank God?"

"Well, by that point, it was like I was programmed to hate my foster family, no matter who they were."

Defense mechanism, she thought, but she knew better than to say it.

"If they had gone through the official channels, I would have had to push them away."

"Why?"

"Because they were part of the system."

Of course.

"So how did you—"

"The day after I turned eighteen, Craig asked if I wanted to come live with them."

Ah. The happy ending was in sight.

"But," Boone hurried on, "I was Mr. Tough back then. I said thanks but no thanks. I had some jackass idea about finishing out the year and then getting a job, a place of my own, all that shit that sounds so possible when you're eighteen and stupid." He twisted to face Jamie. "Stay in school, kid. You hear me?"

"Don't worry. If I have to Super Glue him to the seat, I'll make him stay." She leaned forward, fascinated. "Don't stop there. What changed your mind?"

"Craig broke his arm."

She blinked. "Say what?"

"Yeah. He was carrying some boards and he tripped. The next day, Jill corralled me in the hall. She basically told me I was coming to live with them because Craig had put his ass on the line for me more times than I knew, making sure I didn't get in trouble, and now it was my time to pay him back." He shrugged. "So I moved in with them."

"You're saying you owe your life to a broken arm?"

"Yeah," he said with a wry laugh. "That's about it. If Craig hadn't tripped, God only knows where I'd be now. Rotting in jail, most likely."

She squeezed her eyes tight to block out the mental images. Some possibilities should not be examined. "Were they planning to go to Peru even then?"

"It wasn't definite. At least not officially. But I think they were pretty certain of it."

"And were they looking to bring you along right from the start? Because I have to say, any-one looking at it from the outside could say, hmm, a kid with no family, they needed muscles and dedication—"

"They had a daughter." He swallowed hard. "She died."

Oh, God.

As if by unspoken agreement, they both turned to watch Jamie, who responded by delivering a wide, drool-filled grin.

"When she was a teenager, she got into drugs in a bad way. It went downhill fast. Jill and Craig did everything right, got her into rehab, got counseling. They thought they had it behind them."

"Please don't say it."

"She slipped up once," he said gently. "That was all it took."

"Turn off the recorder, please."

It wasn't until she felt the slide of his palm against hers that she realized she had taken his hand. Regret washed through her.

"Jamie and I need to get down to Peru as soon as we can make it," she said. "We need to meet them."

"They'd like nothing better."

She nodded, stood and moved to check Jamie's diaper, simply because it was the only thing she could think to do that would keep her away from Boone.

From taking his hand again.

From kissing him again.

From giving him all of her in a misguided attempt to make up for his past.

ONE WEEK LATER than originally planned, it was finally time for the family gathering at Maggie's place. Boone was looking forward to it about as much as he'd relished that five-mile trek from an outlying village to Ollanta that he'd had to do a couple of months ago. The trek he'd had to make because the village had no phones, no internet and no way to tell Craig and Jill that he needed a ride back. Because he'd picked up a parasite that was seriously complicating life in a place with no indoor plumbing.

So, yeah. Dinner was going to be great.

Kate buzzed around the house, gathering the small army's worth of baby supplies she deemed necessary for a couple of hours away from home. He watched as she raced back and forth, checking on the contents of the diaper bag and muttering to herself.

"Wipes, okay, plenty in there. Diapers, oops, need another one. Boone, can you grab a diaper from the changing table, please?" She frowned into the depths. "Better make it two. Or even three. I'll get a spoon and his dish and the box of... Bibs! He'll need a bib!"

Boone walked past the bouncy seat where Jamie watched the activity with his hand in his mouth.

"Did you know that you require more equipment than most of my friends in Peru have in their entire homes?"

"I heard that!"

He rolled his eyes and leaned a little closer to Jamie, whose eyes were now firmly locked on him. "Good luck sneaking anything past her when you get to be sixteen."

The drive took less than twenty minutes. He suspected it would have been faster, but Kate seemed to be taking him on a guided tour of Comeback Cove's finest attractions.

"Now that I can walk again, we'll have to go to River Road and poke around," she said. "It's not tourist season yet so a lot of the shops are still closed, but it's pretty, and Jamie will love the ducks on the river. Maybe we'll get fudge, if the Flip-Flop store is open."

"The who?"

"The Flip-Flop Fudge shop. Best fudge in the universe. They make one kind…it's vanilla, really creamy, with little gummy flip-flops in it. So good. You have that smooth yummy sweetness and then the chewy, sour candies, and it's like, OMG. Food orgasm."

The silence that followed wasn't one that anyone would describe as comfortable.

It wasn't just her words that got to him. It was the way he was suddenly and painfully aware of her at his side, their arms almost brushing in the confines of the car. He was swimming in her: the sound of her breath, suddenly sharper and faster; the smell of baby powder and lemon that surrounded her; the curves and dips hovering at the edge of his vision, the ones that had become so familiar to his hands and his lips when they were together.

And in the back seat, the living, kicking proof of their togetherness gnawed on his own hand and made soft snuffling sounds.

Kate bit her lip and stared out the window.

"Do you want to pretend I didn't say that?" she asked. "Or should we talk about it?"

He took his time answering. He needed to get these words right. Not the easiest task, given that the more they were together, the more difficult he was finding it to keep his distance.

"Talking is probably not a good idea. Especially not while we're driving, and definitely not when we're about to go to your mother's place."

"I don't know." Kate's words were light, but there was an edge to them that told him she wasn't as carefree as she was trying to appear. "In my experience, hanging with Mom has never been much of a mood enhancer."

Like he needed the help?

She pulled up to a stop sign and breathed in deep. He wished she wouldn't. It drew attention to places he wasn't supposed to be noticing, unless his son was attached to them.

"So in a minute, you'll be able to see the river," she chattered. "On a really clear day you can see the island where Daisy…" Her voice trailed off. She sighed. "Boone, I… Look, please understand, this isn't easy for me, either. But I don't think… No. I know. Being…together again. It would be… I'm not going to lie."

She probably should. His sanity might depend on it.

"There's a definite appeal to the thought of going back to where we were. You, um, made quite an impression."

Damn it. He really wished she'd kept talking about the river.

"But I have to think about the future. And even though, yes, we had some pretty unforgettable moments—"

Blue. He spotted a streak of blue. That would be the Saint Lawrence.

"I need to think long-term. If you and I were to start up again, it would just…" She sighed.

I'm not you. I want to have more kids. I would like to have them with someone I can build a life with.

Right. Her life was here and his was there, and he was supposed to be making things better for her. So far, all he'd done was send her through a rotten board.

I shoulda named you Mosquito, said his mother's voice. *'Cause that's about how annoying you are."*

He stared at the window, searching for that bit of blue again. If it was close enough, he could jump in and have some sense shocked into him.

KATE ALL BUT jumped out of the car the minute she pulled up beside the sign that said Daisy's Place Bed-and-Breakfast. She was an A1, first-class idiot.

Though for the life of her, she wasn't sure what was worse—trying to resist Boone, or trying to talk like a reasonable adult when she was walking around feeling like some warped fairy godmother had sprinkled her with aphrodisiac pixie dust.

She had a sudden image of a fairy wearing a feather boa and smoking a cigarette in one of those '30s holders, pouring glittery powder from a can marked Horny Dust so it landed all over Kate.

She crawled through the rear door to unbuckle Jamie, breathing deep. Ah, yes. Nothing like the smells of stale back seat mixed with Eau de Diaper to ground a gal.

Unfortunately, she was still acutely aware of Boone standing behind her, no doubt watching her butt as she leaned and stretched.

A year ago, she wouldn't have hesitated to give

a teasing little wiggle. Now the only wiggling she allowed herself was that of her fingers in Jamie's face as she sang "Itsy Bitsy Spider."

Even though she and Boone had never even pretended that they had a future, watching him go back to Peru had done a number on her, and not just because she'd been pregnant. She had missed him. More than she'd expected, more than she could believe. It had scared her to see how long it took to stop reaching for him in the night, to stop grabbing her phone to text him a funny message or an update whenever she thought of him, which was basically all the time.

She couldn't go through that again.

She wanted a full family. A husband who lived in the same house. Getting back into Boone's bed, letting him back into her heart—neither of those would help her in the long run.

She refused to think about how utterly amazing the short run would be.

"Here." She shoved Jamie into Boone's arms. "You carry him. That way my mother can't throw anything at you."

"Oh, that was reassuring."

"I try."

She kept one hand under Boone's elbow as she half guided, half propelled him forward up the walk to her mother's porch. Daisy's Place, like Kate's house, was one of the older buildings in

Comeback Cove. Unlike Kate's house, though, her mother's was in immaculate condition. No loose shingles or sagging floorboards were allowed to exist here.

"Mom has a local contractor practically on retainer," she said as they walked the weed-free stone slabs leading to the steps. "I hired him to do a couple of the most urgent things when I first moved in. He does great work but he's pricey."

And maybe if she kept babbling, she could forget about the warm strength of Boone's arm beneath her palm.

A door closed. Kate looked to where Maggie waited on the porch, watching them with the assessing eye of a ruling monarch inspecting the fleet.

She gave Boone's elbow a sustaining squeeze.

"Hi, Mom." Kate bounded up the steps first, determined to show her mother the benefits of having Boone around to help with the lugging. She gave Maggie a quick kiss and hug. "Is Allie here?"

"She and Cash are in the dining room. They came early to help." Maggie shot a quick glance in Boone's direction. "Cash is very helpful."

Kate looked back. Boone rolled his eyes.

Quickly, before she could talk herself out of the instinct, Kate took Maggie's arm and pulled her away from the door. "Go on inside, you two," she called out gaily, as if she wasn't ready to blow her top at any second. "Boone, just yell and Allie will give you the tour. Mom and I will be right behind you."

With that, she marched her mother to the corner of the porch farthest from the windows.

"Katherine Joy, what are you—"

"Mom." Kate came to a halt beside one of the many flower planters lining the porch banister. Crocuses and grape hyacinths already filled it to overflowing. "This has to stop."

"Oh, really."

"Really. Boone has never lied to me, as I reminded you many, many times over the past year. We are both happy with our arrangement, and you know damned well that Jamie deserves the chance to know and love his father."

"I—"

"Hang on." Kate leveled one finger in her mother's direction. "Boone is a good and honorable man who is working to make the world a better place for people. I knew that when I got involved with him. And not to gross you out or anything, but I was the one who did the seducing, okay? So you can stop acting like he took my virginity and tossed me out like old laundry. I want him in Jamie's life and I will thank you to stop making him feel guilty for not doing what *you* think he should have done."

Maggie's eyes were bright and her cheeks were pink, but her lips were still set. "I can think whatever I wish of him. It's still a free country."

"You can think whatever you want, Mom. But he is the father of my son and I would appreciate it if you treated him with common courtesy and respect."

"Fine. I'll be the soul of tact." Maggie pulled herself to her full height. "But you just remember that when I go in there, everything I'm saying to him is a lie."

"Oh, there's a surprise," Kate muttered as her mother marched back to the door.

"Surprises are highly overrated," Maggie snapped and yanked the door open.

Kate sagged against the post and focused on the glints of sunset bouncing off the river. Couldn't anything ever be simple?

At that moment, Allie poked her head out the door.

"Oh, good," she whispered. "You're still alive."

The laughter that burbled out of Kate was most welcome.

"Of course I'm alive, you nitwit. Did you leave Mom alone with Boone? He's the one we need to worry about."

Allie waved the words away. "Not necessary. Mom is in there fussing over Jamie, and Cash is an excellent diplomat. He'll make sure no blood is spilled." She scooted closer to Kate and lowered her voice. "What did you say to her? She came in looking like she was ready to rip off heads, but she practically oozed sweetness and light."

"To Boone?"

"Yes, to Boone. Though come to think of it, he's looking kind of shell-shocked. Like he's braced for attack." She shuddered. "Boone isn't my favorite person, either, but he doesn't deserve the Wrath of God treatment."

"Nobody deserves that. And at the moment, I bet Mom is more pissed off at me than at him."

"Why, did you threaten to cut off her Grandma privileges if she didn't make nice?"

"Almost."

"Katydid. You didn't!" Allie practically bounced out of her totally nonsensible heels. "I wish I'd been here to watch the show."

"Yeah, well, if dinner is exceptionally horrific tonight, you can blame me."

"Not to worry. Cash will sweet-talk Mom into behaving before she even knows what hit her."

"Speaking of Cash, have you figured out a solution to the moving in dilemma?"

The bouncing came to an abrupt halt. "Not yet. Part of me wants to take the plunge. And part of me wants to take it slow. And the rest of me is hoping that the perfect answer will be hiding inside my next fortune cookie."

"Well, I'm no cookie, but I had a thought." One that Kate couldn't believe she had needed so long to figure out, because from what she could see, it was the perfect solution. "Why don't you move in with me?"

Allie blinked. "With you? But you're going to sell."

"Yes, I am, but not right away. Even with everything Boone is doing to fix things up, I'll need more time to get it completely market-ready, and who knows how long it will take to sell. I've been thinking it might make sense to get things in shape, stay through the winter, then list it in the spring when the market is so much better." She pointed at Allie. "If you moved in and split the bills with me, it would be cheaper than buying yourself out of a lease *and* I could definitely afford to stay through winter. Plus you would have more flexibility. You could take your time about making the next big step with Cash. Believe me, nobody ever regretted taking the time to be sure of a decision." She grinned. "And if you don't make it home at night, I'm not going to interrogate you the way Mom would."

"Oh, dear God, don't make me think that. She's already dropping hints about Cash, and how much time I'm spending with him, and hoping I learned my lesson with Luke."

Well, it was nice to know that Boone wasn't

the only one on Maggie's radar. "I thought she liked Cash."

"She does. She adores him. But you know Mom. She's going to reserve final judgment until the minister says *husband and wife.*"

Yep. That sounded like vintage Maggie.

"So, what do you think?" Kate asked. "I'm game if you are."

"I think it's a great idea. Plus I'm all for having more time with Jamie. But are you sure you're okay with it? I can be a bit of a slob."

"I wouldn't have offered if I wasn't certain. I'll whip you into shape. Plus it'll be nice to have an extra set of hands, you know?" Not to mention that she was already dreading the way the big house would echo once Boone was gone. Saying goodbye again would be a lot easier if she knew there was going to be someone else around.

Also, having Allie at home would help her focus on the future. On the next steps in her life. Maybe she could even start dating again, while she had a sitter on hand. Surely she would feel like being with someone else eventually, right? Maybe in winter, when the divorce would be well underway and she was used to Boone being back in Peru. Once she knew that the marriage was truly over, there would come a day when she would feel ready to see someone else.

Certainly.

Someday.

CHAPTER TEN

BOONE HAD SAT through his share of uncomfortable meals. His first dinner with Craig and Jill… the awkward airport breakfast with the flight attendant who had helped him make the most of an unexpected overnight in Lima…the oh-so-proper tea that Kate's grandmother had insisted they have after their wedding. Yeah. He was still convinced that Nana's presence was the only reason Maggie hadn't poisoned him.

This dinner wasn't the worst meal he'd endured, but it was definitely in the bottom ten.

Hadn't Kate said something about a secret passage in this house? He wished he knew where it was about now.

At least they had Jamie to keep things light. Every time the conversation dragged or Maggie's sighs became too loaded, someone would comment on Jamie's outfit or marvel over the way he was sitting so straight on Kate's lap, and the oohing and aahing would begin anew.

He definitely owed the kid an amazing first birthday present. Could he ship an alpaca to Canada?

Cash, at least, seemed to be on his side. He was full of questions about Peru and Machu Picchu and Project Sonqo—not the interrogation that Boone had been braced for, but questions that, he knew, came from genuine interest.

"My brother runs a charitable foundation associated with the family dairy," he said at one point. "You might want to apply for a grant through them."

"Wouldn't that be a conflict of interest? I mean, given that—" Boone broke off, unable to think of a simple way to say that Cash was dating Boone's sister-in-law. Though given that Boone and Kate's marriage was a mere formality, soon to be ended, maybe Cash didn't see that as an issue.

Kate, however, seemed to know the dangerous waters that this conversational canoe was headed for. She sent him a sympathetic smile and turned to Allie.

"I totally forgot to tell you—Boone and I opened up that cupboard that you and I found."

"What cupboard?" Maggie asked. "Have some more ham. I'll be eating it for three weeks."

Boone reached for the platter. Maggie scowled. Very deliberately, he forked a large slice onto Kate's plate.

"It was in the middle bedroom upstairs," Kate said. "The one I had before we moved here."

Then, as Maggie watched, Boone gave Kate a wink and took more ham for himself, as well.

Under cover of the table, Kate poked Boone in the thigh. He stared at his plate to hide his grin.

"It was built into the wall," Kate continued, all innocence, "and someone had papered over it a couple of times. Allie was with me when I stumbled across it, scraping the walls."

"And why were *you* doing that job?" Maggie's word choice made it very clear who she felt should have been wielding the scraper.

"Because Boone was wrestling with a toilet."

Boone was impressed. He'd had no idea that Kate could lie so quickly or effectively.

"So, was there anything in it?" Allie asked.

Kate was momentarily distracted by Jamie lunging for a dinner roll—he had just learned the joys of grabbing everything within reach—so Boone answered. "There was a painting of the house."

"Of my parent's house?" Maggie's eyes softened, and for a second Boone glimpsed the sentimental woman he'd suspected was hiding behind her Mama Bear coat.

"The colors are different," Boone said. "And the turret isn't there. But it's definitely the same place."

"No turret?" Maggie stared at him as if she suspected him of trying to trick her.

"That's right. It threw me for a moment, too. But it's definitely the same house. The window details and the porch are hard to miss."

"And it was a different color?" Allie asked.

Kate picked up the story. "Mmm-hmm. The porch was silver and the shutters were white instead of yellow, and the rest of this house was a gorgeous shade of blue. Not navy, not robin's egg, but something like…" She glanced around the room, then sat back in her chair, squinting at a quilt hanging on the wall behind Allie. "Like that line in the middle of the ruby quilt."

Everyone turned to check it out. Boone, who had given it only a cursory glance before, was now caught by the detail work in the quilt. It was a riot of colors—a brilliant yellow background with the vibrant blue line outlining the center. Green circles seemed to be randomly sprinkled throughout while gray rectangles clustered in the middle. Deep red diamond shapes all around the outside edge were, he assumed, the reason Kate referred to it as the ruby quilt.

Something she had said tickled his memory.

"Didn't you say that Daisy was a quilter?"

"Right." Kate handed Jamie a spoon. "Here you go, Jamiekins. You can't choke on this. Daisy made that quilt, right, Mom?"

"Yes, she did."

"It's beautiful." Boone wasn't trying to butter

up his mother-in-law, at least not this time. The quilt truly was a work of art. "Project Sonqo works primarily with weavers and knitters, so I don't have much knowledge about quilts. But there are different patterns and designs that are used over and over, aren't there? Or does everyone reinvent the wheel?"

Maggie's expression was guarded but her voice was surprisingly neutral when she answered. "That's right. Gran—Daisy, that is, she was always Gran to me—generally used the traditional patterns, but there were times when she went out on her own. Story quilts, they're called. When you make one that's designed to tell a story or remember an event."

Allie was following the conversation intently. "I didn't know that."

Maggie shrugged. "You never asked."

Boone came close to choking on his mashed potatoes. Had he just been the recipient of a sort-of indirect compliment from Maggie?

Kate caught his eye over Jamie's head, her own pleased surprise all over her face. There was a brief tap on his thigh—so quick it was as if she'd started to give him a pat, then remembered the ground rules.

He liked it better when she forgot.

"So that one is a story quilt, Mom?" Kate

rushed into the question. Trying to keep herself on track? "What's the story behind it?"

Maggie turned sideways to study the quilt. "You know," she said, drawing the words out slowly, as if she were physically sifting through her memory banks, "I don't think she ever told me. In fact, I know she didn't. I asked her a couple of times while she was working on it, but she laughed and said that if I was supposed to know, I would figure it out."

"That's not fair," Allie said.

Maggie shrugged. "Gran set her own rules."

Boone thought he heard Cash mutter something about it running in the family. He focused on the quilt to keep from snorting.

That blue line... Something about it kept beckoning him. He could swear he had seen it before.

"Gran did say," Maggie said, then stopped, a serving spoon of corn suspended in her hand. "Now, that's odd. I haven't thought of it in years, but I know there was something about Uncle Fred. Well, he was my great-uncle, but he was the only one I had, so he was just Uncle. Anyway, I have this memory...it's all foggy. But I remember her showing the quilt to Fred and him looking it over and saying something about her getting it right."

"Maybe he was just examining her needlework."

Maggie sniffed. "Hardly. Fred couldn't care less

about things he considered women's work. Food, maybe, but other than that, nothing."

"Sounds like yet another unsolved Hebert family mystery," Cash said. "Right up there with whatever Charlie might have—"

"It's the house."

Boone's outburst startled him almost as much as it did everyone else at the table, but he was too excited to worry about politeness. He practically jumped from his chair and circled the table until he was in front of the quilt.

"This line." He traced the route of the blue line, making sure to keep his finger far enough away that there was no fear of accidental grease marks. "Look. It's the shape of the house. The foundation. The footprint."

Kate saw it first. "Without the turret. You're right." She bounced in her seat, pointing to the quilt. "That's the porch at the bottom, and there's the little alcove off the bedroom, and the mudroom at the back."

Cash whistled. Allie squinted, but he could see the comprehension dawning in her face. Even Maggie seemed…well, not impressed. But intrigued? Absolutely.

"So we have a painting of the house without the turret, and a quilt that sure seems to show the same thing from a different approach." Kate, ever practical, ticked points off on her fingers. "So—coincidence?"

"Since Uncle Fred was the one who lived there," Maggie said in an oddly strained voice, "I don't think so."

Boone had spent the last decade-plus in a town built on ruins. If there was one thing he knew, it was that sometimes the past had a strange way of making itself known in the present.

He grabbed his phone. "Maggie, could I get a picture of this?"

"What for?"

"I want to compare it to the painting."

"Oh. Well, I guess that would be all right. As long as you don't copy it or anything."

"Mom, really?"

Boone grinned at both Maggie's reluctance and Kate's impatience as he snapped the photo.

"So Fred and Daisy were in cahoots. Do you think they were trying to tell you something?" Allie asked.

"Sure." Cash snickered. "It's a treasure map. Boone, look carefully and see if you can find the hidden X."

Boone joined in the laughter as he made his way back to his seat. But when he glanced at Kate, he noticed her expression as her gaze lingered on her great-grandmother's work. She'd looked the same way while debating opening the cupboard—like a kid on Christmas morning who'd just opened the gift she didn't know she wanted until she saw it.

And he couldn't help but wonder if there would ever be a way that he could be the one to make her look like that.

A FEW DAYS LATER, Boone eased his aching self into a kitchen chair, inhaled about half his glass of lemonade in one draw and sighed.

"I hurt all over," he announced to whatever dust motes might have sprouted ears.

It had been a productive morning. Kate and Jamie were running errands, so he'd doubled up on work, trying to make up some of the hours lost to Kate's ankle. Not that he begrudged the time. Other than the frustrations caused by helping Kate undress that first night, it had been kind of a trip to live her life for a few days. And it had definitely forced him to step up his game with Jamie—a prospect that had scared the crap out of him at first, but which he now gave thanks for every time that little mouth flashed him a one-toothed grin.

But with the house to himself, he'd spent much of the morning on the roof, prepping it for shingling. It wasn't a job that lent itself to interruptions. He'd lost count of how many times he'd gone up and down the ladder, but the burning in his legs told him that the number was up there in the three-, maybe four-aspirin range.

Unbidden, he remembered the time last year when he went for his first post-Canadian-winter run. This was worse. Not just in agony, but because last time his healing had been spurred by a seriously welcome massage from Kate. He could still hear the way she'd laughed as she'd teased him about his lack of conditioning, could still feel the sweet heat of her hands moving up his calves and thighs and...

"Torture yourself much, Boone?"

He downed more lemonade and opened his laptop. Distraction. That was what he needed. He'd rest his legs, check his email, maybe even hear back from the bank about his loan application.

It was almost a relief when he saw how many Sonqo-related requests and reports were waiting for him. He had a decent break ahead of him. Better yet, there was an email from Jill, updating him on the events and people he'd left behind.

The social media interns had some great plans for their Facebook page... Everyone was doing well... They'd had another one of *those* tourists, the ones who want everything to be just like home but with alpacas...

Boone read it all with a smile. All those familiar names and places, all those situations he understood. He might be sitting in a green kitchen, savoring lemonade while he read, but in his mind he was back in Ollanta, listening to the voices rolling in from the streets, smelling the potatoes that would usually be cooking around this time of day. It was almost a shock when he looked up and noticed the collection of glass bottles on the windowsill. Part of him had expected to see the familiar photo of Jamie that sat on his desk in the Project Sonqo office.

He returned to the email, rereading more carefully. Jill was skilled at writing everything she wanted him to know and hiding the items she wasn't ready to reveal. Boone had always suspected she was a master at sleight of hand, but he had developed a new appreciation for her ability last year when he was in Ottawa. Jill and Craig had been dealing with Craig's illness for months before they let Boone know that anything was amiss. Since then, he'd made sure that no email was taken at face value.

Though, as Jill had pointed out when he said something to her about wishing they had told him sooner, what would have been the point?

"You couldn't have done anything differently," she'd said. "Your job was to finish that course. You could hardly have done that if you had come bouncing back down here. It's not like you're a doctor, Boone. Besides, you had your own affairs to attend to." Which had sounded perfectly innocent until she'd elbowed him in the ribs.

He laughed silently to himself. Jill was the ultimate romantic. She hadn't said anything, but Boone was well aware that she was certain he and Kate were actually madly in love but simply didn't know it yet. He knew that she was dying to have Boone bring his wife and child back to Peru so she could spoil Jamie the way she spoiled the kids that wandered in and out of the project office.

Huh. He had to admit, there was something about that picture that appealed to him, too.

For a moment he let himself wonder. What if he were to suggest it to Kate? Not a move there, God no, but she herself had said that she wanted to meet Jill and Craig soon. Maybe in the fall? Before she went back to work, before winter made travel complicated…

He shook his head. What was he thinking? Kate's life was here, in this town, in this house. His job was to make sure she could continue that way.

You're supposed to make things better for her, remember?

"Back to work," he told himself. "The sooner you get through these reports, the sooner you can get back to working on the house, the more you can do for Jamie and Kate."

With the goal in mind, he returned to the task

at hand. He reviewed a couple of résumés from potential interns, looked over the grant application prepared by their current co-op student and checked on the plans for their major fund-raising drive to be held in June. There were emails from the medical foundation in the same village to discuss some joint activities, a couple from various funding agencies in need of periodic updates and—his favorite—a picture from Jill, of her and Craig laughing in the office while modeling scarves. She looked relaxed. Craig still looked a bit frail, but better than he had a few months back. Simply seeing their smiles eased the part of himself that was wound tighter than he'd realized.

They were doing okay.

Better yet, once he saw that picture, it was like he'd received permission to ease up. To relax. And to think about himself and his other responsibilities a bit more.

He'd suggested twice-yearly visits when he and Kate were discussing the separation agreement. Finances and his wariness about his parenting ability meant he didn't dare commit to more than that. The way he figured, it was better to show up more often than expected than to do it the other way around—not that he had any personal experience with parents who didn't deliver on their promises, no, not at all.

But they hadn't discussed how long each visit

would last. Now, though, working his way through the remarkably large chunk of items that he was able to tend to from afar, he had hope that his times in Canada could be along the lines of a month, maybe even a month and a half at a stretch. Just like this one. That shouldn't overwhelm anyone, should it? If he could do that two or three times a year...

Okay. It wouldn't be like having a father around all the time. But it could still be good. He could still be a dad to his son, the kind of dad he wanted to be. Could still be a help to Kate.

And what about when she meets someone else? What about when she remarries and has other kids?

He pushed those thoughts firmly away. He refused to cross that bridge until there was no other choice.

Instead, he clicked through to the next email—and saw that his loan application had been denied.

THAT FRIDAY, KATE sat in her lawyer's waiting room and realized that this was the first time she had been truly alone in almost six months.

She was a wreck.

Even though she knew she hadn't received any new messages, she pulled her phone from her purse and checked. Boone had tried to hide his nervousness about pulling solo parent duty. She had swallowed her own apprehension and assured him he would be fine, reminded him yet again that there was expressed milk in the freezer if needed, then stopped herself just before she gave him a kiss for luck. She'd slipped up enough times already. She wasn't about to add to the total.

Allic, of course, would assure her that her slips were undeniably Freudian in nature. Kate had an unsettling suspicion that in this, at least, old Sigmund might have had a point.

Since she'd taken her phone out anyway, she scrolled through some of the pictures of Boone and Jamie that she'd been taking almost nonstop. She went back to the first ones after Boone arrived, melting a little at the worry lines around his eyes when she had insisted on him holding Jamie. Compare that to the most recent—Boone at the kitchen table, Jamie on his lap. One hand curled around the baby's tummy while the other tapped on the laptop in front of him. Best of all were the matching expressions of concentration on their faces, complete with two indrawn bottom lips.

That shot was going in this year's Christmas card.

She flicked through a few more, mentally chiding herself. For almost six months, she had dreamed of being able to do a solo dash to an appointment or the library or just go for a walk. No diaper bag, no mountain of equipment, just her and freedom. And what was she doing with this long-anticipated time? Looking at pictures of her baby.

Though in fairness, this wasn't the kind of me time she had longed for. Because other than the hours of labor, when the world had shrunk down to just her and her body and the midwife's voice, she had never felt so alone in her life as she did in this waiting room.

This is wrong.

The words kept sliding through her awareness. They'd been filling her head for days now, every time she thought of this meeting to start the divorce. Look at the calendar—note the date approaching—be filled with dread. Look in the closet—try to figure out what to wear to the appointment—close the door fast. Look at Boone—listen to him telling Jamie about alpacas—imagine that voice on the phone, interrupting this appointment, telling her to stop. Telling her he'd changed his mind about the divorce. Telling her to come home to him and their son.

This is wrong.

She grabbed the folder with the paperwork she'd prepared, double-checking with unsteady hands. Marriage license. Birth certificates. Financial disclosures. Preliminary separation agreement.

Everything was there. Everything was organized and prepared and checked off the handy-dandy list provided by the lawyer.

It was too easy. Divorce shouldn't be this easy. A few discussions, some signatures scrawled on papers and then just a matter of time?

There should be more…well, she didn't know what. She didn't want this to be a long, antago-nistic procedure, not for her or for anyone. It was good that she and Boone were being so practical and cooperative. It was very good that uncon-tested divorces were possible, that no one had to be blamed or smeared or turned into a scapegoat. She and Boone had decades of coparenting ahead of them. This was sensible and smart and exactly what she had known would happen from the min-ute he had said, "We could get married," and then added, "Temporarily, of course."

She had known this wasn't a forever thing right from the start. She had sworn up and down that she was good with this, that it made sense, that it was an excellent stopgap measure. This had been for Nana.

There was no need to feel like she had lost something precious—and yet she did.

This is so, so wrong.

She returned to her phone. Pulled up the pic-tures again, this time truly registering another change in them. They went from all Jamie a month ago, to Jamie and Daddy two weeks ago, to equal parts Jamie, Jamie and Daddy, and Boone. Solo Boone.

When she'd first started snapping those Boone-alone pics she had told herself they were for Jamie. He needed to see his father as an independent person, not just as the dude with the goofy smile who was always holding his kid.

Yeah. Because Jamie really needed to see this shot of Boone frowning at whatever he was cooking on the stove. Or this picture of him alone on the porch, hands in pockets, silhouetted against the sunset.

Or this one of a shirtless, muscled Boone hammering up a sweat in the upstairs bathroom.

There in the waiting room, surrounded by fake greenery and muted telephones, she looked the photos and herself in the eye and gave in to the truth.

She wanted Boone to change his mind. From the moment he had walked off the plane, she'd been waiting for him to drop everything, pull her into his arms and announce that he had been an idiot to leave. And if he were to follow it up with a promise that he would never leave again, at least not for longer than a couple of weeks, she would be ecstatic.

Not for Jamie. Rather, not just for Jamie.

For her.

Because somewhere in the past—weeks? months?—she had fallen in love with her husband.

CHAPTER ELEVEN

BOONE WAS READY to sell his soul for functional breasts.

He'd spent the last half hour walking the floor with Jamie, who had made it abundantly clear that he had as much interest in the bottle as he would have in, say, pizza, or beer, or anything that wasn't attached to Kate. Boone had promised himself he wouldn't cave at the first sign of distress. Kate had put on a brave face, but he'd known she was nervous enough about leaving as it was. However, they were rapidly approaching the forty-five-minute sobbing limit he had set for himself when the first tears had appeared.

If he'd known it would go on this long, he would have set that deadline a lot lower.

"Come on, kiddo. You're fine, really. Stop chewing your hand, bud, you're gonna hurt yourself."

Jamie's response was to look up at him, blink, and crumple once again.

Singing. Singing had worked last time. The thing was, thirty-plus minutes of howling had driven every tune Boone knew out of his head. He tried to remember the songs he'd heard Kate crooning as she went about her day, but other than wheels and buses and bunnies, he was lost.

"Maybe something by someone who knows their stuff?" He jiggled Jamie over to his laptop, did a one-handed navigation to YouTube, and clicked on the first playlist that came up. It wasn't until he heard the repeated doorbells that he realized he was entertaining his son with the soundtrack from *The Book of Mormon*.

Oh, that was Father of the Year material, for sure.

Except—it seemed to be working. The sobbing didn't exactly stop, but it did dial down a bit. Only for the first song, though. Once the doorbells of the "Hello" song stopped, Jamie's lip started quivering again.

"Whoa whoa whoa, buddy. Hang on. You want the bells again?"

Back to the first song. Back to the chimes.

Back to a semihappy kid.

Jamie shoved his fist in his mouth and chewed again, but the most pitiful cries had stopped. As long as Boone kept a solid loop of the doorbell song playing, life was grand.

"That's it, buddy. We're getting this. You're doing great, aren't you? You want to try the bottle aga—whoa, whoa, no, don't cry. I'll take it away."

He moved the bottle out of sight, then stopped as a crazy idea came to him.

Two shakes of the bottle, and there were a few drops of milk on his thumb. He brushed it over Jamie's lips.

"Maybe you need to taste skin, too, huh, Jamie? You have a refined palate that can't be fooled by—"

One little mouth fastened around his thumb. One little human vacuum cleaner switched on.

"Holy—good God, kid. And your mother has that attached to her…"

But Jamie had figured out that he was being fooled. And he was far from happy about it.

Things couldn't possibly get worse, so Boone slipped the bottle into the open and protesting mouth. Maybe it was because there was milk on the nipple already. Maybe it was because the doorbells were still chiming in the background. Maybe it was because Jamie had finally decided that something was better than nothing. But this time, he began to suck. Just a couple of times at first, punctuated with enough stops and sobs to convey the message that he was seriously pissed off about this development, but he drank.

The relief that washed through Boone left him looking for a place to sit, fast. He lowered the two of them into a kitchen chair, adjusted his grip around Jamie's stomach and kissed the top of his son's head.

"That's my boy," he said softly. "That's my Jamie."

Jamie grunted but continued eating.

"Okay, kiddo. That's the end of the song. Shh, I'm gonna start it again, don't worry. You're not watching the screen, are you? Mind if I check my email?"

Receiving no protests, Boone carried on.

"Let's see. We have some ads for real estate investment. Yeah, their marketing department needs to work on refining their search skills, don't they? Something from Jill—oh, it's just more stuff about Fashion Week. Okay. And what's this?" His pulse jumped a notch. "Hang on. I applied for a consulting job with these folks. That was... Oh."

Thank you for your interest in our organization. Unfortunately, at this point we are unable to...

He closed his email, just stopping himself in time before he accidentally ended the music, as well.

"That's the third one this week, Jamie. I'm not even getting interviews."

Like you seriously expected anything different?

He knew there were other jobs out there, that he could surely find something to boost his pitiful income. He had years of experience helping mold Project Sonqo into the established organization it was. There had to be other groups, other charities that would be willing to pay for some of that expertise.

But logic was having a hard time making itself heard over the steady drumbeat of *not helping, not helping, not helping* that was even louder than Jamie's cries.

KATE WAS DRIVING home in a slight daze when she realized she had made the mistake of going too long without something to drink. It hit the way it always did, in the form of a wall of fatigue. Luckily for her, she figured it out when she was just a couple of blocks from Bits and Pizzas.

Five minutes later she walked through the door, waved to Allie and Nadine behind the counter and headed straight for the cooler.

"Oh, wow," she said after draining half a bottle of water in one never-ending swallow. "That was seriously overdue."

"Someday you're going to listen to me and set an alarm on your phone to remind you to drink every hour." Allie's tone was that potent mix of exasperation and ridicule that only sisters could pull off.

Kate wanted to protest but figured it would be a

waste of breath, what with the way she was going through more water than Sea World.

"Where's the cutest little guy in the whole world?" Nadine asked.

"Home with his dad."

Nadine crossed her arms. "So it really wasn't a virgin birth?"

"Seriously, Nadine?" Allie grabbed more water and a ginger ale from the cooler. "Come on, Kate. Let's hang out in my office for a minute."

"I don't want to drag you from—"

Allie rolled her eyes. "Oh, please. It's the middle of the afternoon, there's three people here, and Nadine knows how to yell if she needs me. Right, Nadine?"

"I don't know, Allie. You might be setting the bar too high."

"Also, if anyone did give Nadine trouble, she would sass them into submission while waiting for help." Allie pushed the drinks at Kate. "You want a slice?"

"No thanks, I'm—"

"Nadine, could you please bring us a couple of slices of the house special?"

"Sure thing. But it'll cost you an extra hug from Jamie next time he's here."

"Deal," Allie said, while Kate listened with astonishment.

"Did you really just use my baby's affections as a bargaining chip?"

"Damn straight," Allie replied with cheer while pushing Kate toward the back rooms. "So, is this your first time leaving the munchkin with Boone?"

"Yep."

"And your first outing is to my place? I'm honored."

Kate was on the verge of telling her the truth— *Well, I actually went to the lawyer, but then I figured out I was in love with Boone. So even though I kept the appointment because I was already there and I have to talk to Boone about it all and everything is a mess, it might have been a colossal waste of money*—then decided she couldn't do it. Not yet. For one thing, it was all too fresh and new. For another, Allie worried enough already. There was no need to give her more reason to fret and fuss.

"That's right. You were the chosen destination." She waited for a beat while Nadine scuttled in with slices on plates, set them on the battered metal desk and saluted Allie on her way out. "So. You and Cash. Have you told him about our plan?"

"I have."

"And?"

"He's disappointed, but he understands."

"Well, yeah. You're awesome. Who wouldn't want to have you around nonstop?"

Allie blew her a kiss. "He likes the thought of me being with you, though. Said something about that working to his advantage."

"What did he mean by that?"

"I'm not sure. I asked him, but he just laughed and then…um…" Allie raised her eyebrows, Little Miss Innocent. "He got distracted."

Distracted. That seemed like the word of the day. Because Kate was certainly incapable of focus. Well, on anything except going home and putting Jamie down for a nap and getting a little *distracted* herself.

Because her whole reason for keeping things platonic with Boone was to stop herself from falling for him, but she had done that anyway. So what was the point of continuing to deny herself?

"Oh, and you can't change your mind now, because I broke the news that I wouldn't be renewing the lease. Shattered my poor landlady's heart."

Kate had been trying to protect her heart. But now, everything that lay ahead—Boone's departure, the divorce he probably still wanted, his insistence that he wasn't made for a real family—pointed to a guaranteed broken heart in the very near future.

"I've even done some packing. Some stuff is

going to Cash's, but can I start moving things into your place?"

And since she was already in love…and since she was going to get hurt, no matter what…what, precisely, was the point of separate bedrooms?

"Absolutely." She picked up her pizza, already anticipating the pleasure that awaited her. "I'd say it's definitely time to get moving."

KATE KEPT QUIET about her change of heart for the rest of the day. Very, very quiet. The last thing she wanted was to tell Boone she'd changed her mind, only to decide that making love would be a mistake after all.

Well, actually, the *last* thing she wanted was to have to wait until nighttime before she jumped him. But leading him on was a close second.

She decided to use the interminable hours to make sure of her decision. It didn't take long. Any doubts were swept away in the late afternoon, when she left Boone in charge for a few minutes. When she returned, she found him balancing Jamie in one arm, while with the other hand he "helped" Jamie hammer in a nail.

"That's it," Boone said. "You've got it. Soon you'll be fixing things all by yourself."

Neither of them had any idea that she was watching, so she let herself soak up the sight while she could. In those moments, two things became very clear to her. The first was that she didn't think it was humanly possible to love anyone more than she loved the two of them.

The second was that Boone was lying.

Oh, not deliberately. She had no doubt that his past had led to all kinds of reasons he feared parenthood. But after spending years watching teachers and parents interact with children, she could spot a natural with no problem. Boone had it. No one could go from being afraid to touch their child to this moment—in this short a time—without having that solid core of caring and comprehension of what kids needed. Boone had all the instincts to become an excellent father. He just had to believe in himself.

Easier said than done, she knew.

But once she had reaffirmed that she truly loved him, the rest of the equation was a no-brainer. If she had only a few weeks to be the family she wanted to be, then she wasn't wasting another night.

The one decision that remained was to figure out how to get things going.

An hour later, paintbrush in hand, she debated. She could take the direct approach: put Jamie down for the night, walk up to Boone, and say, "Hey sailor, want to have a good time?" There was a certain simplicity that appealed to her.

But while her body was all for anything that

would reduce the distance between upright and horizontal as fast as was humanly possible, her heart resisted. In many ways this would be their first time. She wanted it to be memorable, filled with as much wonder and laughter as their initial close encounter of the awesome kind.

The answer came to her as they finished dinner.

"I think I got more paint on me than on the walls today," she said, as casually as she could manage. "How about if you give Jamie his bath while I grab a shower?"

First hint, delivered. She knew it had hit home by the way he glanced toward her and then dragged his gaze away, so slowly and forcefully that she knew he was imagining her beneath the water, the same way she pictured him in the clanking upstairs shower. Slick skin and firm muscles and a whole lot of soaping going on.

"Sure," he said, but she heard the thread of need in his voice and grinned. Only to herself, of course.

She made a fast lunge around her room before she hit the shower, gathering a bucket of bath supplies which she carried out to the kitchen.

"Here you go," she said. "You guys have fun."

Boone kept his eyes steadily on Jamie as he said, "You, too."

"Oh, I will." She sighed. "It's been months since I was able to have a shower without worrying about someone waking up or crying in his crib. I intend to take full advantage of it. There are parts of me that haven't seen a loofah since I don't know when."

Was it wrong to revel in the way he closed his eyes and breathed in, sharp and fast?

She sashayed out of the kitchen and made a beeline to her bedroom and the tiny en suite bathroom, where she immediately stripped and jumped in. She hadn't been kidding about the paint. More than that, she wanted every bit of skin to glow, to smell the way it had that first night—not like powder and spit-up, but like primrose and promises.

Thoroughly scrubbed, she turned her attention to her nails. The purple streak might be long gone from her hair, but she could still rock the Electric Violet polish on her toes. She left the water running as she worked, sending a mental apology to every drought-stricken part of the world.

"Just this once," she whispered. "Just so he has longer to imagine me in there and get truly desperate."

Toes properly pimped out, her next task was her hair. It was, alas, too short now to pull off the cinnamon-bun effect. But she could still fancy it up. The rhythm of a French braid came back to her fingers quickly.

She crossed her fingers that other rhythms would return just as easily.

A spritz of cologne. A hint of lip gloss. And then, at last, the white bathrobe she had worn that night she crashed the convention. Except this time, the only thing she was wearing beneath it was herself.

She turned off the water, opened the door a crack and listened. She couldn't make out words, but the steady rise and fall of Boone's voice told her that all was well. She stepped into the bedroom, made sure all the essentials were within easy reach on the bedside table, and patted the pillow.

"Be back soon," she promised the bed, and off she went.

Heart thudding, she padded barefoot into the kitchen. Boone had Jamie on his shoulder, walking back and forth while doing the Ward Off Trouble jiggle.

"A few more minutes, buddy," she heard him say as she approached. "I know you're hungry, but your mom really needs a chance to—"

"Hey," she called as she entered. "Everyone survived, I see."

Boone turned. She assumed he had planned to say something. But he stopped in his tracks, mouth slack, eyes wide, as he took her in.

She waited, letting him look. She needed this.

He needed this. This moment when nothing was said but everything was understood, when she was pretty sure he was physically incapable of speech or movement, when need thickened and perfumed the air as strongly as the first lilacs of spring.

"Kate?" he said at last, and the hope she heard there told her that she had been so, so right to play it this way.

"Come on," she said, crooking her finger. "You're going to learn how to put Jamie to bed."

But he didn't move. "Jesus, Kate," he said. "Are you sure?"

"Not a doubt in my mind."

"But you said—"

"I was wrong." She couldn't let him list the reasons she had given. If that happened, she would have to explain. And even though she longed to tell him the truth, that she loved him, she knew he wasn't ready to hear those words. She wasn't going to do or say anything that might push him away.

Instead, she padded into the kitchen, reached for Jamie, and slid one hand up Boone's chest.

"You go ahead and shower while I feed him."

He nodded and turned. Too late, she realized he was headed for the upstairs bathroom.

"Nuh-uh. Down here." She hooked a finger over the neckline of his T-shirt and backed toward her room, pulling him in her wake. He still seemed befuddled, but when they stepped over her threshold he seemed to catch the mood.

"Maybe I'm just forgetful," he said, "but I think we've already had a few lessons in how to put Jamie to bed. Are you saying you haven't taught me everything?"

"More like parceling out the lessons. Teaching you each piece as you're ready."

"And you think I'm ready now?"

She deliberately dropped her gaze, then raised it to meet his with a smile. "Oh, I am one hundred percent positive of that."

With that, she let go of his shirt, gave him a little nudge to turn him around and—slowly, deliberately—planted a kiss in the middle of his back. Even through the woven cotton she could feel the way every muscle tightened.

"Go," she said, giving him a little push toward the shower, where she knew he would be surrounded by the lingering scent of her body wash.

"I'll be teasing him without even trying," she whispered to Jamie as she settled in the rocking chair. "Two points for efficiency."

But it was more than that, she admitted as she rocked and hummed, burped and relocated. She might be used to having Boone watch while she nursed their child, but tonight, she didn't want him to see her as a mother. Tonight, she wanted to be just Kate and Boone. She wanted the night to close down around them the way it had before, blocking out everything else but them.

She couldn't wait.

In one of his rare instances of excellent timing, Jamie finished and she could put herself back together before Boone opened the door. Someday she would remember this and forgive the kiddo for forgetting to make his bed or pick up his toys, and he would never know why.

She realized, belatedly, that she hadn't thought about fresh clothes for Boone. Though as she let herself openly and eagerly drink in the sight of his bare chest above the towel riding low on his hips, she couldn't say she was complaining about that oversight.

He hovered in the doorway. Waiting to see if she had changed her mind? Oh, no, no. She was going to disabuse him of that notion right away.

"Come here." She crooked her finger, drawing him over, pointing to the bed. Once he was perched on the edge she and Jamie snuggled in beside him. "Ready?"

It was a safe bet that the slightly strangled sound he made meant he had passed *ready* a long time ago.

"See, you know how to give him a bath and change his diaper and all that good stuff, but I haven't done anything about the songs."

"There are songs?"

"Yes, indeed. They're the most important part of bedtime. At least, they will be until he's ready for stories."

"I can think of a few things that might be even better than stories."

"Really? You'll have to tell me about them later."

Oh, how she had missed this. Sex was wonderful and awesome and mind-blowing and all those good things, and she was most definitely looking forward to having her entire being hijacked by everything that was Boone, but this playing, this teasing, this drawing things out—this was just as important in its own way. She was having fun.

"It's not just wedding DJs who need to know the right song for the right time," she explained with mock seriousness. "It's one of the major parenting skills. Now, we can't do any of the bouncy ones, because he just ate." She refused to have her second First Time be accented with Eau de Spew. "But there are plenty of others. Like 'Itsy Bitsy Spider.'"

"I think I've learned that one." He raised his palms, stared at them for a moment, then added, "But I'll be dipped if I can remember what to do with my hands."

"Like this." She held her hands in front of her—awkwardly, since she was reaching around a bobbing baby—and touched opposite thumbs to forefingers. "That's right. Then you twist, like so."

It took him a couple of attempts but he caught on. "Oh, yeah. Now I remember. Like riding a bicycle," he said.

"Mmm-hmm," she agreed. "Now." She used her hand to draw circles in the air. "Next one. 'The bum-ble bee, goes a-round the tree, with a *bzzzzzz*!'" She took Boone's hand and guided it to Jamie's tummy. Two sets of chortles—one deep, one delighted—surrounded her.

Oh, if she could freeze a moment to live forever, this could be the one.

They moved from spiders and bees to monkeys jumping on the bed and swinging in the trees, then to slower, quieter ones. Her pulse jumped as she felt the familiar heaviness against her arm that meant Jamie was on the verge of slumber.

But there was one last song she had to get through first.

"This is the one we do before I put him down every night. No actions, just words. And if Paul McCartney ever hears this, I won't be responsible for the consequences." She gathered Jamie onto her shoulder and swayed back and forth while she launched into the words she had cobbled together over long sleepless hours when the only songs she could remember were oldies. Which was why her son's favorite lullaby was a slowed-down take on "She Loves You."

"Mommy sings to you, and she loves to teach you ga-a-ames. Daddy's in Peru, but he loves you just the sa-a-ame."

She caught Boone's eye. "Chorus," she whispered, and he got the message, joining in.

"We love you, yeah, yeah, yeah. We love you, yeah, yeah, yeah. We love you, yeah, yeah, yeah, yeah."

When she finished, Boone whispered against her ear, "I am never going to be able to listen to the Beatles again."

A heady mix of anticipation, nervousness and uncertainty bubbled in her veins as she eased off the bed and settled Jamie in his crib. All of a sudden, she didn't know what she should do next. The playfulness that had brought her this far seemed to have been sucked out of the room, leaving a giant looming pile of hesitation in its place. Not about whether or not she should do this. Oh, hell, no. But it had been so long that she wasn't sure she remembered how to get from point A to point B.

"He, um, usually falls asleep pretty quickly," she said in a low voice—easy, since Boone was standing directly behind her with his hands on her shoulders. "But we should probably move out of his sight."

"Any place in particular we should go?"

CHAPTER TWELVE

THE BED WAS the logical location, but Kate found she wasn't ready for that. Not yet. Instead, she took his hand and guided him to the pillow-lined window seat. She started to sit beside him, both feet on the floor, but he shook his head.

"Hang on." He positioned himself sideways in the window, bracing himself at one end, then tugged her down so she was nestled against him. Her back was against his chest and his arms were around her waist and his legs stretched out on either side of hers. She closed her eyes and melted into him, not sure if it was more calming or arousing to be cradled against him this way. It felt as if bubbles were pushing out of her veins and popping against her skin, leaving it prickly and keenly aware of every breath he took, every play of his muscles against her.

This. I have to remember this.

For a few breaths they stayed silent. Anticipating. Reacquainting. Their right hands were laced together, but her left one rested on his thigh and his was nestled tantalizingly close to the underside of her breast, and just sitting there, she could swear the Eagerness Meter was jumping by the second.

"I don't know how to say this without sounding like I have a one-track mind." His words were low against her ear, the vibrations tickling her back and rippling through her. "But right after I booked my flight—before you set the, um, ground rules for while I was here—I did some reading. About, you know." He kissed the spot below her ear. "The first time after having a baby."

"I'm glad you did. It cuts down on how much I'll have to explain."

"Oh, consider me educated. And mildly terrified." He laughed against her hair, sending sparkshivers down her spine. "Some of them made it sound so scary that I started to wonder how anyone ever...and then I reminded myself how many couples have second or third kids, and I thought, okay, this must be survivable."

Second or third kids. "Kind of like labor," she said, keeping it light to cover the sudden twist in her heart. What she would give to have another baby with Boone, to see what miracles their genes could produce another time...

No. She wasn't going to waste time on *who knows* and *if only*. Not tonight, not for the rest of their time together.

Instead, she tipped her face up to look at him as directly as was possible.

"I'll tell you if there's a problem. I promise."

He kissed her forehead. "I don't want to hurt you, okay?"

"I'll be *fine*."

"Just swear to me you won't let me hurt you."

Wrapped in the cocoon of his arms, it was easy to feel the muscles of his biceps tensing, to hear the apprehension in his voice. And while a part of her was blown away by his concern, something about it felt off. Too much. Like that moment when she'd first handed Jamie to him in the bathroom and he'd stepped back.

But this was different.

Or was it?

What if I drop him?

I'm sorry I made you back up.

Swear to me you won't let me hurt you.

She pulled herself out of his embrace and spun to face him, kneeling before him, her hands on his shoulders and her eyes locked on his. "Listen to me, Jackson Boone, and listen up good, okay? I trust you. No—I *know* you. I know that you have overcome odds that would have left other men knocked to the ground. I know that you're full of care and compassion, even though there was practically none of it in your life for so long. And I know—well, I suspect—that you think your past is some sort of guarantee that you're going to hurt me or Jamie or both of us."

His fast intake of breath told her she'd hit that nail straight on the head.

"But let me tell you this. I might have spent most of the last year on a different frickin' continent, but before that I spent an awful lot of hours with you, and never once did I see anything that made me fear for my safety. Not. Once. Just like I've never worried about you with Jamie." She placed her palm on his chest, spreading her fingers wide. "All I've seen is a truly amazing father who keeps getting better every day."

He wasn't convinced. His doubts were reflected in his clouded eyes, in the tight line of his jaw.

"You have to believe me, Boone. I know what I'm talking about. Day care director, remember? I've been trained in recognizing problems. I've had to make the calls to Children's Aid, and trust me, I've never been wrong about a situation. Do you honestly think I would let you near Jamie if I had any fears about you?"

"I…I guess I hadn't thought about that." He swallowed. "But—"

"But nothing. Boone. Listen. Do you have any idea how easy it would have been for me to send you back to Peru without ever telling you I was pregnant?"

The light dawning in his eyes gave her hope that she was getting through.

"I could have, you know. And I would have.

Don't think for a minute that I wouldn't have kept it a secret if I had even the teensiest, tiniest worry about you." She crept forward, sliding her hands back to his shoulders, daring a light kiss on his forehead. "But I didn't do it. I told you right away. I did everything I could think of to make sure you were a part of our son's life, and I'm still doing that, and I'll keep on doing it, because you are a wonderful, loving, totally together father. And Jamie is beyond lucky to have you in his life, and I am damn lucky to have you as my—"

Husband. She wanted to say *husband* but caught herself in the nick of time.

"My partner," she finished, sliding higher and closer, curling forward to kiss his chin. "In parenting. And in laughter. And in bed, because, Boone, if you had any idea how much I want you right now, you—"

The rest of her words were crushed out of her by his swift embrace. Silenced by his kiss. Sent squeaking when he swung his feet to the ground and grabbed her around the waist and tumbled her onto the bed, falling beside her, around her, above her. He grabbed her wrists and pulled them above her head and stared down at her, his gaze filled with all the heat and need she remembered in every aching cell, but this time there was more. She couldn't place it until he kissed her again. Slowly this time. Tenderly. Gentle and lingering and yet with more emotion than she could ever remember.

"Thank you," he whispered, and she had to swallow down the sudden rush of tears.

God, she loved him.

She wrapped her arms around him and pulled him tighter, clinging to the rightness of being with him again and pushing aside the truth she hadn't dared say—that nothing he could do would compare to the pain she was going to face when he left.

WHEN BOONE WOKE the next morning, his first thought was that he couldn't remember the last time he'd slept so soundly.

His second thought was that his deep slumber was only partly due to the sex, though he wasn't going to discount that. But he was pretty sure the main reason he'd slept so well was because of Kate's ability to hear beyond his words.

Do you have any idea how easy it would have been for me to send you back to Peru without ever telling you I was pregnant?

He had never thought of that. And the thing was, she was absolutely right. She could have broken up with him as soon as she knew Jamie was on the way, or at least before things became obvious. He could have gone back without ever even suspecting. And given her own experience with

her father, Kate would have known that sometimes silence was the best choice.

Instead, she had given him both the gift of their
son and the gift of her trust.

He had no idea what he'd done to deserve any
of this. But he was damned well not taking it for
granted.

In the early morning light, he drank in the sight
of this woman who had upended everything about
his world. She lay on her side half under the covers, the blankets pulled haphazardly across her
torso and one arm tucked beneath her pillow.
There was a thin blue line on her thigh, like a
vein suddenly made visible. He stared at it in lazy
surprise. Had that been there before? Or was that
one of the changes brought about by nine months
of carrying their son?

He hadn't been around to watch her stomach
grow large except via video feed, had never placed
his hand on her abdomen and felt the kick from
inside. But he could look now.

Slowly he eased the blankets back and gently
touched his finger to her stomach. Was it softer
than he remembered? Yeah. A little. The pink
lines running up and down her lower abdomen
were new, too. Were these stretch marks? He tried
to remember everything he had read while she was
pregnant. There had been something about those
lines, something that made them sound almost

like a trial to avoid, what with all the discussions of how to prevent them and the reassurances that they would fade over time. He didn't know why. Other than looking like they might have hurt a bit, he didn't see any problem with them. They were like a tattoo to him, an unspoken message to anyone who saw them that this body had made a miracle.

His gentle touch hadn't seemed to bother her so he flattened his palm over her abdomen, wondering how it had felt to house someone inside her. She had tried to describe the sensation of Jamie's kicks and twists, but it was still beyond his imagination. Not the physical part as much as the thought that there was another person living within. How the hell did women walk around and carry on with their everyday lives as if this was just a regular thing, when they were busy making another whole person? Jesus. If it were up to him, pregnant women would be entitled to nine months of nonstop massages and pampering, complete with a steady stream of fresh fruit and personal chefs.

This body—this woman—had given him the most amazing gifts in his life. He had to let her know how much it meant to him.

He had to make sure she was able to stay in the house she loved.

A sense that he was being watched had him

shifting his focus from her body to her face. She watched him with a lazy smile.

"My eyes are up here," she said, tapping the side of her temple.

He grinned. "Yeah, but I've spent a lot more time looking at those since I got here than I've spent looking at these." He tickled the valley between her breasts. She giggled softly and reached for the blanket.

"You might want to keep the exploration to just your eyes at this point. Things are ready for the morning nursing session, if you get my drift."

He wasn't too worried about it, but since she seemed concerned, he happily shifted position to lie down and pull her flush against him.

"So," he said against her hair. "I think we got a little carried away last night."

"Do you know that was the first thing you said to me the morning after our first night together?"

"I did?" His memories of that morning centered around a whole lot of bliss and a boatload of thanks that it was a Sunday and neither of them had to run off anywhere.

"Mmm-hmm. I have to tell you, as morning-after lines go, that was a pretty good one. Especially because you didn't vanish in the night."

Funny, that. He had never been one for simply disappearing—he always said goodbye, in a note at the very least—but staying all night hadn't been his usual style. Never the first time he slept with someone, for sure.

Not until Kate.

"I had to stick around. Had to make sure I'd made a good impression on you."

"Oh, trust me, you had." Her smile softened. "But you made an even better one by staying."

"Best nonmove I ever made."

"Really?" She hesitated, then added, "I'm serious, Boone. I know nothing turned out the way we planned, but for me, even though I could have lived without the shock, I just can't imagine what it would be like without Jamie." She snuggled closer to him. "Or without seeing what it did to you, how you stepped up, how you're trying so hard to be the best dad you can."

He didn't even have to think. "Yeah. I mean it."

Even he could see that he was making amazing strides in the fatherhood department. But it was killing him that he had yet to find a way to keep her and Jamie in the house.

The loan was a bust. He could try another bank, but realistically, finding one that would say yes was as likely as winning the lottery. Jill and Craig were already paying him as much as Project Sonqo could spare. Consulting jobs... Yeah, that had been a fail so far, though he was going to keep trying. Maybe if he applied for more grants...or if the project could find a celebrity in need of a cause…

A soft cry from the crib had Kate letting out a little moan.

"It awakes."

Boone laughed softly. "Don't let him hear you. He'll get a complex."

"That's my job as his mother." She stretched and frowned as another cry sounded, more insistent this time. "Make you a deal. I'll go to the bathroom. You do diaper duty. Meet you back here in five."

"You got it."

He hopped out of the bed and padded over to the crib, where Jamie rocked from side to side, hand in his mouth. To say that his son was less than thrilled to see Daddy instead of Mommy would have been an understatement.

"Believe me, buddy, I know. I think she's all that and a side of fries, too. But we have to cut her a break every once in a while, you know?" He carried Jamie into the office and placed him on the changing table. "She's more than just your favorite feeding mechanism. Believe it or not, there are babies all over the world who like bottles just as much as—"

He froze, the diaper half off.

The bottles beneath the porch.

Before Boone fixed the porch, he had widened the hole enough that he could lower himself through it and fetch the bottles. Despite his jokes that he'd been hoping to find a treasure map in one of them, they had all been empty. A quick online search told him that even though they appeared to be from the Prohibition era, they weren't worth enough to even try to sell them to an antiques shop. Kate had insisted on keeping them, claiming they would make perfect containers for flowers and candles, but it seemed that was as useful as they would be.

"But why were they there in the first place?"

Jamie's response came in the form of a perfect arc of pee that shot straight into the air and just missed Boone's arm.

"Holy—okay, wait, hang on." He slapped the diaper back into place and grabbed some wipes to deal with the damage. But even as he mopped and fake-scolded Jamie, his mind whirled.

Kate saw the bottles as proof that Charlie had worked on the house, but did that make sense? Charlie wouldn't have left them lying around on the ground. If he was using them to transport booze, he needed them to be clean. And if he'd needed a place to hide them, there had to be places where it would be easier to retrieve them.

"No one would build a porch over a pile of bottles," Boone said as he lined up the fastenings on Jamie's sleeper. "So someone had to put them there later."

It could be that someone had simply been trying to hide evidence of some surreptitious nips.

But there was also a carefully hidden painting. And a quilt with a hidden footprint. And if someone—say, Great-great-uncle Fred—were to stumble across something secreted away in the house built by his brother the bootlegger...and if Fred didn't dare reveal his findings, maybe because there could be something illegal about them... but if he wanted to leave a few clues for future generations...well, what would be the one item that everyone would associate with a rumrunner?

"Jamie, I might be totally off the wall here, but I have a feeling your Great-great-whatever-uncle Fred might have left us one of Charlie's calling cards."

BOONE SPENT THE next few days pondering the treasure.

When Kate ran to the library, he accompanied her, grabbing some local history books. "So I can appreciate where Jamie will be growing up," he said when Kate looked at his reading material with raised eyebrows.

When she was busy with Jamie, he grabbed his laptop to research legends, lost treasures and people who had stumbled across unexpected things hidden in their walls.

When he was on the roof, he pulled out his phone and examined the photo of Daisy's quilt, comparing it to one he managed to snap of the painting.

His first inclination was to check the turret. He could understand it not being in the painting, being a later addition and all, but why wouldn't it have been included in the quilt? After all, Maggie remembered Fred inspecting Daisy's work and deeming it correct. Unless the turret had been added significantly later in Fred's life, that is, which struck Boone as highly unlikely.

No. There had to be something more to it.

He spent hours going over every inch of the house, stomping on floors, pounding on walls. He even poked his head into the small space at the roof's peak, the equivalent of an attic, but all he'd found for his efforts was a lot of dust and the rodent skeletons that Kate had anticipated when she'd opened the cupboard.

When his hunt yielded nothing, he was forced to reconsider. Unless old Fred had been hiding money between the studs, there simply wasn't enough space anywhere. And since the legend said that whatever Charlie found was of interest to American authorities, Boone thought it must be something more significant than cash.

No. Whatever Charlie had found, it had to be something major. Probably bigger than the proverbial breadbox. The only place to hide something like that would be in the basement.

Boone waited until Kate was settled upstairs with her paint and her roller before he headed down the carved stone steps into the place she had referred to as the crypt. It was an apt name. He hadn't been this creeped out since the time his mother had locked him a closet because he'd got into her wallet.

Halfway down the steps, he froze. He had forgotten all about that.

"Probably a good thing," he said out loud. Because it sure as hell wasn't a memory anyone would want to keep.

He thought of Jamie. Imagined him at five or six or seven. Imagined pushing him into a closet and closing the door and walking away from the sound of small fists pounding against the door, away from the crying and the pleas and the—

He jerked away from the thought, so violently that he almost lost his balance. What kind of person could do that to a kid?

Back when Kate was pregnant and he'd had to deal with the fact that he was about to be a father, he'd forced himself to read up on what makes a parent abusive. He knew that it was likely someone had done something equally heinous to his mother. It was cold comfort.

He wondered if she had ever vowed to never do anything like that to her kids, only to crumble when things got rough.

Kate believed in him. That helped. But still he wondered if he was strong enough to break the family tradition.

"Enough." He picked his way down the remainder of the steps, ducking his head to avoid whacking himself on a giant wooden beam.

"I'll give you this much, Charlie old boy, you sure knew how to build a house that would last."

But had Charlie built anything special into the place? That was the question.

Boone cautiously crossed the stone floor, wishing he'd thought to grab a sweatshirt. Everything was so gray. So cold. So harsh. He almost hoped he didn't find anything down here, because he could think of a whole lot of other places where he would rather spend his time. Like upstairs, holding Kate. Bright, warm, soft Kate.

Yeah. That was better.

The turret was located in the northeast corner of the house. It took him a few seconds to get oriented, and then a few more to figure out why the stone walls didn't veer away from their straight lines to take the circular shape he'd expected.

"A crawl space? Seriously?"

Sure enough, the corner where the turret should branch off was as square as anything else in the basement, at least most of the way up. But the top quarter opened up to a yawning darkness that was guaranteed to be the stuff of nightmares.

"Great," he muttered. "Just ducky."

Now he knew how Indiana Jones felt when he pried up the stone and saw the Asp and Cobra Welcoming Committee.

"Hot shower," he said, boosting himself up. He was definitely going to need some kind of reward to get himself through this. "Long hot shower. Cold beer. Soft Kate." He forced a grin. "Hot Kate. Needy Kate."

At least now he had a more pleasant explanation for the blood pounding in his ears.

He wriggled forward, forcing himself to go slow, reciting the alphabet in English, then Spanish, then Quechua, just so he'd have something to hear other than the rustling sounds that could only mean rodents of the live and frightened kind.

"Just so long as you're not rabid," he said, aiming his light in a slow path along the floor, the walls, the cracks.

Nothing.

He made himself keep going. He wasn't coming this far only to miss something important because he was too chickenshit to go the distance. But he had to admit that it was nothing but sweet relief when he was able to say nope, nothing in there. He had no idea he could wriggle backward as fast as he did on his way out.

His feet hit the ground. He straightened with the kind of groan that came from the deepest parts of him, turned—

And let loose with a totally unheroic yelp when he came face-to-face with a frowning Kate.

"Jesus, Kate," he said when he could breathe again. "You almost gave me a heart attack!"

"You? How do you think I felt when I came down here and saw feet sticking out of the crawl space?"

"Where's Jamie? And why are you here?"

She crossed her arms. "Napping, and I should ask you the same thing."

He could try to talk his way out of it, but he had a feeling she was going to put it all together anyway. "Looking for the treasure. Can we finish this upstairs? If I don't have a shower in the next three minutes, I think I might self-destruct."

He stepped past her in a beeline for the stairs. Behind him, the silence stretched, pulsed, and then—

"Hang on. What do you mean, looking for the treasure?"

Despite himself, he grinned.

This was gonna be interesting.

CHAPTER THIRTEEN

LOOKING FOR THE TREASURE? What the heck was he talking about?

Kate paced back and forth outside the bathroom, listening for the sounds of clothing hitting the ground. Boone had refused to say anything. "After I shower," was his answer to all her questions as she followed him up the stairs. She had trailed him into the bedroom just in time to see him enter the bathroom and close the door, leaving her with a sudden, painful insight into how it felt to be four years old and begging for Christmas hints.

But she wasn't a little kid. And she had a very adult arsenal of weapons at her disposal.

So as soon as she heard the rush of the water and the scrape of the shower curtain being pulled back, she stripped out of her own clothes and let herself into the bathroom.

She'd never thought she would be grateful there was no lock on the bathroom door. Huh. First time for everything.

She crept across the floor, grabbed hold of the curtain and gave it a yank.

"What the—"

But Boone's question died as she stepped into the shower.

"Slide over," she ordered. "The crypt always makes me cold."

Smart man that he was, he took a step back. She moved forward, positioning herself both beneath the spray and flush against him.

"Now," she said sweetly, "tell me about your treasure hunt."

"Is that the only reason you're in here with me?"

"Absolutely." She dipped slightly at the knees, rubbing ever so slightly against him. "Though you know, I do need to get cleaned up."

With that, she reached over and past his shoulder, aiming for the body wash on the shelf. As she had totally expected, she was intercepted before she could grab it.

"You might have to drag the words out of me," he said against her ear.

"Is that a promise or a threat?"

"Which one do you want it to be?"

She laughed and licked water from the crook of his neck. "Talk treasure to me, Boone."

"I think it's in the house. Have you ever done this before?"

"Done what?"

"This." His hand slid between her legs. "In the shower."

"Can't say that I have. Why…um…are you serious about this? Why do you think it's in the house?"

It took him a minute to answer, probably because she was kissing the corner of his mouth. "Why is what in the house?" he said at last.

She dragged her mind away from the rhythm taking over her body and back to the matter at— no, not hand. Bad word. Well, very good word, but not if she wanted to…

"The treasure," she managed. "You think it's— wait, I'm supposed to be torturing you—"

"Trust me, you are."

She wrenched herself away from his probing fingers. "I haven't even started."

With that, she began kissing her way down his chest, her lips sliding over a muscled landscape until she hit his belly button. She was swimming in a sea of water and skin and steam and soap, and she couldn't decide if she should prolong the moment or rush forward the way her body wanted.

On the other hand, who said she had to choose?

"Tell me about the treasure, Boone." Her tongue swirled around his belly button. Her hands gripped his hips. His hands tightened on her shoulders and she grinned. All this and she'd barely even started.

"The bottles," he said. "The quilt. The…the… the round thing."

"This round thing?" she asked with a strategic squeeze.

"Turret."

Okay, she hadn't expected that. She glanced up, unsure if she had heard right or if the rush of blood southward had robbed him of all his mental faculties. "You think Charlie hid the treasure in the turret?"

He shook his head back and forth, slowly. It might have been a negative. But since his movements were in perfect sync with those of her hand, it was difficult to be sure.

"It's not there. I checked."

"So you looked under it. In the crawl space."

He gripped her under the arms, hauled her upright, and sandwiched her against the wall of the shower. "I have a thing for exploring places. Empty…hot…spaces."

She would have pointed out that the crawl space was anything but hot, but he was kissing her and pushing against her, and the water was pounding, and breathing was almost impossible. So she wasn't going to quibble about something like a *word* when there were so many better things to do with her time. And mouth. And hands.

She wriggled sideways, searching for a better

angle, but her foot slipped and her arm flew up and her elbow bashed into the wall.

"Ow!"

He stopped kissing her neck. "Are you okay?"

"I just wish the shower was bigger," she said before realizing the golden opportunity she was missing. "I mean, no. I'm horribly wounded. Boo-boos everywhere. You'd better kiss them."

"Everywhere?"

"Everywhere."

Boone was as good as his word. And soon, Kate learned that when it came to shower stalls, size most definitely didn't matter.

THEY WERE LYING in the bed, where they had collapsed after dragging their wobbly-kneed selves out of the shower. Boone ran a lazy hand over her arm while images of the last half hour or so floated through his memory. She had said something in the shower. Something that had actually pierced the fog of desire surrounding his brain, something that had made him think, *Wait, that could be important.*

But then he'd given in to the best distraction he'd ever known. He could honestly say that he had absolutely no regrets.

"Ouch." She rubbed her elbow. "I really whacked this."

"If you're trying to get more kisses out of me, you're—"

He stopped as the memory he'd been hunting for crashed into his brain.

I just wish the shower was bigger.

"Why is the shower so small?"

She blinked up at him. "What?"

"Your bathroom. It's built in that space behind the hall, but it feels smaller than that."

"Isn't that just an optical illusion? You know, because there's so much shoved in there."

"No." He sat up, staring through the open door into the bathroom, trying to measure it against the bits of the hall that he could see. "Even with the pipes behind the wall it should be bigger."

"Maybe that was all the space Nana and Poppy thought they needed."

"But are they the ones who added it? Or did Fred do it as part of the turret project?"

She shook her head. "Boone. Do you seriously think that whatever Charlie found, it's hidden in this house?"

He didn't even hesitate. "I do."

"Okay, but—I mean, I know it's always been this possibility in the back of my mind, but... She rolled backward to peek at Jamie, who had started rustling around, then scooted in closer to Boone, her voice lower. " I can follow your logic about the turret, and why you were poking around down in the crypt. But Boone, why… I mean, yes, it's cool to think there might really be something, but—"

He had to tell her the truth.

"I want you to stay in this house."

It was easy to follow the train of her thoughts by the expressions racing across her face. Confusion…hesitation…disbelief, and then, suddenly, comprehension.

Followed immediately by resistance.

"Boone. Why would you… I mean, I—we—have a plan. I'm fine with selling this place. Really I am."

"You might be fine with it. But is it what you want? And what about Jamie?" He knew he'd scored a point by the way she jerked, slight but unmistakable. "This house is such a huge part of your family's history. Don't you think Jamie deserves to grow up here?"

"Honestly…okay. I admit it. If I were queen of the world, moving wouldn't be my first choice." She ducked her head. "But since I don't see a crown on my head, I guess I have to be like everyone else who can't get what they want all the time and just…deal."

"Not if I have anything to say about it."

She sat up straighter. "Boone—"

"Kate." The words stalled in his mouth. *I can't be here with you. I can't give you the family you want. I can't be the husband you deserve.* "You love this place."

"I love a lot of things that I can't have."

His heart skipped a beat.

"But I'll be fine," she continued with a defiant lift of her chin.

"I want you to be more than just fine." His hand closed over hers. She gazed down at their meshed fingers and swallowed hard.

"I applied for a loan," he said quietly.

"You *what*?"

"Turned down in record time. I applied for some consulting jobs, things I can do part-time from Peru. No idea if any of them will come through, though a couple of 'em have potential. But if we could find the treasure…"

"Which probably doesn't exist."

"Your logical head tells you that." He tapped her chest. "But what about here?"

Her silence was all the answer he needed.

"I don't have a lot I can give to Jamie," he said. "Especially when it comes to things like family history."

Her eyes softened.

"But you—you have history all around. Memories. In every nail and board of this house."

"Boone." She bit her lip. "Those are important, I won't pretend they're not, but…"

"*But*, think of it this way. If there's something

here…and if I can find it…then I'll have given Jamie something, too. It will be from you *and* from me."

He hadn't even known how important that was to him until he said it, but as soon as the words were out, he recognized their truth.

She watched him, her hand clutching the sheet to her breasts, her face unreadable.

"I don't think there's anything here, Boone." Her words were gentle, as if she were telling a kid that his dog had run away. "And even though I understand what you're saying, and it's kind of the sweetest, most amazing thing I've ever heard, I think you're chasing rainbows here."

"Maybe. But you know what they say is at the end of the rainbow."

"If you don't find anything… I don't want you beating yourself up if we can't stay here."

His pulse quickened. She was going to say yes.

"There's something here. It's too much to be a coincidence."

"So let's say you find something. A treasure chest, or whatever Charlie might have stashed somewhere. Who's to say that it's worth anything?"

"Who's to say that it isn't?"

Her nod was slow, but hey. Agreement was agreement.

"Kate." He tipped her chin up so he could look

her in the eye. "I saw you when we were opening up the cupboard. You can't tell me that you don't want to do this."

"I…" She sighed, but he was pretty sure it was directed at herself, not him.

Then he remembered the rest of what she had said when they were opening the cupboard. "You don't want to lose the dream, do you?"

"It sounds so silly."

"It does. But dreams are what make us human, right?"

"Now you sound like an anthropologist or something."

"Hey. When you live near Machu Picchu, you hang out with a lot of those types." He waited a beat before adding, "Make you a deal. I'll be okay with not finding anything if you're okay with letting go of all the possibilities."

Her nose wrinkled. "That didn't really make sense."

"That's what happens when you climb in the shower with me. All ability to think, totally gone."

"Ooh, now I feel powerful."

"You should." No one else had ever had this impact on him before, that was for damn sure.

"So whad'ya say? Want to see what's behind the bathroom?"

"Okay." She placed a hand on his arm. "But I

swear, if there's anything alive back there, you will be dead meat."

"You got it, babe."

It took Kate exactly thirty-three minutes to regret her decision. That was the point when Boone finished pulling on his jeans, making some rapid measurements that confirmed his suspicion that the bathroom should have been bigger and slammed a sledgehammer into the wall of the office.

"He's lucky I love him." Safely out on the porch, well beyond the line of destruction, she soothed Jamie, who had been peacefully resting on her shoulder until the ominous *whack* made him startle. "Because this in itself could be grounds for that divorce I don't want anymore."

Which, she admitted, was just as contradictory and messed up a statement as anything Boone had said while talking her into this harebrained scheme. But what could she say? She'd been a goner the moment he'd said he wanted to have some sort of family history worth passing on. No one with a heart could have resisted that.

Plus, Boone hadn't been the only one still feeling the effects of the shower.

"At least he made the destruction totally worth my while," she said, then remembered who she was talking to. "Oh. Scratch that. I didn't say anything inappropriate."

At this rate, she would forget everything she knew about how to talk to kids right around the time her maternity leave ended.

Then she remembered that Boone would be back in Peru when her leave ended, and there wouldn't be anyone rendering her speechless or senseless.

Crap. She wasn't supposed to think of that. She was supposed to be filling herself with joy right now, not counting the days in dread.

Except they had only a couple of weeks left. And she probably should start preparing herself.

"It's still about six months until I go back to work," she said, patting Jamie's back. "Maybe we could convince Daddy to come back then. To help with the transition, and all that."

She allowed herself a moment to imagine what it would be like, having Boone here to help get Jamie ready in the mornings. To come home after those first days back at work to find the fridge stocked and dinner waiting and Boone eager to take Jamie from her so she could pour a glass of wine and stare at the ceiling for half an hour. To listen to Boone giving Jamie a bath while she washed the dishes, and know that there was still time to sit down together, just watching the hockey game or reading side by side. To roll over and kiss him good-night, and then maybe kiss him again, and again, and...

"Kate? Katie, you're gonna want to see this!"

Startled out of her reverie, she hurried into the office. Boone had decided it made the most sense to begin the assault there. It would still be a mess, he'd said, but it wouldn't interfere with any pipes or damage the bathroom. Since Kate was a big fan of functional indoor plumbing, she was in full agreement.

She still wasn't prepared for the sight of the gaping hole in her wall. Or the pile of rubble on the floor. Or the dust that had Jamie sneezing and her coughing and doing a frantic mental search of materials in old walls that could be dangerous to tiny lungs.

She took a step back. "I don't think Jamie should breathe this in."

Boone's smile dimmed. "Shit. I never thought..."

"It's okay," she rushed to assure him. "I didn't think it would be this intense."

He nodded and set the sledgehammer on the ground. "Here. I'll take him back outside. You have a... Wait... It's all over my shirt." With that, he peeled off his T-shirt, pushed past her into the kitchen, and ducked his head under the faucet. He came up sputtering, dripping and laughing.

"There. Now I can take him."

Oh, God. Just when she thought she couldn't

love him more deeply, he did something so goofy, so thoughtful, and she fell a little harder.

She handed Jamie over, pausing to give Boone a lingering kiss. "Good call, Dad."

"Just doing my job. Now, go look. You're not gonna believe what's behind there."

Her imagination kicked in as she picked her way over the hunks of wall now scattered on the floor. "Sorry, Nana," she muttered as she braced herself against the edge of the hole. She peered… blinked to make sure the dust wasn't making her see things…then looked again.

"Stairs?"

Laughter from outside the window had her turning toward the yard. Boone was there, Jamie in his arms, watching her through the glass. She hurried through the mudroom at the back and yanked the door open.

"There are stairs there!" She practically jumped down the steps to where her guys waited. "Boone, you're right. I don't believe it. A hidden staircase! Did you see where it goes yet?"

"Nope. I wanted you to see it first."

She drew a long breath to slow the hammering of her pulse. "It's probably just another entrance to the crypt. That makes the most sense."

"It's not. For one thing, it's only, what, two or three meters from there to the stairs you use now, right? Why would anyone have two sets of stairs that close? It's not like there were servants here."

"True. And I guess if it led down there, we would have seen it at some point. Not that I spend any more time in the crypt than necessary, but still."

"Besides," he added with that nerf herder grin she loved so much, "these steps go in a different direction."

Oh. She'd been so blown away by the discovery, she hadn't noticed that detail.

"We have to see where it goes," she said, but he shook his head.

"Remember where I live? There are ruins all over the place. Rule number one when you stumble across something new—refrain from rushing to see what's there. The first thing you have to do is make sure it's safe."

"I like it better when I'm the sensible one and you're the one chasing rainbows."

His grin was slow, lazy and utterly wicked. "New positions are always worth a try, Princess."

MUCH AS KATE hated to admit it, Boone was right. They had to be sure the stairs were safe before they explored them. They also had to make sure the area stayed safe for Jamie.

"God only knows how old these walls are, or what was in them," Boone said as they taped plastic sheeting to the walls to seal off the back half of the room.

"Are you saying that my great-grandfather and his family might have used inferior products?"

"Trust me, Kate. I don't think anyone related to you could ever be accused of shoddy workmanship." He tweaked her nose. "But safety standards have changed in the last hundred years or so."

"Smart-ass," she grumbled, but then he caught her in a kiss and she ended up laughing against his mouth and for a second her world was so perfect that she didn't think it possible to be happier.

Don't get used to this, she warned herself, but it did no good. She wanted to freeze time, to stop the progression of days and keep them the way they were. Together. Laughing. Dizzyingly happy. The family she longed for but hadn't believed they could create.

And she started to wonder if they could prolong the miracle.

Whenever she caught Boone at his laptop deep in project work, she made sure to ask him about it later. Not simply because she was interested—though she was—but also so she could get an idea of how much he could do from here. She remembered what he had said about applying for consulting work he could do from Peru and looked up some of the jobs to see if there was any reason he couldn't do it from Canada. She emailed photos of Boone and Jamie to Jill and Craig, sneaking in some questions about how things were running in Boone's absence. As she suspected, he was missed, but nothing had come to a grinding halt.

She was building a case. For what, she wasn't sure yet. She knew Boone couldn't live with them full-time. Even if he could let go of his fears about carrying on the cycle of abuse—fears which, she noticed, seemed to be easing—there was his dedication to Project Sonqo. She couldn't ask him to give up his life's work.

And even if she did—even if she told him she loved him—was her love alone enough?

Boone loved Jamie. Of that, she had no doubt. He was growing as a father, tuning in to his son, learning how to read a situation and respond better than some of her teachers at the day care who had years of experience. And Jamie totally adored his dad. Seeing the two of them together, especially when they didn't know she was watching, was like spying on a meeting of the Mutual Adoration Society.

But what about Boone and her? She knew she loved him, but did it go both ways?

And if it didn't, no matter how much she loved him, was that enough? Would she be willing to live alone most of the time so she could stay married to a man she loved but who might never love her?

CHAPTER FOURTEEN

THE HOUSE WAS SILENT.

Boone was at the hardware store, Jamie was down for his nap, and Kate was debating between painting the porch and feeling virtuous, or sacking out on the sofa with a book and feeling indulged, when the decision was taken out of her hands by the slam of a car door. She peeked outside just in time to see Allie hauling two stacked boxes up the porch steps.

"Do you need help?" she asked as she raced to hold the door.

"Nah, I'm good." Allie set her load in the foyer. "One more trip, and then I'll take them up to my room. And if you touch them, I will totally forget that I stopped at Tim Hortons and grabbed you an Iced Capp on my way here."

"Not fair, Al," Kate called as her sister bounced back down the steps. Her reply came in the form of a laugh floating back in her direction.

Kate glared at the boxes. "I should be able to do this. It's not like I'm some fragile flower."

The boxes stayed silent.

Kate lifted one. It wasn't heavy. Her ankle was completely back to normal. Allie was simply being a mother hen.

But was it worth risking an Iced Capp?

Kate sighed, sat on the living room sofa and grabbed her book, which she deliberately raised to hide her face when Allie returned.

"Oh, good. You can be taught."

"Dite mo, Allie." Kate lowered the book and glared. "That drink better be maple flavored."

"Would I get you anything else?" Allie started up the stairs. "Wait here like an obedient sister. It'll be in your hands before you know it."

Kate made grumbling noises but obeyed. Not that it was so difficult. Once in a while—not often, but sometimes—it was nice to be indulged and pampered.

Besides, if she stayed on the sofa, then Allie would stay with her. Which meant she would be less likely to spy the plastic sheeting blocking Boone's work area. Which greatly reduced the chances of Allie asking questions Kate wasn't sure she wanted to deal with quite yet.

As soon as the boxes were out of the foyer, Allie raced back outside and returned with a cup of cold deliciousness. Kate accepted it, took that first throat-numbing sip, and let out a small moan.

"Oh, my God. I haven't had one of these in weeks."

"How have you survived?"

"I've been…distracted." She sipped again, looking up in time to catch Allie's frown. "It's okay. It's only house stuff."

"Yeah, I noticed the work in the bathroom. It's coming along nicely. Good timing, too, what with me moving in."

"It will be." Kate pulled the straw from her drink and licked it lovingly. "This was totally worth abandoning my dignity and letting you boss me around."

"Bought by a frozen drink that isn't even alcoholic. Better not let Boone know you're that easy."

Kate choked.

"Aha. As I suspected." Allie sat back, her expression a cross between delight and concern. "I didn't think Boone's room looked messy enough to be housing him."

"You totally set me up!"

"Yeah, I did. So." Allie sipped her frozen lemonade. "What happened to that whole plan to keep things platonic and build a new relationship around Jamie?"

"We're doing that."

Allie snorted. "That's not all you're doing."

"Is Cash going to be having sleepovers here after you move in?"

"I don't—look, totally different situation, okay?"

"Yeah, but I'm a respectable married woman."

"A respectable married woman who's boinking the man she's divorcing."

"I like to forge a new and creative path."

"Kate." Allie leaned forward. "Have you really thought about this? I mean, he's a hunk, no argument there, and since he's been here I've gotten to see a new side to him that makes me like him a lot more than before. But you said yourself, he's not going to be able to give you the kind of family you want."

The tight numbness in Kate's throat had nothing to do with the frozen concoction in her hand. There was no one Kate trusted more than her sister. But if she talked about what she was feeling, what she was contemplating, then it would be real.

She wasn't sure that she was ready for reality yet.

"Maybe I was overcome by lust," she said, hoping she sounded defiant and not desperate. "Maybe I thought, he's a damn good time and I would be an idiot to not take advantage of him being here. Maybe I thought, he's like pizza and ice cream the night before a diet."

"Yeah, maybe. But if that was all true, you wouldn't have locked him out of your bedroom in the first place, because it would have been just about the sex, and there's nothing scary about that." Allie tipped her cup toward Kate. "But you've been kind of quiet the last week or two. You talk about the repairs, and Jamie, and you slipped in just enough about me moving in to keep me from getting paranoid that you'd changed your mind, which I appreciate. But you haven't said squat about you, or you and Boone, and that's what worries me. Because it makes me think that you blew past simply having sex a long time ago."

"I didn't lock him out." It was the only part of Allie's statement that she trusted herself to respond to.

"No, you just told the husband you hadn't seen in almost a year that you wouldn't be sleeping with him. Which, don't get me wrong, totally your call and for good reason, and I completely supported that move. Didn't think it had a snowball's chance in hell, but I supported it."

"You're seriously ruining my Iced Capp."

"You know us little sisters. Always barging in where we don't belong." Allie twisted sideways, one hand fiddling with the clip on her baggy denim overalls. "Don't get pissed, but I have to be sure. This change was your decision, right? Boone didn't—"

"What? Oh, God, no. He was totally—I mean, I practically had to draw up a contract promising that I wouldn't end up regretting it. He showed amazing restraint."

Allie's low whistle bounced off Nana's walls.

Kate waited for the echo to die out, swishing her straw from side to side in the icy confection, buying time and trying to come up with an answer to the question she knew Allie would ask.

"So, what made you change your mind?"

Damn it.

"And before you try the ice cream line again, or some variation on it, let me point out that I have known you, oh, all my life, and you have never been the type to be impulsive or impetuous, or get swept away."

"Except when we're talking Boone."

"Right. I forgot there was a precedent already set there. But I still won't buy it, because there's more on the line now than just you. Anything you do now, especially involving Boone, is going to impact Jamie, as you well know. Maybe I've read you wrong all these years, but I can't see you giving in to something that could make future interactions with Boone more complicated. It's just not you."

Kate stared into her cup, searching for inspiration among the swirls of brown deliciousness.

She may as well have saved herself the effort.

"Oh, Katie. Sweetie."

Just the twist in Allie's voice was enough to tell Kate that Allie had figured it out on her own. And that she was almost as heartbroken over it as Kate herself.

"Tell me I'm wrong. Tell me you didn't."

The deep breath that Kate took to steady her voice was a total waste of oxygen. "Sorry. No can do." She lifted her head and looked her sister in the eye. "I fell in love with my husband."

It was the first time she had said it to anyone— well, anyone other than Jamie. She had expected the words to leave a trail of sorrow in their wake. Instead, as soon as she said them, she felt the most unexpected lightness. Kind of like the way she'd felt when she first told Boone she was pregnant. It should have been terrifying, and at some level— the logical, detail-oriented, practical one—yeah, it was. But below that, at the point where it mattered most, there had been the most amazing feeling of delight. Of wonder.

She was pretty sure the tears welling up in Allie's eyes had nothing to do with joy or delight.

"I know you're worried about me," she said quickly. "And I appreciate it and understand it, because in your shoes, I would feel the same way. But the thing is, Allie Cat, I'm okay. More than okay, actually. I'm happy," she said, letting the amazement seep into her words. "I know it doesn't make any sense and it screws things up so much, and if I was remotely sensible I would have avoided it, but... I'm so happy, Allie."

"Ooo-kay." Allie nodded slowly. "Let me get this straight, so I know what I'm working with.

You slept with him again, and you figured out you love him, and—"

"No. Wrong order. I slept with him again *because* I figured out I was in love with him. And I thought, well, heck. The only reason I was trying to keep him at arm's length was to avoid falling for him, but since that was a fail, then why was I depriving myself?"

"That makes about as much sense as divorcing him to stay friends."

"I know."

"But you don't seem bothered by it."

"I'm still in the giddy carried-away stage, okay?"

Allie's smile was reluctant, but at least it was a smile.

"Okay," she said softly. "You're in love with the father of your baby, and you're happy and giddy and life is wonderful. And I have to say that it's pretty awesome to see."

"Thank you."

"But someone has to ask the obvious question, and since I'm your sister and you're going to love me no matter what, I think I need to be the one to do it." The smile slipped from her face. "What happens when he has to go back?"

Kate stared into her drink. "Did I mention I'm still in the giddy stage?"

"Yeah, I know. The future doesn't matter, right? Living for the moment, following the dream?"

"That's the plan." And maybe if Kate squared her jaw just a bit more, she could convince herself.

"I'm asking anyway."

That was the trouble with sisters. They insisted on doing what was best for each other, even when it hurt.

"When he has to leave, well, he has to leave."

"Okay, but…forever? Are you still getting a divorce? Are you going to try to make this work?"

"I don't know."

"God help us, Kate, if I have to be the practical one. I promise it won't end well for either of us. You'll be screwed and I won't recognize myself."

Well, at least that got them laughing.

"Some things just can't be practicaled," Kate said. "Sometimes you have to see how things unfold."

"Yeah. It wasn't so long ago that I was telling that to myself. You know, back when I was getting ready to marry the wrong guy?"

"Totally different. You didn't love him and you knew it."

"I didn't love him, but my head said I should, so I convinced myself I did."

"You're talking in circles." Kate stopped to consider. "Either that or I'm a lot more sleep-deprived than I thought I was."

"It means, goof, that sometimes everything looks like it *should* be love, and the evidence is so strong that we talk ourselves into it. Like, Luke was awesome and fun and one of my best buds, and I felt horrible for him being alone after his mom died and I wanted to help him, so when he said he loved me, my head said, *Hey, falling for him would make life so much better for everyone!* And I believed myself." Allie shook her head. "I know. I picked a really stupid time to start using twisted logic."

"No denying that. But, Allie, this is about me, not you. I don't see how—"

"Here's how it relates to you, okay? And don't get pissed with me if you don't like what I'm going to say. Because you know damned well that Mom is going to say the same thing, and if I say it first, you'll have time to come up with a really excellent answer to shoot her down."

"So you're going to say something that's going to make me furious, but you're doing it for my own good. An act of mercy, essentially."

"Exactly."

Kate looked into her almost-empty cup. "You really should have spiked this."

"If I'd known you were going to drop this on me, believe me, I would have. Anyway. My point is, it would make a whole lot of sense for you to fall in love with Boone."

"Oh, yeah. Because everyone I know wants to give their heart to someone who doesn't think he can cut it as a husband, but that part barely matters because he lives on a different continent."

"This isn't about him, it's about you. You like things neat and tidy, Kate. You want—no, you *need*—to be able to dot those i's and cross those t's. You want a perfect family, and the easiest way to do that would be for you and Boone to stay together."

Well, so much for the worry that Allie needed to be the practical one. "Did you hear the part about different continents?"

"That's almost irrelevant."

Kate laughed harder than she had in days.

"I'm serious," Allie said. "Living in different countries would be a challenge, no doubt about it, but that's just logistics. You wouldn't be an average family but you would still be an intact nuclear one. And *that* is what matters to you, Katydid. Not being physically together but being emotionally together."

Oh, God. Why did that have to sound so terrifyingly true?

"All your life, hon, you've wanted family. You wanted it so much that you tracked down the father Mom told you to ignore. You wanted it so much that when you got pregnant, you married a man you barely knew."

"That was for Nana."

"Sure. Part of it was. But honestly, Kate, you could have lied to her. Or you could have just pretended. But you did the real thing."

"Because..."

Why *had* they gotten married for real? Allie was right. It would have been easier, and a whole lot less complicated, to simply make Nana believe they had done it. But when Boone had suggested it, Kate had needed less than a day to take him up on the offer. Actually, she had known she would say yes as soon as the shock had worn off, but she had forced herself to wait so she could assure her future self that she had indeed given it thought.

"I thought we were being sensible." Her words were soft, muffled by her bowed head. "It just felt like the right thing to do. But maybe..."

"Maybe you were already in love with him but you just didn't want to admit it yet?"

"No. I wasn't." She paused, turning the thought over in her mind. "But maybe I was slipping over the cliff at that point."

"There's nothing wrong with that." Allie leaned over and gave Kate's hand a fast pat. "People live their whole lives hoping it will happen to them."

"Yeah, that would explain the giddiness." Too bad she wasn't feeling any of it at the moment. A little gaiety would have been welcome. "Of course, it doesn't give me insight about what should happen next."

Allie raised her hand, the model schoolchild. "Question."

"Yes, Miss Hebert?"

"Why do you have to figure it out now?"

"Because he's leaving soon? Because I gave a lawyer a whack of money I can't spare to start a divorce?"

"How about because you want to know what's going to be happening with the rest of your life?"

Oh.

"Remember when you said I should move in here and nobody ever regrets taking the time to be sure they're making the right decision?" Allie leaned back with a smug smile. "Boone might be leaving, but he's going to be back. And divorces aren't granted overnight. Which means, big sister, that maybe you should listen to your own advice."

SATURDAY MORNING, BOONE woke up early. He tried to convince himself it was because of the sun shining in through the curtains they'd forgotten to close the night before, but the hollow sensation in his gut told him the real reason.

He was leaving in exactly one week. And he'd be damned if he was going to waste a minute more than necessary in sleep.

Kate lay curled on her side, one hand tucked

beneath the pillow as always. A lock of hair had slipped over her face. He longed to brush it back but stopped himself. He would have plenty of time to sleep once he was back in Peru, but she didn't have that same luxury.

Jamie was still out cold. Boone paused a moment to soak in the sight. Skype was a godsend, but since the whole point of those calls was for him to interact with his son, the odds were that these were the last days he would watch Jamie sleep until the next visit. By then, he would probably be rolling over on his own and even sleeping on his stomach sometimes. In his own room.

But not in a different house—at least not if Boone had anything to say about it.

He crept out of the room, grabbed the jeans he'd stashed by the sealed area of the office, and pulled on his work boots. Kate had no idea that he was close to clearing through the end of the stairs. A couple of places had filled in with dirt and stone, and there were some twists in the path that made it difficult to know what part of the house was above him. But today was going to bring some answers. He could feel it.

Well, that, and if the tunnel went on much longer, he was pretty sure it would come out in the neighbor's yard.

Ten minutes later he was underground once more. He'd grown accustomed to the coolness.

This tunnel wasn't as damp as the basement, thank God, but he still felt the chill in his bones after a few minutes. Since Jamie would wake soon—meaning another Kate-enhanced shower was out of the question—he was going to have to suck it up and deal.

"Charlie, old friend, you had better have a damn good reason for leading me down here."

It had to be the treasure. Why else would anyone go to this trouble? It had to be tied to Prohibition. To Charlie. To the treasure.

The real question was how it had stayed a secret. Charlie couldn't have done all this himself. His father, his brother, anyone else who worked with them—someone had to have known about this place. If not all of them, at least the brother who had lived here.

On the other hand, if Boone had had a brother—one who'd died while trying to get away to a new life—would he have wanted to preserve the proof that his brother had been doing something illegal? Or would he have sealed it off from the world and hoped that time would fill in both the tunnel and the hole carved in his heart?

There were rocks at this end of the passage. Boone had moved a few yesterday, but he'd had to stop before Kate grew too suspicious and followed him down here. Now he started hauling again, his body warming up with the exertion.

Each rock had to be tested before he could move it. There wouldn't be much good in finding a lost treasure if Kate had to use it all to pay for Boone's funeral after the tunnel collapsed on him.

When he got back to his laptop, he was going to have to check to make sure he had enough life insurance.

He allowed himself twenty minutes at a time down here. After that, he started getting claustrophobic and imagining all the different toxic gases that he could be inhaling. But his timer had yet to go off when he set down one rock, turned to test another, and came to a sudden stop.

There was a door behind the rocks.

KATE KNEW SOMETHING was up the moment Boone burst back into the bedroom. One minute she was snuggled against the pillows with Jamie, enjoying a few lazy post-nursing stretches. The next, Hurricane Boone flew in and landed on the bed.

"What time does Cash get up?" he demanded.

She blinked. "I have no idea. And good morning to you, too."

"Good morning. Right. Okay, how about Allie? She would know, right?"

"What's with the interest in Cash? Do you have a sudden burning need for some male bonding? Because if so, I'm pretty sure your son needs his diaper changed."

"What? Oh, right. Sure." Boone whisked Jamie off the bed and headed down the hall toward the changing table. With a last lingering look at the bed, Kate pulled on her robe and padded behind. She spared a second to admire the efficiency with which Boone was attacking the job in front of him. Was this really the same man who had been terrified to touch his own son just a few short weeks ago?

"So what has you so excited?"

"I found a door."

CHAPTER FIFTEEN

Kate stared at Boone in disbelief. "You found a what?"

"Down the steps, Kate. At the end of the tunnel. There's a bunch of rocks, and I cleared some of them away, and there's a door back there."

"No way."

"It's true." He paused to flash her a grin over his shoulder. "There's something down there, Kate. I can feel it."

Oh, wow. If it was true...

But she couldn't let herself get excited. Not yet. There were too many steps between here and there to let herself start planning ways to tell her mother that all those stories were true, and that oh, by the way, Boone was the one who put it all together.

Though she did let herself have a couple of seconds to consider the possible reactions.

"Okay," she said slowly. "But why do you need Cash?"

"Some of those rocks are heavy. I've cleared away all I can manage on my own. The rest will take muscles, and don't take this the wrong way, but Cash has the advantage over you."

"I'm not getting bent out of shape over facts, Boone. As long as you don't start comparing me to Cash in other ways, I'm good."

"Not to worry there, babe." His wink had her imagining possibilities that she knew might not be wise but which she couldn't quite keep at bay.

"Allie's an early riser, but this might be much even for her. I don't want to freak her out. Let me grab a shower and coffee, and by then it'll probably be safe."

"Sounds good."

Allie was indeed awake when Kate touched base with her, and yes, she just happened to know that Cash was also awake. It didn't take long before they were both at the house, listening with wide eyes and open mouths as Kate and Boone filled them in on what they had uncovered.

"So you want to get the last rocks out of the way and see what's behind the door," Cash said.

"Right." Kate nodded. "That's where you come in."

"What can I do?" Allie asked. "I admit, I'm no weight lifting champ, but I can carry a tray loaded with dinner for four on one shoulder, and that's not exactly a feather." She wrinkled her nose. "Especially when the high school hockey team drops in."

"Would you hate me forever if I asked you to stay up here with Jamie while I go down and explore with them?" Kate knew it wasn't the fairest of questions, but she already had to be sensible about letting Cash be first assistant. And since she was the one who'd had to live with the mess, she felt she deserved something.

"How about if we trade off, fifteen minutes at a time?"

"Deal." Kate looked at Boone. "You heard her. Work fast."

Fast turned out to be optimistic. *Steady* and *cautious* were more the words of the hour. Much as she wanted to be on hand when the door was cleared, Kate had to admit that the regular breaks were welcome. Three people made for a cramped and claustrophobic tunnel, especially when they were moving rocks out of the way.

"And you say you do stuff like this all the time in Peru?" Cash asked at one point when they all ventured upstairs for a drink and fresh air.

Boone shook his head. "Not a lot. Just enough to know that I definitely would never make it as an archaeologist. Or a coal miner, come to think of it."

"Yeah, I used to think it would be fun to explore

caves." Allie rolled her eyes. "One misconception, totally cured."

The adults laughed, which made Jamie giggle, which started everyone laughing all over again. Everyone was dusty, knuckles were scraped, they were all going to hurt like hell tonight, and yet the moment was so utterly perfect that, again, Kate wished she could stop the clock.

This. I want this.

The laughter. The companionship. The under-standing. And the way they were all so easy to-gether, the way everything just fit. A month ago, she wouldn't have believed it possible. But now she and Boone and Allie and Cash were acting like those couples who form lifelong friendships. At any moment, she expected one of the guys to suggest that they barbecue something for dinner.

It could be like this again. They could make it work. Not all the time, but if she and Boone were to stay together, then they could plan. They could have regular times like this.

You like things neat and tidy, Kate... You want a perfect family...

But this longing was more than that. Kate was sure of it. She hadn't gone searching for this couple-companionship. It had simply happened on its own. No one had engineered it. And that, she decided, was all the proof anyone needed that it was meant to be.

It took another hour, but at last the door was cleared enough. Kate was on tunnel duty when Boone turned back to her.

"Ready?"

The dim light and the lousy conditions couldn't touch the excitement in his eyes. He reached behind him and squeezed her hand. She squeezed back, then tugged him close and kissed him. Not a quick whisper of lips, either, but a serious kiss that she hoped conveyed all the love and appreciation and joy she was feeling at that moment.

"For luck?" he asked when she finally released him.

"I don't need luck," she said, low and close, for his ears only. "I've got you."

It was too dim to read his reaction. His sudden jerk didn't offer any clues, either.

But then he clasped her shoulder. "Here's to Charlie."

"Look, you two." Cash's voice boomed in the close quarters. "Either open the door or get a room. I don't care which."

So it was that they all were laughing when Boone put a shoulder to the door and pushed.

Nothing happened.

"Is there something behind it?" Kate asked. Cash groaned. Boone laughed.

"Back up," he ordered, and this time he pulled instead of pushing.

"Holy—" he said.

Kate stood on tiptoe to peek over his shoulder. "More bottles?"

There was another crawl space–sized opening behind the door. From what Kate could see, it seemed to be filled with row after row of bottles similar to what they had found beneath the porch.

"Hang on," she said. "We're under the porch here, right?"

Boone nodded and tapped the closest container. "I have a feeling those other ones we found might have been more than just the leftovers from someone's party."

"You think they were a marker." The quietness of Cash's words couldn't hide his amazement.

"Who thinks there's something behind those bottles?" Kate asked. Their grunts sounded affirmative.

"Ninety-nine bottles of hooch on the wall, ninety-nine bottles of hooch," Boone sang out. "Take one down, pass it around…"

And so he did, handing it back to Kate, who held it for a moment, one finger tracing the edges of the cool glass.

I'm sorry, Charlie. I should have believed.

Then she passed it back to Cash and took the next one from Boone.

The fifteen-minute switch-off timer had just beeped when Boone shouted that he'd found something.

"What?" Cash asked, but Kate shook her head. "Can you lift it? Can we take it upstairs?"

A few more grunts, then—

"Got it." Boone backed out of the hole cradling some kind of rectangular container. Very carefully, he tipped it sideways, allowing him to turn and face the exit.

"Come on," Kate said. "We need to show this to Allie."

Once upstairs, there followed a few minutes of logistics and one long silence when Cash asked if they should wait and open the—whatever—with Maggie in attendance. Kate and Allie shared a look.

"We probably should," Allie said, but Kate shook her head.

"I have her only grandchild. She won't kill me. I say let's open it now."

Jamie was secure in his playpen on the other side of the plastic sheeting. Boone ran upstairs for his toolbox. Kate felt like a fool but made everyone tie rags over their mouths before they opened it, just in case.

"I can still see your eyes rolling above the rag," she said to Boone.

"I bet it doesn't do anything to muffle sound, either," he said before breaking into long, loud guffaws.

"Can we please open this?" Allie begged. "I'm already an hour late. I called in Nadine to cover for me but she has to leave soon, and I'm dying to know what's in there."

Boone took one of the extra rags Kate had fetched and used it to wipe dirt from the container.

"Is it wood?" Kate asked. Boone shook his head.

"It's some kind of metal," he said, reaching for the latex gloves Kate had unearthed from the first aid kit.

She expected him to pull them on. Instead, he handed them to her.

"Wait. No." She pushed them back to him. "You're the one who should do this, Boone. You put the pieces together and did the work. This is yours."

"It's your family history. You and Allie should open it."

But you're my family.

The sense of rightness that swept through her at the thought told her it was the truth. Boone was her family. Boone and Jamie and her, the three of them, their own little part of the world that filled her heart. How had she ever thought that anything else could ever be better than what she had found with this man?

So they wouldn't have a conventional family. They would deal. *She* could deal. For in that moment, she knew that she would rather have part-time with Boone than full-time with anybody else. This was the family she wanted. This was the love she wanted. Boone might not think he could do this, but he hadn't known how to be a father, either. She could teach him.

Especially if they had a lifetime to figure it out.

"You guys." Allie's impatience pulled Kate back to the moment. "The clock is ticking."

Kate made a fast decision. "Cash, would you do the honors?"

"Me? But I'm not a Hebert."

"No, you're not." Kate met Boone's gaze. "But you're part of the family. And all the parts should have a role in this."

"Whatever." Cash shook his head, but he adjusted his rag mask, snapped on the gloves and ran his finger along the edge of the container. As he did, more of the greenish growth came loose.

"Is it silver?" Allie knelt down to look. "Whoa. Yeah. Definitely silver."

"Look." Boone pointed to a spot in the middle of one of the long sides. "That looks like it's inset. Maybe a latch?"

Cash slid his fingers over the spot Boone indicated. He pressed. The container opened ever so slightly.

Kate reached for Boone's hand. Or was it the other way around?

It didn't matter. They were together. This was happening.

BOONE WASN'T SURE he was breathing anymore. Not because of the silly rag tied round his face, not even because of Kate's hand in his, wonderful though that was, but because this was it. This was the key to giving her and Jamie the house, the security, the life he longed to provide for them. It had to be. He couldn't have been led to this for any other reason.

Cash eased the top of the container open. Inside were several bundles wrapped in some disintegrating fabric. Boone caught a glimpse of silver. His heart thudded.

Allie made a squeaking noise. Kate squeezed his hand so hard he thought she might break something.

It was really happening.

Cash pushed aside some of the fabric and pulled out something that flashed gold and red, something Boone couldn't comprehend until Kate said, "Dear God, those can't be real rubies."

Rubies.

Boone's head started to spin.

"It's a necklace." Cash held it out for them to view. Boone knew as much about women's jewelry as he did about brain surgery, but he was pretty sure he was looking at something that could pay for three whole aisles down at Village Hardware.

"I think there are earrings that match." Cash pushed aside fabric scraps. "Yep. Someone had good taste."

"Do you think... Daisy's family had money." Kate spoke softly, almost reverently, as she touched the necklace with one finger. "Do you think this might have been hers?"

"That doesn't seem likely," Boone said. "She was a single mother who supported herself by, what, making quilts and doing seamstress work? If that was hers, wouldn't she have sold it to provide for her son?"

"Good point." Cash unrolled another bundle and let out a low whistle. "Anybody into emeralds?"

Kate gasped. Allie squeaked again. For himself, Boone had lost the ability to vocalize.

But he could still see. And astonishing as the necklaces might be, to him they didn't hold a candle to the awe in Kate's eyes as she watched Cash's every move.

"This one feels heavier." Cash said as he lifted the next packet. "More solid, too. Almost like—"

Whatever he was going to say was lost in the rip of aging cloth and the tumble of a pile of spoons to the tabletop.

"Spoons?" If Kate was disappointed, it didn't show. "Are the others knives and forks?"

Cash checked. "Yeah, I'd say you have a complete dinner service here, kids. Anyone want to have a party?"

"Let me see one." Allie took one of the spoons and peered at it. "I think they're real silver, all right. Look at all that tarnish." She rubbed at it with the hem of her shirt. "There's some design on the handle. Kate, do you have any—"

"If you're going to ask for silver polish, stop and think about who you're talking to," Kate said drily.

"Actually, I was going to say toothpaste. I remember reading once that you can use it as an emergency replacement for polish."

"The things you learn," Boone muttered. He reached for one of the knives. Allie was right. There was a design etched into each of the handles.

"This one isn't as tarnished." Kate reached past him and lifted a fork. "Look, you can sort of see it. It looks like…a bird?

"I think it's just the head." Kate squinted. "It looks like an eagle."

Charlie had made a deal with the American authorities…

"Let me see something." He squeezed between the sisters to take in the array spread on the table. He counted the silverware, then counted again to be certain.

Twenty forks. Twenty spoons. Ten serving pieces. Nineteen knives.

He gave a piece of it to the Americans...

"Is silverware even worth anything?" Cash's voice seemed to come from a distance, muffled by Jamie's squeals and the pounding in Boone's ears.

All he told Daisy was that it would be immensely valuable to the right people...

"Hang on, Jamie. Mommy just needs a minute on eBay to get an idea of—"

Boone traced the insignia on the handle of one of the serving spoons. He flipped it over and inspected the back. The year 1776 was engraved on either side of the handle.

First the British sat down and ate the meal that was already set out on the tables. Then they torched the place...

"Look up the going rate for silver," Allie said. "Even if it just gets melted down—"

"No one's melting this down." Boone's words cut through the air of merriment in the room. He turned around slowly, forcing himself to make a mental list of the mess he'd created. The gaping hole in the wall. The rocks piled everywhere. The dust that coated the furniture. The yawning tunnel that would have to be dealt with.

The joy in Kate's face, slowly fading as she read his expression.

"Boone? What's wrong?"

His mother's voice slipped back into his head. *You never could do anything right.*

"We can't keep it."

Allie laughed, short and high. "Well, no one's planning to keep it. I mean, wasn't the plan to sell it to fix up the house?"

The house that Kate loved. The story and history. The endless possibilities she was kind of embarrassed to imagine.

All gone now. All because of him.

"Look on the back of the handle," he said, tossing his piece to the table. "We have to call—I don't know. Someone in Ottawa."

"Oh, my God." Kate breathed the words out, lifting her gaze from the fork, to Allie, then to Boone. "Oh, my God. Charlie's treasure was stolen from the White House?"

Boone nodded. "We can't keep it," he said again, looking at the wall, the mess, the whole goddamned house. "We can't sell it. We have to hand it over." He stared at the floor. "It's over."

CHAPTER SIXTEEN

KATE WENT THROUGH the rest of the day in a daze as the implications of their discovery sank in, one bit at a time. Maggie was called to come see the treasure. Kate tracked down an old boyfriend who worked at the Museum of History, who put her in touch with someone from the National Archives, who must have had a Mountie escort to get to Comeback Cove as fast as she did. Forget that it was a Saturday in May, soon the house was hopping like River Road at the height of tourist season.

And through it all, Boone stayed in the background. Silent. Flinching whenever anyone congratulated him.

Kate ached for him. He had pinned so much on this quest. Sometimes she had thought he was almost obsessed with the need to let her stay in the house.

He wanted to take care of them. She understood that, and his desire to give Jamie a past to be proud of.

But was he determined to give them the house because it was easier—safer—than giving himself?

She wandered upstairs to the room with the hidden cupboard, the one that had been hers before Maggie married Neil. Her mom had been right next door in the room that had housed Boone, albeit temporarily.

A small smile crossed her lips. Boone in Maggie's room. No wonder he had said it always felt cold to him.

"Charlie," she said, "Daisy, Nana, Poppy…if you're listening, I want you to know, I love you all. And I love this house. I promise I won't sell it to anyone who wants to tear it down."

She moved to the little cupboard. Boone had removed the door and added shelves, and she had painted it a deeper blue than the powdery shade on the walls. It was now a built-in bookshelf, one that echoed the colors of the river that could be spotted from the window when the trees were not in full leaf.

"So many secrets." She ran a hand over the shelf that Boone had sanded to be almost as soft as Jamie's cheeks. "So many memories."

She was going to miss it, no doubt about it. She was very grateful that she could stay here a little bit longer, that she and Jamie and Allie would have time together under this roof.

But time moved on. Rivers flowed. Things

changed. Some possibilities ended, but others opened up.

She sat in the window seat and stared out at the activity below. So many people coming and going. Thank heaven Maggie was here to deal with them, because right now, Kate had more important things on her mind than the fate of possibly stolen, possibly historic silverware. Like figuring out when and how she would tell Boone that she loved him. That she wanted to stay married to him. And that, wonderful as this house was, she didn't need turrets or stained glass or secret staircases.

She needed her home. Her family. Her husband.

Those she could have anywhere, as long as Boone was in her life.

It FELT LIKE forever but at last the hordes had departed and it was just Kate and Boone once more. Kate thought she had never been so happy to see the door close behind anyone as she was when the last Mountie left.

"Wow. That was a day."

"Yeah, that's one way to put it," Boone said from behind her. Too far behind her. Why wasn't he up here sliding his arms around her waist? Maybe he was holding Jamie, though that had never stopped him from delivering a one-armed squeeze before.

When she turned around, she saw that his hands were in his pockets. His face had that closed-off expression she'd seen only on the rare times when he had let something slip about his mother.

That wasn't exactly encouraging.

"Boone," she began, moving toward him, but a squawk from the floor pulled her attention to Jamie, struggling against the confines of his bouncy seat.

"Right," she said. "I forgot it's your dinnertime."

"There's a first." A hint of a smile tugged at the corners of Boone's mouth. "You take care of him. I'll make something for us."

"Good plan," she said, then reconsidered. Jamie needed time with his father. She needed something to keep her hands busy while she talked, because she knew she had to have this conversation now, in daylight, with Jamie present as a constant reminder of how amazing she and Boone could be when they worked together.

"Actually, let's switch it up. I'll chop and cook if you take cereal duty."

He nodded, scooped Jamie into his arms and headed for the kitchen. Jamie was strapped into his high chair and given a spoon to bang. Kate started water boiling and pulled vegetables from the fridge. Boone mixed cereal. It could have passed for any other night except for the silence hanging over them.

And the way Boone's gaze kept straying to the plastic sheeting at the entry to the office. Kate knew that though his body was in the kitchen with her, everything else was on the other side of that semitransparent covering.

"Heck of a mess," she said softly. Better to get the undeniable facts out of the way.

"Yeah." He turned swiftly, taking himself and the bowl of cereal to Jamie. "Yeah, that's for sure."

"But we'll put it back together."

"I shouldn't have done it, Kate."

She winced at the guilt in his voice, the way his shoulders hunched forward as he offered the first spoonful of food.

"Look. You —we—took a chance. Sometimes chances pay off, and you end up with something wonderful like a baby. Other times, they don't turn out the way you hoped." She set bread on the table, squeezing his shoulder as she moved past. "Win some, lose some. But it will be—"

"Don't you dare say it'll be fine."

"But it will be. Boone, listen to me. Jamie and I will be happy wherever we land. I love this house, but I'll love the next one, too, as long as it has the two most important things in my world. Jamie." She turned to face him, bracing herself against the counter as she finished the thought. "And you, whenever you can be with us."

Even from across the room it was impossible to miss the immediate contraction of every muscle in his body.

The heck with keeping her hands busy cooking. She needed to touch him, to try to smooth away some of that tension. "Boone," she whispered as she slipped behind him and wrapped her arms around him. "I know you're still worried about what kind of father you can be. I know you have a life in Peru that you want to keep. But I've seen the way you've fallen in love with Jamie. I've watched you learn how to read him and understand him and give him what he needs, and I know that you are killing it as a dad. I want you here as much as you can be. I want Jamie to keep a calendar where he crosses off the days until you come back to us. I want…" She buried her face in the unyielding rigidness of his back, breathing him in, filling herself with him to give her strength. "I want us to stay together, Boone. Because Jamie loves you. And so do I."

His hands closed over hers. For one second she thought he planned to give them a squeeze before turning around and kissing her and telling her that yes, God, yes, he loved her, too, and wanted to be with her, too, and was willing to take a chance on the kind of family, the kind of marriage, they could make.

Instead, he pulled her hands apart and then blindly pushed the spoon forward, totally missing Jamie's mouth.

"Boone. I know it wouldn't be the easiest way to live, but we have something so—"

"No."

She stopped. Stopped speaking, stopped breathing, stopped understanding.

"What?"

"No." He stared into the bowl of cereal. "I can't stay married to you, Kate."

Coldness slammed through her, as raw and numbing as a January gale. The world receded for a second, like she was seeing everything through binoculars. Everything was out of her reach. The house. Boone. Hope.

I can't stay married to you.

She moved to the counter, stared out the window, searching for some flicker of light in the dusk. Her hands curled around the worn edges of the counter where her mother and grandmother had washed and chopped and stirred. Where they had undoubtedly also talked and wept and prayed.

Help me, Nana.

She replayed his words in her mind, listening for some shred of possibility against the background of Jamie's babbles and the steady *clank, clank* of the spoon against the bowl.

"I can't stay married to you."

He had said *can't*. Not *won't*, but *can't*. That was better, wasn't it? *Won't* would mean he didn't want to. But *can't*…that just meant logistics and obstacles, and wait, she knew how to handle those…

"But you can," she whispered to the window. "You can, Boone. I know it won't be the usual kind of marriage, but military families, they do this all the time. They make it work."

Clank.

"I'm not asking you to give up Project Sonqo. I know how important that is and I'm proud of you for being part of it. But it doesn't have to be…" She squeezed her eyes tight, breathed deep to push away the heaviness pressing on her chest. "You have so much love in you, Boone. I see it there. Just like…like you knew that the treasure was here, even when the rest of us—"

Clank. Clank.

"We can do this. I know we can, because I love you, Boone." No more staring into the darkness. She made herself turn around. "I love you, and what we have is too—"

Her eyes registered the sight in front of her before her feet did. Her eyes saw Boone blindly holding the spoon in front of Jamie and her ears told her that Jamie wasn't making any noise and her eyes saw the jerky movements of Jamie's jaw and the frantic wideness of his eyes and her brain said, *Jamie, choking, move*, but her feet took longer to get the message so for one never-ending second she was rooted in place while everything in her screamed.

Then her feet took flight. Her hands reached for Jamie, tugging at him, but the straps were secure and she let out a cry of fury while Boone reared back and she barked at him to call 911 while she fumbled with the fastener and then it was loose, Jamie was loose, and her training kicked in and she placed him over her knee. *Tummy down, support his head, five back slaps. One, two, three, four—*

Something warm hit her foot. Jamie squirmed. He coughed.

And then he let loose with the most welcome cry she had ever heard since the one that had signaled his arrival into the world.

"Jamie!" She scooped him close, pressed him to her, breathed him in. "Jamie, oh, my baby, you're okay. You're okay, it's okay. Shh, sweetie, you just choked on your cereal. I know it was scary but you're okay now, I promise, Mommy is here, Daddy is—"

Boone.

She blinked back her tears long enough to catch

a glimpse of Boone, hovering at the edge of the table. She held out her hand.

He didn't take it.

"Jamie?" he asked in a strained voice.

"He's fine. Really. Did you call 911? If you did, we should call back, tell them everything is—"

"Are you okay?"

She nodded, unable to speak past the emotions rushing back into her throat.

Boone stared at the floor. When he raised his head, she wished for her tears to return and act as a veil between her heart and his utter lack of expression.

"Good." He turned on his heel and started walking away. "Let's keep it that way."

ONE MINUTE HE was in the kitchen, using every bit of strength he possessed to stay pulled together while he killed the best thing that had ever happened to him. The next, he was upstairs in the bed he hadn't used in weeks, lying on his side and staring at the clock on the bedside table.

He had no idea how he'd gotten there. No memory of turning his back on Kate and walking up the stairs.

Yet here he was, fully clothed, watching the numbers change on the clock and willing them to go faster. He needed to get out of here. Needed to get on that plane and get back to Peru and return to the one place where he knew how to make things better, where he didn't destroy everything he saw and touched and loved without even trying.

I want us to stay married.

She would never know that when she'd said that, some wall inside him had shifted. No, it had fallen down. He was Humpty Dumpty and the wall between him and everything he wanted had tumbled down, but he had still fallen and had still broken apart on the ground.

The hell of it was that for one second, one heartbeat, he had thought about saying yes. For the space of one breath, everything he had ever wanted had been his.

Then he had remembered.

I want to have more kids. I would like to have them with someone I can build a life with.

He'd said no because he knew, knew the same way he'd known that old Charlie had stashed something in this house, that she hadn't been lying. She might want him now. But what she really wanted was the same thing she had longed for before he'd blown up her life: a family. More kids. A husband she could rely on, one who didn't walk around like a ticking time bomb no matter how much she insisted he was a good parent.

So he'd said no.

And then, because he had to do something, anything to keep from saying, "wait, no, actually," he had focused on Jamie. On feeding Jamie. On making sure he got that spoon into that mouth every time, because that was what good parents did. They made sure their kids were safe and warm and fed even when their own insides were being shredded.

But he'd been so shell-shocked, so blind to anything but what was happening inside, that he forgot to look. He just kept shoving and pushing and doing what he thought was right, because that was all that mattered, wasn't it?

Jamie could have died. If Kate hadn't been there, hadn't known what was happening and what to do...

He forced himself to relive those moments. The way Kate had flown across the room. The unholy sound she'd made as she'd pulled Jamie out of the chair. The way she had known exactly what to do when she'd flipped him over and started counting, one, two, three. And then the way she had sagged and cried and clutched Jamie to her. And God, dear God, it had all been over before he'd even really grasped what was happening.

He didn't need to be his mother's son to hurt his own child. He was able to do it without even trying.

He stared at the clock. How many minutes until he was on the plane? How long until he could let himself feel the loss that was already lodging inside him?

How long until he could be certain that he wasn't going to destroy anyone else?

KATE HAD THOUGHT that no days could be as long or as lonely as the ones after Neil's death. She hadn't thought it possible that any hours could stretch on, bleak and joyless, the way they had after his funeral, when all of a sudden it was just her and Allie and their mother, and nothing was right anymore.

It turned out that a broken heart would always have that effect, no matter the reason it had shattered.

In some ways this was worse. No, there wasn't that abrupt demarcation that had come when the principal called her down to his office to find Nana waiting to tell her that Neil wouldn't be coming home that night. But this—this week in which she was forced to see Boone all day, to watch him hide upstairs each night, to watch him with Jamie and see the love pouring out of him and know that there was no love there for her...

No. He loved her. She was sure of that. He had never said it, never even hinted at it, but she knew it was true, the same way she knew that he would never deliberately hurt her or Jamie. Love was what had made him want to keep the house for

her. Love was what had made him extract her
promise that she wouldn't let him hurt her when
they made love again. Love was what had made
him curl around her in the night, what had made
him watch her in the early mornings when he
thought she was still asleep.

He loved her. She knew he did. But it wasn't
enough to make him push past the fear.

Every minute hurt. Every breath hurt.

They stayed civil. Polite. They said *please* and
thank you so many times that the house could
have been a Victorian tearoom. Oddly, though,
the one word that was never spoken was the one
she needed most.

Sorry.

Outside, the world went on. Word came from
Ottawa that while further study was needed, it
seemed that Charlie's treasure was indeed a collection of items that had been taken from the
White House before it was burned. Kate was ad-
vised to keep a date in June free, as there would
likely be an official ceremony to present the items
to the American ambassador. She circled the date
on her calendar but made no promises.

Maggie informed Kate that the Mayor was
walking around town refusing to tell anyone what
had happened. Not that she needed to—everyone
had heard the tale already. But it seemed the Mayor
was hoping against hope that the items would be

proven fake or that another legend would appear, one that would easily replace the treasure in Comeback Cove's tourism campaigns.

Kate took Jamie to the pediatrician for his six-month check-up. Boone had planned to join them. That was one of the reasons she had scheduled the appointment during his visit. But he had said something about plumbing and she had simply nodded.

"Fine," she'd said, and the part of her that wasn't numb had been oddly glad to see the way his jaw clenched at the simple word. It meant he wasn't indifferent to her.

Back in college, when Kate had been studying attachment in abusive families, her professor had compared a child's need for love to that of a starving man faced with a soggy potato chip. It wasn't nourishing. It wasn't what anyone would choose under normal circumstances. But when the choice was that or nothing, the chip would win every time.

That clenched jaw was Kate's soggy chip.

The worst moment came when she woke up in the middle of Boone's second-to-last night and heard him talking. At first she thought he was on the phone with Jill or Craig. But three in the morning in Comeback Cove was two in the morning in Ollanta, and she doubted that there was any emergency that would require a call at this hour.

Besides, when she listened more closely, his voice was going on and on, steady, without the pauses that would come with a phone call.

She had to know. She slipped out of bed and moved to the foot of the stairs, where she waited. And listened.

And died a little inside when she realized that he was singing into the recorder. "Carry On Wayward Son," the song he had sung over and over while walking Jamie the night of the ankle and the tooth. The night when she had figured out that he was going to be better at this family thing than he thought possible.

Why the hell wouldn't he believe her?

When Saturday morning finally arrived, it was almost a relief. She packed Jamie's diaper bag and had the wild thought that this was how she had felt while getting ready for Neil's funeral. The time of bracing for the worst was almost over. Once she got through this, she could stop saying goodbye and start crawling forward into her new reality.

Of course, her twelve-year-old self had had no idea that the days and weeks and months after the funeral would be the hardest as she learned what it truly meant to live without the only father she'd known. And yet here she was, thirty years old, still clinging to that same belief.

Boone had offered to take the bus to Ottawa and then taxi to the airport, but Kate had refused. Jamie deserved every minute with his dad, she said.

She ordered herself to stop listening to the little voice inside that kept reminding her that every moment they were together was another chance for him to change his mind.

But there was no hesitation as Boone stowed his bags in the trunk.

And no sounds of regret as he said that he would sit in the back for the drive, so he could keep Jamie amused.

And no words for her as they drove, other than those related to their son.

When she turned in to the airport and started to switch to the lane leading to the parking lot, he said, "Just drop me at the curb."

"But I—"

"Kate. Jamie fell asleep. Just drop me. It'll be fine."

She pressed her lips tight and steered toward the Air Canada departures area.

When she pulled up to the curb, he sat motionless. She had the oddest feeling that he hadn't truly understood what was happening until this moment.

On the other hand, she was barely going through the motions herself.

She didn't trust herself to turn around. She watched in the rearview mirror as Boone's hand hovered over Jamie's cheek, longing, she knew, for one more touch, but reluctant to disrupt the nap.

He was such a good father.

Then he looked up. For one second, their eyes tangled in the mirror. And even though she knew she shouldn't, knew it was probably the worst thing to do, she said it anyway.

"I love you."

His eyes widened, then closed, fast. He turned his face away from her, just like a child refusing comfort.

He opened the car door.

"I know," he said softly.

And then he was gone.

CHAPTER SEVENTEEN

"BOONE, WHAT THE hell are you doing?"

He dragged his attention from the computer screen to Jill, framed in the office door. Behind her he spotted flashes of color and heard the unmistakable cries of kids running past. He swiveled slightly in his chair to follow their path as they flitted from side to side down the road, chasing and laughing and reveling in life.

Enjoy it while you can, kids.

In the doorway, Jill tapped her foot and gave him the over-the-glasses glare she had perfected over decades of herding jackasses like him.

"I know you heard me," she said. "Your ears might have got plugged up on the plane, but you've been back a solid week now, so I know there's something else clogging your head. Not to mention that's the fifth time I've walked through here and seen you staring at the same game of FreeCell." She shook her head as she walked to her own desk. "If you're going to slack off, just leave for your place and do it right. I have plenty to do in here without needing to babysit you."

"Don't sweet-talk me too much, Jill. It'll go straight to my head."

"You're such a pain in the arse."

It felt good to have her berating him again. He'd learned long ago that the only time he needed to worry with Jill was when she wasn't giving him hell.

"I'll leave soon. But the Wi-Fi at my place was spotty this morning, and it's Saturday, so I need to—"

"Oh, that's right." Jill checked the clock. "You need to call Jamie."

The dread that had filled him from the moment he opened his eyes this morning multiplied faster than rabbits in spring. "Yeah."

"Can you give me five minutes?" she asked. "I just want to find a couple of files. I'll take them back to my place and put a sign on the door so you can have privacy." Her eyes met his and softened. "Unless you'd rather have company."

Would he? Oh, hell, yes. He was pretty sure that this call was going to be as rough as the whole drive from Comeback Cove to the airport. Or the never-ending time waiting for his flight, when he knew that all he had to do was make one fast call and everything could turn around. Or that whole last week when every waking moment, and most of his sleeping ones as well, was spent drowning in the awareness of what he had lost. Which was nothing compared to what he would have lost if Kate hadn't been there.

You've lived through worse, he told himself. It was what he'd always said.

The difference was that this time he didn't believe it.

"I'll be okay," he told Jill. He would survive this call. And the next one, and the one after that, until they became more joy than torture once again. "But thanks for the offer."

"No need for thanks," she said with something closer to her usual briskness. "I'm just dying to get another look at that little cutie of yours. You haven't been flashing near as many pictures as I'd like since you got back."

"Trying not to be an obnoxious father."

"Good Lord, Boone. Like anyone could ever get bent out of shape over a man in love with his child."

He didn't like the way she looked at him when she said that. It made him feel like he was back in her grade nine algebra class, trying to convince her that he'd done his homework but simply forgot to hand it in.

Craig had welcomed Boone back with a hearty back slap and carried on as always, but Jill had been giving him the eye since he walked into the office. If he didn't do something to convince her he was okay soon, she was going to start asking questions he didn't want to answer. Either that or she would bypass him and talk directly to Kate.

That could not be allowed to happen.

"Here." He pulled his phone from his pocket, opened the photo gallery and handed it to her. "There's about fourteen thousand shots of Jamie on this. Knock yourself out."

He turned back to his laptop, trying to shut out the comments and coos coming from behind him. Email. He would check his email. So what that he had already checked it eight times in the last hour? So what that, once again, there had been nothing from Kate other than the usual brief rundown of Jamie's day, accompanied by a new shot of him being adorable?

It was better for everyone this way. He was here, doing what he knew he could do best. Jamie was growing and thriving and surrounded by enough love that it didn't matter that his father wasn't physically present. And Kate—well, she might believe that she loved Boone, but time would help. Now that he was gone she could get back to her regular life. Her safe life. Allie was moving in soon and Kate could watch her and Cash navigating their way to a family, and Kate would remember what she really wanted.

Maybe Boone should email Eric from the hardware store, the one who had gone to school with

Kate. He'd been awfully interested in how she was doing. Boone suspected that if asked, old Eric would be more than happy to deliver something to Kate, or give her some advice on finishing the jobs Boone hadn't been able to get through. Eric would know how to patch the holes and smooth off the rough edges and make sure everything was the way it should be. And when the jobs were done, Eric would still be there, in Comeback Cove, part of Kate's regular world.

Yeah. That might be a good thing. And maybe, in about fifty years, Boone would find the strength to do it.

"Here you go."

With a start, he realized Jill was at his elbow, holding his phone out to him while he sat there like a zombie in front of his screen. He really needed to get a grip.

But even as he thought it, he knew he was screwed. Because the only way he could pull himself together was by getting a grip on the only two things that mattered.

Jamie. And Kate.

"I'll get out of your way now," Jill said quietly. He nodded his thanks. She slipped out the door and closed it firmly behind her, leaving him alone.

After a lifetime of being on the empty side of a door, Boone should have been used to it.

Yeah. He really should.

KATE SETTLED JAMIE on her lap, hit the button to start the Skype call and pulled up the smile she'd been practicing all morning. She could do this. Fifteen, twenty minutes, and this first sort of contact would be behind her, and then she could breathe again. She had her list of things to tell Boone, all about the new tooth coming in and that they had started tasting vegetables, and that Jamie had figured out how to sit up by himself and grab the stuffed alpaca Boone had given him. Jamie was wearing his cutest shirt and Kate had combed her hair and brushed her teeth—total win—so she was as ready as she would ever be.

She would be fine.

"Hi there." Boone's voice came through first, meaning she had one millisecond to catch her breath at the arrow of longing that hit her straight in the heart before the video portion of the call kicked in and she had to put on her happy face. "Hi, Jamie!"

On her lap, Jamie's head swiveled back and forth. Searching.

You're not the only one, sweetie.

"Hi." Crap. She had never felt this awkward before, like no matter what she said, it would be the wrong thing.

Though maybe that was because there was nothing right about this situation. All of it was wrong. They should be—okay, not together in the same house, but together in intention, in their hearts, in love. As wrong as the situation had felt when she was waiting for the lawyer, this was infinitely worse.

"Well." She sat up straighter and brightened her smile. "We've had a busy week around here. Did I tell you that someone has learned that he can screech? Like, really loud?"

She chattered on, glancing at her notes as needed, keeping it all about Jamie. She was doing this for Jamie. Her heart might have been ripped out of her chest but her little boy still deserved to know his father, and she would make that happen, damn it.

Jamie, however, seemed to have other ideas. He twisted around on her lap and stared at the door.

"Look, Jamiekins." She tapped the monitor. "There's Daddy, right there. See? He's waving at you."

Boone waved obligingly. Jamie's lower lip stuck out.

No. Not more tears, not now.

Boone must have seen the oncoming threat as well, for he leaned forward in his chair. "It's okay, buddy. I miss you, too."

Oh, sure. He misses *Jamie*.

She blinked, not sure where that had come from. She wanted Boone and Jamie to love each other. She wanted them to look forward to visits, to cherish their time together.

It seemed there was a part of her that was too weary and bruised to remember those conditions didn't have to apply to her, as well.

Jamie slapped the monitor. Kate pulled his hand back but not before Boone's hand had also come up to press against his screen.

"I got the official invitation to the presentation," she blurted out, desperate to say something, anything, before reality caught up with her again.

"What presen—oh." Boone's expression flipped from curious to closed faster than the sign on an ice cream shop at the end of the hottest day of summer. Too late, she remembered that Boone wouldn't want to know about the ceremony to officially present the White House silver to the American ambassador. In Boone's mind, that was nothing but another sign of his inability to be the kind of father Jamie deserved.

"Right. Well. Allie brought another load over yesterday." That was better. "Her landlady still refuses to believe she's leaving and keeps offering her new deals. I think the only thing that's left would be for her to pay Allie to stay."

"She's moving in at the end of the month, right?"

Oh, he was good. No one watching would have any idea that he already knew all of this, that he had been in the kitchen with her and Allie as they'd talked about what would come to Kate's and what would go to Cash's and what might need to be—God forbid—stored in Maggie's garage.

"That's right. We're looking forward to that, aren't we, Jamiekins?"

And she was. Once Allie was here, things would be better. There would be another adult on hand to simplify showers and dishes and laundry. The house wouldn't echo the way it did. There would be a new person using the upstairs bathroom, so Kate would have to put out fresh towels to replace the ones she found herself crying into often.

"Well." Boone's smile seemed almost as fake as hers. "Sounds like everything's rolling along pretty smoothly there."

Jamie whimpered. Kate steeled herself.

"Absolutely," she said with all the fake cheer she could muster. "Everything is just fine."

IN THE MIDDLE of his second week back, Boone found an unexpected email in his inbox.

Ian North... Cash's brother... Northstar Foundation...

That was right. Cash had said something about his brother heading up the charitable arm of the family business. He had said something about getting Boone and this brother, Ian, together, but nothing had happened.

Looked like Cash had mentioned Boone and Sonqo anyway. Nothing wrong with that.

Expanding...looking for field operative...equal parts Canada and travel...salary...

Boone stopped breathing.

He checked the salary again.

He did a mental calculation of how many heating bills it could cover, even for a house as needy as Kate's.

Boone had never been hit by lightning. But he wouldn't be surprised if it felt a lot like the jittery sensation that had him all but jumping from his seat to prowl the edges of the office.

Jill paused in the middle of a line in the flow chart she was preparing for an upcoming seminar and took in his actions.

"Ants in your pants?"

Her voice brought him back to reality. What was he thinking? He belonged here. If Ian had been talking something part-time, something that could be done from Peru...but no. This was a full-time position. And it wasn't even a real offer, just an email to let him know about it and invite him to apply.

A job like that would get hundreds of applicants. Boone wouldn't stand a chance.

"Whatever is going on in that twisted mind of yours, it certainly seems to be interesting," Jill said. "Because I swear you just zipped through every emotion in the human experience in about thirty seconds flat."

He couldn't tell her. He wasn't going to apply, and even if he did, he wouldn't get it. So why make her think that he might be leaving? He couldn't leave. This was his life.

Even if it didn't feel as alive as it once had.

"Interesting email," he said.

"From Kate?"

"Of course not." Jill knew that he got the Jamie report at the end of each day. Why would she think anything had changed?

"Oh." She waited.

He didn't offer.

She turned back to her flow chart.

He resumed pacing. Once around the desk… twice, with a stop to refill his coffee en route… three times, with ideas and options and what-ifs dancing through his head…

"Boone?"

"Yeah?"

"Are you going to tell me what's bothering you, or are you going to haul your restless arse out of here so I can concentrate?"

Mierda.

He headed for the door. His hand was on the knob when she said, "Running away never solved anything, Boone."

Well, that stopped him in his tracks.

"I'm not running anywhere. I'm leaving so you can do your…"

His voice trailed off, withered by the glare she was sending his way.

"Don't you dare insult either of us by pretending you don't know what I'm talking about," she said softly.

He let go of the doorknob. The mask of bravado he'd been wearing since he came back slipped away and he sagged, every bit of him, like a tent when the frame had been removed.

Jill set her marker on the desk.

"Boone." She spoke gently. "I know you love this place. I have seen how much you've poured into it over the years, and I know how much you have given it, and us. But do you honestly believe that we want you here at the expense of your own family?"

The last thing he needed was for Jill to start badgering him about what was going on.

"We're not a family," he said. "Not a real one. So don't—"

"And where in the hell did you come up with that idea?"

Okay, that was definitely not the response he'd expected.

"Jamie is your son. Kate is your wife. Tell me how that doesn't make a family."

"Oh, I don't know. Maybe because I'm here and they're there? Or because the divorce has been started? Or because—"

"Because you're too chickenshit to try for real?"

He wasn't sure where this conversation was coming from, but one thing was certain: he didn't like it.

"The email wasn't from Kate, okay? So don't waste your energy coming up with fairy tales about—about any of that."

Jill watched him, her eyes unreadable behind her glasses. At last she nodded, slowly, like she had been deliberating and then come to a decision.

"You're fired."

He went numb. No. More than that. He clearly and distinctly felt himself step outside his body. He stood off to the side, keeping himself safe from harm while a piece of his life splintered and died. And the strangest part, other than the fact that he was watching it all from an oddly removed distance, was that he knew this feeling. He hadn't lived it since he was a kid, but oh, God, he'd lived it enough times then for it to be carved into his very core.

"You can't fire me." He had to speak slowly to get the words out, because his mouth was still operating independently of the part of him that wasn't participating in this.

She shrugged. "I probably should talk to Craig, true. But once I explain everything to him, he'll back me up."

"Really."

"Absolutely."

"Then maybe you could explain it to me. Because I sure as hell don't know where this came from."

"Sure." She grabbed her marker and rubbed it back and forth between her palms, the way she always did when she was leading a seminar or a class. "Let me lay it out for you. Craig and I are the executive officers of this foundation. We have the final say in all employee matters. Your work has not been up to par since you came back. You're distant and snappish and not doing your job the way it needs to be done. Therefore, your employment is being terminated."

"That's bullshit." Bullshit was good. It meant he could argue his way back in, and everything would be right again, and he could stop watching himself from a distance. "You have some crazy idea that I don't want to be here and I need to go back to Canada to be with Kate and Jamie, because you're sure that we're really a happy family that just needs time to work things out. So you think that if you fire me, I'll have to go back there."

"Oh, is that what I'm thinking? Good of you to tell me. I had no idea."

A thin line of sweat broke out along his upper lip. This wasn't supposed to be happening. "Jill, come on. Look, I…okay…yeah. I haven't been up to snuff since I got back. I admit it. But that's… you can't just fire me. You wouldn't. I know you. If you really had a problem with my work, you would talk to me about it, the same way you have God knows how many times in the past."

"Maybe I've given you all the chances I can give." The marker clacked against her rings as she rolled it. "Maybe I've reached my limit."

"That is so—"

"You weren't supposed to come back here."

He stepped back. "What does that mean?"

"It means, Boone, that you're messing up bigtime." She looked toward the ceiling, beseeching the heavens for guidance, no doubt, before leveling that teacher-gaze at him once more. "You don't need us anymore. We love you. God knows you're like my own son. But Boone, sometimes your skull is thicker than the rocks in the ruins. You shouldn't be here. You should be back home—"

"This is home."

The words burst out of him. He didn't mean to say it, didn't mean to feel it, but as soon as the words were out there, he knew it was true. This was home. He had known it but never admitted it, because he knew what would happen if he did. It was the same thing that had happened every goddamned time.

Home was the place that sucked you in and then spit you out. Home was the place you had to leave.

"Oh, Boone." Jill's voice did a 180—almost mocking one second, total sympathy the next. "Boone, having you here—having you with Craig and me—it saved us. I know you think that we were trying to help you, and yeah, that was part of it. But you...you gave us a new focus. You gave us new hope. We wanted to build this community and make this place work, and we probably would have done it anyway, but when you came to live with us...it gave us a new reason to be here. We knew that you had so much promise. That all you needed was a fresh start in a place where nobody had hung any labels on you, where you didn't have a past that sucked. But we needed that new beginning just as much as you did." She paused. "Probably even more."

He closed his eyes, reliving Jamie's wide, confused eyes; the guttural sound Kate had made as she'd flipped Jamie onto her knee; the hot fist of fear that had grabbed his own gut and twisted it as he'd grasped what was happening and then the crippling assault of what-ifs.

He couldn't begin to comprehend what Craig and Jill had gone through when their daughter died. But if those two or three seconds of terror were any clue, then his wonder at their ability to go on had become limitless.

"But, Boone, you're wrong about something. This isn't your home. It was, for a long time, and I can understand, a bit, how hard it would be for you of all people to have to leave the only real home you've known. But nobody is kicking you out this time. Nobody is dragging you away. It's your own heart that's leading you away, because it isn't here anymore."

That kick in his gut? Yeah. Recognition.

"Oh, I know a part of you will always live here. But the biggest piece is precisely where it should be. In Canada. And that's where you should be, as a father to your son and maybe even, God willing, building something with his mother, because it's obvious to everyone that you're in love with her."

Well, so much for thinking he'd kept that hidden.

"You're not going to leave me with any illusions about privacy or keeping things to myself, are you?"

"Of course not. Mothers never do." She tipped her head, her eyes twinkling. "You might as well tell me what was in that email. You know I'm going to worm it out of you anyway."

Since it seemed he was no longer allowed to hold on to any of his delusions, he didn't bother answering. He simply pulled up the email, pulled out the chair and gestured for her to sit.

She read it.

She sat back.

She folded her hands primly in her lap.

"You want to tell me why you're wasting time pacing like an idiot when you should be polishing up your résumé?"

"Because I—"

"And if your excuses have anything to do with Craig and me, or Project Sonqo, or any idiotic notion that you're not qualified for the job, you can stop right there."

And there went his dignity, too.

"There's no guarantee that I'd get it."

She rolled her eyes. "Of course not. But if the head of the foundation is encouraging you to apply, your chances are definitely up there." The chair squeaked as she leaned forward. "If you're looking for guarantees, Boone—in jobs, or life, or especially in love—well, I'd say you picked the wrong planet to live on. The brutal truth is that none of us get out of this unhurt. Some of us get slapped around a lot more than the rest. But the only alternative is to spend the rest of your days living the way you are now. Running. Hiding. Terrified. I don't know about you, but I'd rather take the chance and see what happens. Because you could get hurt, yeah. Or you could end up in the middle of the messiest, happiest kind of life that you could ever imagine."

He didn't need to imagine it. He knew.

Just as he knew precisely why he didn't dare grab what had been offered.

"But what if I'm the one doing the hurting?"

She sat up so straight and so fast that the chair scooted backward. "What the—where on earth did that—"

Then she got it.

"You think that history is doomed to repeat itself."

He couldn't answer. Not with words, not even with a nod. It was too shameful, too terrifying to admit to this woman who had never been anything but an amazing mother and had lost her child anyway.

But Jill wasn't having any part of that.

"Is this a hypothetical fear? Or did something happen?"

It took him three tries before he could get the answer out there. "Yeah. Something..."

It was like a faucet had been opened. No, more

like a fire hydrant. Once he'd started, he couldn't stop. He told Jill everything, from the worries that had gripped him the minute he'd stepped off the plane until that moment when he could have killed his kid without even trying. By the time he was done he was back in his chair, slumped in the seat, staring at the floor so he wouldn't have to see Jill's reaction.

When he finally finished, he made himself sit straight, though he still couldn't look at her.

"Are you done?" she asked, not unkindly.

Done. Yeah, that was the word of the moment.

"Guess so."

"I have a question for you. How did you spend the months before you went back home? Not here at work, but when you were off duty."

"I—the same as always, I guess. Cooking. Hanging out. Reading."

"I saw what you were reading, Boone. Don't pretend you don't know what I'm asking. There were so many books about parenting and child-care in your place that you could have stocked your own aisle in a major city bookstore."

He didn't have to look at her to know she was rolling her eyes.

"Next question. How the hell do you think Kate knew what to do when Jamie was choking?"

"She had training. Right. But Jill, I—"

"You think it's different with you. You think

you can't learn anything that really matters, like how to take care of your own son. You think you're not smart enough or strong enough to do the things everyone else can do, or that there's no way you'll ever do it right so there's no point in even trying." Her voice hardened. "In other words, you think everything your mother ever said about you is true."

Good God. If Jill didn't stop driving the breath out of his lungs, he was going to hit the floor at any moment.

"Parenting isn't something you're born knowing, Boone. It's learned. Some people have more of a natural inclination, true, just like some weavers have a better eye than others. But it's a skill. It can be learned. And if you were taught wrong by your first teacher, then guess what? You can learn new skills."

"It's not that easy."

"Who said it was?" She leaned forward, one finger leveled at him. "But you know damned well that it would be more than worth the work."

She was missing the point. "For me, it would be worth it. But what about Jamie? Say I got this job and went back. Say I tell Kate, hey, I want to give this a shot after all. How does Jamie play into that? He's the one who's going to pay the price when I mess up. He's the one whose happiness is on the line, Jill, and there's no way I'm going to risk—"

He stopped. Not because he was out of words, but because of the silly, goofy smile on Jill's face.

"Do you hear yourself, you idiot? You're not worried about you. You're worried about Jamie. You're putting him first. That right there tells me everything I need to know about your ability to be a good father."

"But—" he started, then stopped as her words sunk into him.

"Good." She nodded. "You've stopped talking and started listening. Best move you've made all day."

He wanted to glare, but he couldn't quite pull it off. Probably because he was too busy listening to the small whisper of hope her words had fired inside him.

Jill rose from her chair with a groan, shuffling over to him and bending so her face was level with his. "Keep listening, Boone. And while you're at it, polish up your résumé and apply for that job. It's time for you to find your own Project Sonqo."

What the—

Oh. Right. How could he have forgotten?

In Quechua, *sonqo* meant *heart*.

CHAPTER EIGHTEEN

KATE HAD COME to hate Friday nights.

Most nights she was so wiped out that her only sleep issues were courtesy of little Mr. Jameson. But Fridays were the night before her call with Boone, which meant that she spent half the night making lists of what she needed to tell him, and then the other half making lists of what she couldn't tell him. When she wasn't reminding herself what she could and couldn't say, she was giving herself the pep talk she delivered every week.

Come on, girl. You can do it. You survived last week, even though Boone needed a haircut and you spent the whole call wanting to push his bangs back. You'll make it through this one.

There were times when she felt she should really get a dog. Because, heaven knew, she was talking to herself exactly the way she would address a pup. At least if she had a dog, she would have someone else to talk to while she spent the night in the rocking chair, cursing herself for wasting precious sleep hours.

And then Saturday nights were almost worse.

She had survived, yes, but she also had a whole conversation's worth of fresh reminders of how much she missed him. And how angry she was at him. And how much joy he was stealing from all of them, just because he was—what? Too scared of the past to give them all a shot at happiness?

On the one hand, her heart ached for him.

On the other hand, if he were to walk in the door she couldn't decide if she would kiss him or give him holy hell.

It was probably a good thing that she was still nursing. If she could drink, she would be developing a bottle-a-night habit, and who could afford that? Thank God Allie had both moved in and was in the habit of bringing home leftovers. There was something decadent and cozy about wandering the empty house, distracting herself from the memories and hurts by nibbling on a slice or forking up a little spaghetti.

On the third Friday after Boone's departure—well, technically, it was a little after one on Saturday morning—she was sacked out on the living room sofa, sitting in the dark and snacking on garlic bread while she watched the tree branches swaying in the moonlight, when she became aware of a sound from upstairs. It was a sound she hadn't heard in years, but it was one she had lived so many times in the aftermath of Neil's death that there was no mistaking it.

Allie was crying.

Big sister instincts kicked in immediately. Kate grabbed the monitor, threw it in the pocket of her robe, and made it up the stairs in record time.

"Allie?" She knocked on the door. "Allie, what's wrong?"

Allie's response was muffled but there was no doubt that the words she had just uttered would have earned her a swipe of soap across the tongue when they were kids.

Kate had a moment of panic. She'd been so intent on getting up here quickly that she hadn't even thought that Allie might not be alone. Much as Kate liked Cash, she wasn't prepared to see him while she was in her jammies. Especially because she was ashamed to admit that her so-called night-shirt was really one of Boone's T-shirts that she'd pilfered while they were still in Ottawa.

But if there was one thing she'd learned after years of working with little kids, it was that an air of confidence compensated for a multitude of sins.

"Allie." She knocked again. "Come on. Open up."

She heard the rustling of covers, the shuffle of feet, the rattle of the doorknob.

"Go back to bed." Allie crossed her arms. "I'm fine."

"Really."

"Yes. Really."

"That's interesting, seeing as how you were crying loud enough that I heard you all the way downstairs."

"Maybe I wasn't crying."

Kate peeked over Allie's shoulder. The bed was empty, Allie was in pajamas, and her eyes and cheeks were puffy and wet.

With one finger, Kate teased a tear from her sister's cheek. "You want to tell me about what's not wrong?"

Allie's lips clamped together.

Silence.

"Did something happen at work?"

"No. Kate—"

"With Cash?"

Allie's face crumpled. "No."

She never could lie for beans.

"What did he do, Al?"

"Nothing. Don't you have a baby who'll be waking you up soon?"

"I've spent a lot of time with preschoolers. I know how to use distraction, and let me tell you, that didn't cut it."

"It wasn't a distraction. It was the truth."

"Oh, good. How about spilling a few more truth bombs, okay?" She ran through possibilities in her mind. Maggie was in favor of the sisters living together, so it wasn't that... Cash had joined them for dinner on Wednesday and everything had seemed fine then, though Kate was painfully aware of how quickly relationships could shift... She and Allie had adjusted to each other's schedules, Allie was totally unpacked, her check for the utilities hadn't bounced...

"Is Cash having a hard time with you living here?"

The night light in the hall cast enough illumination for Kate to see the way Allie's gaze dropped.

"Okay, kiddo." Kate took her sister's arm and guided her back into the room, seating both of them on the edge of the bed. "Out with it. What's his problem? Is he—I mean, this is kind of awkward, but is it, you know, not private enough for you guys? Because I know it's not the same as having your own place, but we could maybe put a door at the top of the stairs, or put a minifridge and a microwave in Boone—I mean, in the other room, so you don't have to feel like you're in a dorm, or—"

Allie stared at her for a second before bursting into an odd mix of laughter and tears, punctuated by some serious hiccups. Kate reached for her. Old habits died hard. But Allie shook her head and raised a hand to stop her.

"It's not that, Kate. Cash hasn't said a word, I swear on Nana's grave, and I'm at his place half the time anyway, so it's not like we're teenagers trying to find a way to sneak off together." She grinned, hiccupped once more and stared down at her hands knotted in her lap.

Kate put on her thinking cap. Whatever it was, Allie obviously didn't want to tell her. So, that meant…crap, she wasn't awake enough for logic… It had to be something Allie was afraid would upset Kate. Something that would make her worried or angry or sad or…

Oh.

"It's not *Cash* who has the problem with you living here, is it, Allie Cat?"

Allie tried. She really did. She shook her head, all wide-eyed innocence, but the half sob in her throat betrayed her. "This made so much sense," she wailed. "And I was so excited to move in and play with Jamie, and help you the way you always help me. But—"

"But Cash?"

"Yeah. Cash. Every time I go there, I kick myself. I know that we've only been together a few months and I know that people will talk and I know that Mom is going to blow her stack, but, Kate, I…this is wrong." She grabbed a tissue from the nightstand. "My head knows that living here is the right thing. But the rest of me thinks my head is a horse's ass."

"Oh, my God, Allie, you dipstick. Have you felt like this since you moved in?"

"Um…"

Kate's stomach cramped.

"Actually, it's been since…um…the day after you suggested it."

Which meant that Allie had regretted saying yes almost immediately. "Why didn't you say something?"

"Because it made sense. And it really was the perfect solution. And I figured once I got here, everything would be fine."

Now it was Kate's turn to burst into laughter. "Well that should have been your first clue right there."

"What do you mean?"

"You were talking yourself into it. Just like when you—"

"When I almost married Luke. Oh, hell. How could I be so dense?"

Kate was pretty sure she was supposed to say something sympathetic and bracing. Unfortunately, sympathetic and bracing were beyond her reach at the moment. The best she could manage was sarcastically supportive.

"You could at least have figured it out before you got everything unpacked, you goof."

"I told you it would be scary if I had to be the practical one!"

Kate grabbed more tissues and shoved them at her sister the idiot. "First thing in the morning,

I want you to pack a bag and get your cute little behind to Cash's house where it belongs."

"But—"

"Don't worry about your stuff. Just move it as you can. If you need to leave anything here, that's no problem. It'll make the rooms look more lived in."

"Thanks, but that's not what I—Kate. I don't want to leave you all alone."

Not to worry. Boone took care of that.

"Hey. We both knew this wasn't going to be permanent. The end just came sooner than we expected."

"But what about the house? Will you still be able to stay until next spring?"

The cramp in her stomach intensified.

"That requires math, and right now the only counting either one of us should be doing involves sheep." She gave Allie a quick hug before rising. "See you in the—"

"Hang on." Allie's hand closed on the hem of the T-shirt, halting Kate's departure. "I'm not going to just run off and leave you. We'll work out something."

"Allie, really. It'll be fine."

She tugged the shirt out of Allie's hand and made tracks for the door again, only to be stopped once more. This time, however, it was Allie's words that made her pause.

"Kate. Remember how you said I should have got a clue that something was wrong when I was talking myself into staying here?"

"Right."

"Well, I'm not the only one trying to convince herself everything is okay. Maybe you should ask yourself why you start getting antsy when I ask you simple questions." Her voice dropped. "Or why you keep saying that everything is fine when we both know it isn't."

AT FOUR THIRTY, Kate told herself that if she wasn't asleep in five minutes, she would have to get up. There was no point in staying in bed. She was tossing and turning so much her movement could probably be measured on the Richter scale.

At 5:05 a.m. she opened her eyes to the sound of snuffling and whimpers from the crib.

Crap. She should have dragged herself out of bed while she could. She'd had just enough sleep that now she was more exhausted than she would have been if she'd pulled a true all-nighter.

It'll be okay, she assured herself as she settled Jamie at her breast. Allie would leave for work around ten. And Boone would call soon after that. She always felt some momentary relief after their weekly call was over. Then it would be lunch, and then she'd put Jamie down for his nap, and she would lie down herself and catch a few winks.

If she could just hang on for…um…seven hours, she would be fine.

She winced, and not because of the razor-sharp tiny fingernails curling into her face.

"But I am fine," she said. Quietly, of course, because there was a small chance that Jamie would go back to sleep. "I'm healthy. Jamie is healthy. Boone is…okay, not here, and not part of my world, but he's still happy and healthy. We have a roof over our heads and will continue to have one, even if it's different. Allie came to her senses. Mom is…" She hesitated. "Mom is Mom. I still have a lot of maternity leave, and I have a great job to go back to, and I am fine, just fine, and…"

It occurred to her that someone who was truly fine wasn't likely to be assuring herself of that while sitting alone in the dark. At an ungodly hour. With tears streaming down her face.

Wait a minute. When had she started crying?

"Okay, so I'm tired." She stroked Jamie's cheek. "Of course everything is going to feel more overwhelming. That's just logical. Right, kiddo?"

Since she and Jamie had yet to learn the same language, she didn't get much of a reply.

On the other hand…

"I do say *fine* a lot."

Jamie's hand batted at her cheek.

"I say bad words a lot, too, though. So that's no proof of anything. Right?"

Except no one had ever called her out on her word choice when she was swearing. Other than her mother, of course, and that was just part of the job.

"Fine." She said it again, drawing the word out, elongating the *f* and stretching the *n*, as if testing them to see how long she could make them last.

"There's nothing wrong with saying I'm fine," she told Jamie as she initiated the burp sequence. "I mean, what am I supposed to say? 'No, Allie, you can't leave, I'm counting on you splitting the bills so I can stay here'? 'No, Mom, I don't know when Boone is coming back or how I'm going to finish the repairs'? 'No, Boone, you have to overcome everything you ever learned and leave the only family you've ever known so you can live here with us, because like it or not, we're a team, like Han and Leia or Indy and Marion or—'"

"It's almost like I'm back in that convention hall where I met your dad," she said to Jamie. "Characters everywhere. Everybody in costume. Everyone pretending to be—"

Everyone pretending to be something or someone they weren't. Just like she had been doing when she met Boone.

Just like she had been doing since he went back to Peru, since he left the first time, since she assured herself that she was good with something fast and furious and temporary when she had never been a fast or furious or temporary kind of gal in her life.

So, had she been pretending—acting—for the last year and a half?

"No." That one was out loud—for Jamie, for her, for the universe. "No. Not about everything."

She recognized the truth of that deep inside her. She might have jollied herself through a few moments, like telling Boone that she was pregnant, or her entire labor. But most of the time, she had been herself. A new self, transitioning to motherhood, but still Katherine Joy Hebert.

Except when she was dealing with a situation she didn't like. Such as, oh, when Boone insisted he couldn't be a father. Or when Allie got a clue about where she wanted to live. Or when Jamie woke up at ungodly hours. Though for that one she'd give herself a pass, because who would ever survive parenting if they weren't allowed to fake their way through the scary parts?

But even she, in her half-asleep, half-crying state, could see that there was a thread connecting those situations. It wasn't simply that she was trying to talk herself through things she didn't want to do.

She was trying to make sure everyone else was happy. Even if it meant lying to them about what she felt.

Even if it meant lying to herself.

A giant sob welled up and burst out of her, a choking, shuddering kind that had Jamie pausing in midsuck to stare up at her, his little eyes wide with alarm.

"Shh," she said through ragged breaths. "Shh. It's okay, baby, Mommy is—"

Mommy is so used to making sure everyone else is okay that she barely remembers how to take care of herself.

She rocked back and forth, a little more quickly, not sure if she was trying to soothe herself or her baby, but this time, it didn't matter.

"This has to stop." That one she said out loud, too, because she knew it would take a hell of a lot of forceful repetition to make that message sink in. "I am going to be a single parent…well, it doesn't matter. I can't walk around pretending everything is hunky-dory when it isn't, because then it'll be just like when I don't get enough to drink. I'll crash and burn. I'm not doing anybody any favors by pretending to be fine when I'm not." She reconsidered. "Okay. Sometimes it's acceptable. But not when it's big things, because…because…because for all I know, there might be a compromise, or some other solution. But if I don't say something, we'll never look for it, let alone find it."

She shifted Jamie to her shoulder. He let his unhappiness be known.

"I need to take a page from your book, kid. Not for everything. But for the important stuff. Like… like when I told Aunt Allie that I didn't care about her moving out already. I'm glad for her, I really am, but she's right. This is screwing up the plans I made." She swayed back and forth, patting and rubbing the little body that was already so much bigger than it had been just a few short months ago. "Or like when I said that I would be okay when your dad went back to Peru. The first time, I mean. Because even though Granny and Aunt Allie are wonderful, they weren't your Dad."

But none of those situations held a candle to the big one.

"I never ever should have told your dad that I was good with something temporary, or something long-distance," she whispered against Jamie's head. "Because I'm not. I want him here. And even though I am proud of what he's doing there, and I really do understand how hard it would be for him to take a chance on a family again, we deserve that chance. Me and you, and him, too. Maybe, if I had pushed it a bit, he would have been more willing to give it a shot. Maybe, when I told him I was okay with marriage being just for Nana, I was giving him the excuse he needed. Not because he can't do family, because he can. If he thinks he hasn't found a home and family there in Peru, then he's only lying to himself. But maybe…"

Maybe when she was turning herself inside out to accommodate him, to give him the chance to keep her and Jamie at a distance, it was what the grown-up Boone had needed. But maybe the scared, rejected kid inside him hadn't heard *freedom*, *options*, *compromise*. That kid probably heard *not needed, not necessary, not truly wanted*.

"I might be way off base with this, kiddo." Though it sure didn't feel that way. "But tonight, I'm going to talk to Aunt Allie about finding a fair way to deal with her moving out. And when your dad calls, I'm going to level with him. What the heck, right? It's not like things could get much worse." She laughed softly. "And after a night of no sleep, I might just be exhausted and scary enough to really pull it off."

BOONE COULDN'T REMEMBER ever being so nervous about a Skype call. Well, maybe the one when he'd spilled the news to Jill and Craig that he'd been doing a bit more than studying and sightseeing in his off-hours in Ottawa. But since then, there hadn't been another long-distance communication that had set his heart thumping and his throat humming the way the anticipation of this one did. Even the interactions with Ian North that had made this possible were a blip on the excitement scale in comparison.

He puttered around the office until the appointed time, when he checked to see that Kate had signed on and then hit her number.

"Hello," he sang out, though the last syllable fell somewhat flat as the video came into view. Jamie seemed to be doing his best to crawl up Kate's chest and make the great dive to freedom over her shoulder. Boone had a perfect view of Jamie's butt as he squirmed and flailed. It wasn't the best in terms of scenery, but given the amount of action, Jamie was certainly feeling strong and healthy today.

Kate, on the other hand, was a wreck. Her hair hung wet around her head, as if she'd just stepped out of the shower. Her shirt seemed to be buttoned wrong. The bags beneath her eyes were bigger than the ones he'd packed for his six-week visit, and her usual sparkle, even the subdued version he'd seen since his return, was lost behind a layer of…he wasn't sure what. Exhaustion, yes. That was evident. But there seemed to be more there, something that went deeper than fatigue.

"Hey," she said, her voice as flat as her eyes.

"Rough night?"

The corners of her mouth twitched. He was pretty sure it wasn't supposed to be a smile. "Yeah, you could say that."

The familiar sense of helplessness took hold of him. There was absolutely nothing he could do from here except let her vent and assure her that she was doing an amazing job, that it would get easier.

Easy for you to say.

He pushed the snarky thought away. Yes, it was true. He definitely wasn't doing his share of the work in raising their son.

But this time, at least, he could promise himself—and her—that the situation would soon be changing. That soon, he would be in a position to really make her life better.

"Is he cutting another tooth?"

"Yeah, I think maybe—"

The oddest thing happened. It was as if she forcefully stopped herself from saying whatever she had started to say. Not because she had been interrupted, but because she remembered something.

"No." It came out a little wavering at first, a little questioning, but then she said it again and there was no mistaking the underlying steel. "No, actually. His teeth are fine. I had a lot on my mind that made it difficult to sleep."

Her head tipped slightly. For a second she seemed almost pleased with herself.

Boone didn't claim to know everything about Kate Hebert, not by a long shot, but one thing was

certain: she was definitely showing him a side of
her that he'd never seen before.

"Anything you need to tell me?"

She hauled Jamie back onto her lap while she
considered. "Yes, actually, but let me get through
the Jamie report first."

Yeah, this was definitely up there in the freaky
column. But he couldn't help but think that she
would be a lot more like herself once he told her
his news.

"Okay. But I have—" he began. Kate spoke
over him.

"As you can see, Mr. Frisky here is learning the
wonderful world of transportation. He's sitting all
by himself for long periods now, a good ten minutes at a stretch, and the other day I caught him
doing some wiggle worm type of actions when he
was having tummy time. I think we might have
an early crawler on our hands." She turned Jamie
to face the screen. "Look, kiddo. There's Daddy.
Are you going to wave to him?"

Jamie slapped the screen and turned tail again.

"He's making some different sounds this week.
I'll try to catch them and send you a video. They're
starting to sound more like a conversation, with
the pauses and cadence you would expect, like
he's imitating—"

"Kate, I have a job offer."

He shouldn't have blurted it out that way. But

she seemed so distracted, and Jamie was being so active that he was afraid she was going to have to take off at any moment, and he had to let her know.

"You have a what?"

"Remember, while I was there I applied for some consulting things. Advisory jobs I could do from here. I mentioned it to Cash, just making conversation, and he said his brother runs a charitable—"

"Right. The Northstar Foundation. What about it?"

"Long story short, they've offered me a job. Ian says it's about a fifty-fifty split between being based in Canada and traveling, and the best part is—" he inhaled, drawing it out, savoring the moment "—the best part is that it pays real money. So you and Jamie can stay in the house."

He sat back and grinned, feeling like he'd finally made it to the top of Mount Dad. He laughed and shook his head, leaning sideways in his chair, swiveling in wide side-to-side motions like a kid who couldn't hold in his excitement.

"It'll take me about a few weeks to get finished up here. But—"

"Are you telling me you're leaving Project Sonqo? You're leaving Peru?"

"Yeah." He blew out the breath of disbelief that

always hit him when he thought about that part. "Yeah. I am."

"You're giving up the work you love."

Boone was getting a strong suspicion that Kate wasn't anywhere as thrilled about this turn of events as he had expected her to be.

"And you're doing it…let me get this straight. You're doing it so that Jamie and I can stay in the house."

"Uh—"

"With or without you?"

Without, of course, said the voice of fear.

With, you idiot, said everything else.

Since he wasn't capable of coming up with a coherent answer, he stayed quiet.

"Tell me, Boone. Were there aliens inhabiting your body when I asked you to stay married? Didn't you hear anything I said that night?" She twisted sideways, peering at him around Jamie, who was sprawling across her face like a starfish on a rock.

"I wanted to—"

"No. No, don't you dare say you wanted to help us stay here. I mean, okay, yes. Yes, in itself, that was thoughtful and I understand why you feel it's important, so don't think I'm not—" She rubbed a tired hand over her face, pushing her hair back, pulling Jamie's finger out of her ear. "But my God, Boone. You couldn't leave Peru for me. You couldn't leave for Jamie. But you'll leave because of the goddamned house?"

For the first time he could remember, Boone was glad there were thousands of miles between him and Kate.

"I understood that you couldn't leave there. I knew you had responsibilities and a life, and I... okay, I didn't like it, but I understood. I was proud of what you're doing. And then, when I figured out that I lo— then I thought, okay, living on two different continents isn't my dream, but we could make it work. It would be worth it. But you were afraid. You said no. No. Even though I—"

She cradled Jamie close to her, rocking back and forth in swift, jerky motions that Boone was pretty sure provided no comfort to anyone.

"You know what, Boone? I don't care where you live. I don't care what you do. Not anymore. I was willing to —but you threw it in my face. It's not that you can't do the full-time family thing. You won't. You don't want to even try. Maybe it's because of the way you grew up, and if so, yeah, I'm sorry. But right now, I don't give a rat's ass."

Shit. How had he messed this up so badly?

"I told you that I loved you. I told you that you're a good father and I believed in you, but you refuse to believe me. Not about you, not about the house, not about anything that matters. Like

Jamie. Or the future." Her voice broke. "Or what we could have had."

"Look, Kate, I'm sor—"

"I have to go."

"Kate. Please."

"No, Boone. I'm going. Your son needs attention and love, and I'm going to give it to him, because that's what matters." She shifted Jamie to her shoulder. "Go ahead and do what you want. I don't care anymore."

Before he could say anything else, she jabbed at the button to end the call.

Silence swelled to fill the room. Well, around him was silence. Inside him there was a frickin' hurricane of words and tears and accusations.

And the sick, clear realization that he had destroyed the one part of Kate's life that should have been the safest.

Her heart.

CHAPTER NINETEEN

KATE WALKED THROUGH the rest of the morning very glad that she had years of practice in looking after kids, because the care she was giving Jamie was the parenting equivalent of autopilot. She cuddled and nursed and diapered, she swept rooms and went outside and yanked up every weed she could see in the flowerbeds bordering the porch. She may have beheaded a few tulips while she was at it. The jury was still out on that.

It didn't matter. None of it mattered. All she cared about at the moment was keeping Jamie happy and staying away from her computer. Also her phone, which she deliberately left on the kitchen table, thus ensuring she wouldn't be able to hear it from outside.

There was nothing Boone could say that would make a difference now. She'd offered her life, her dreams, her heart, and he'd made it clear that he wanted no part of them.

"He can take his stupid job and..."

She growled beneath her breath, yanked up another weed and breathed.

At long last, naptime arrived. She settled Jamie in his crib and did a face-plant on the bed, praying that sleep would come swiftly.

Instead, just as she felt that familiar heaviness seeping through her body, the doorbell rang.

"Son of a—"

She could ignore it. She *should* ignore it. She wasn't expecting anyone, and she wasn't interested in supporting the school band trip or the local soccer league, and if Boone thought he could make up for being an ass by sending her flowers, he could eat the damn things. If she was really lucky, they would be covered in nasty, scratchy thorns.

But whoever it was rang the bell again. And Jamie made a little mewing noise that meant he was halfway to waking up. And she knew that if she wanted any chance of getting any sleep, she had to haul ass to the door and stop whoever was there before they hit the bell again.

She closed the door to the bedroom and hurried out front. As soon as she entered the living room she spied the familiar white hatchback in her driveway and immediately started swearing. It was her mother.

It wasn't until she yanked the door open that she realized she had been cursing in Spanish.

Out of my head, Boone. Now.

"Mom." Kate didn't even bother pretending to

be excited about Maggie's sudden appearance. "This really isn't a good time."

Maggie's eyebrows went up. "Will the Queen be dropping in today?"

"No."

"Then you can manage five minutes for your mother." Maggie swept in, her eyes darting back and forth.

"Jamie just went down for his nap. If you wake him, you'll be spending every Mother's Day by yourself for the next thirty years."

"Well, aren't you a ray of sunshine today?"

Kate longed to come up with a snappy reply, but at the moment, she didn't have the strength to snap her bra strap. "I didn't get any sleep last night. I want to have a nap while he's asleep. So excuse me for being rude, but what do you need?"

Maggie stepped back and gave Kate the kind of once-over that used to mean there had been a phone call from the teacher and it hadn't gone well. "Allie stopped by this morning."

Something started throbbing behind Kate's left eye.

"She said she wants to move in with Cash."

Kate braced herself, imagining what might come next. A tirade against living together without even being engaged? A pointed reminder that she had hoped Kate would talk sense into Allie?

Instead, Maggie reached into her pocket and pulled out a folded check.

"She feels very badly about making a promise to you about helping with the expenses and then leaving. But she's still paying off the wedding that wasn't, so she asked if she could borrow some from me."

Exhaustion and amazement swirled inside Kate, filling her eyes. "Oh, my God, Mom. She doesn't have to do that."

"Well, she did start something with you and then decide to cut and run. I understand why she did it, but still, you already had that done to you once. I won't let your sister do it to you, as well."

And there was the Maggie she knew and loved.

Kate pushed the check back. "Not happening, Mom."

"Oh, Katherine. You know I didn't mean—"

"Yes, you did, and please don't insult either of us by pretending otherwise."

Maggie rolled her eyes and sat down on the sofa. Kate stifled a groan. There went her nap.

"Put yourself in my shoes, Kate. How would you feel if someone treated Jamie the way Boone has treated you?"

This was so not the day for this discussion.

"I would probably hope that I did a good enough job raising him that I could trust his judgment.

And know that there might be more to the situation than what I could see."

"Easy to say from here."

"Yeah, that's true. But it's also true that Boone is taking a job with the Northstar Foundation, just so he can afford to keep me and Jamie in this house. And Allie is determined to keep me here. And you are offering money to help me stay here. And that's all well and good and I love you all, but damnation, can't anyone believe that I might want more out of life than this house?"

Oops.

If the break in her voice at the end of her rant hadn't been a clue, she would have known she'd pushed it too far from the shock on Maggie's face.

Kate thought she couldn't get any more tired. Now, contemplating the apologizing and explaining and groveling that lay in front of her, she felt her exhaustion double.

"I'm sorry," she whispered. "I know you all mean well. I know that in the long run, everything will be f—"

Her unfinished word hung between them.

Maggie stood. Kate braced herself, waiting for her mother to pour out some guilt, walk away, whatever.

Instead, Maggie walked over to her and pulled her into a hug.

"Oh, Katie." Maggie's fingers were strong as they stroked Kate's hair. "I'm so sorry."

Kate wanted to laugh and remind her mother that, really, Kate had been the one disparaging everyone, but she stayed quiet. Partly because if she opened her mouth, the lump in her throat was going to emerge in the form of howls. Mostly because she knew that if she really wanted people to listen to her, she had to stand behind her own words.

"It's funny," Maggie said, continuing to play with Kate's hair. "When I came over that day and talked to him—"

Kate tensed and raised her head. "What day? You talked to Boone without me?"

"When you hurt your ankle. You were asleep. Didn't he tell you?" Annoyance crossed Maggie's face. "I brought lasagna. Don't tell me he didn't feed it to you."

"I remember lasagna. He said you left it on the porch."

"Did he now?"

Kate didn't know what had happened between her mother and Boone, but watching Maggie now, she was sure it hadn't been a tea party.

"Mom? What did you do to him?"

"I didn't do anything." Maggie gave her a quick pat on the back before returning to the sofa. "But

I gave him some insights into—well—dealing with you. When you're sick or injured, I mean."

The throbbing behind Kate's left eye had spread to encompass the entire side of her face. "What. Did. You. Say."

"I didn't give out any state secrets. I simply told him that you don't like to be a bother, so he would have to ask you what you wanted. Which seems to be something I forgot myself."

Okay. Kate could live with that. Except that everyone seemed to have forgotten the part about asking and had gone straight to assuming.

"I also told him that if he broke your heart, I would hunt him down and turn him inside out. So, when is he starting this new job? Because I want to know if I need to book a flight to Peru, or if I can save the money and kill him once he gets here."

Kate stared at Maggie, not sure how to take it, then started laughing. Oh, but it felt good to laugh. And if it was tinged with a little hysterical exhaustion, well, that was understandable, wasn't it?

"You can't kill him, Mom. Jamie deserves to have his father around."

"Then why, exactly, are you so upset about him taking the job?"

Either Kate was more tired than she thought, and incapable of saying things so people could understand them, or Maggie was trying to make her think.

Both options sucked.

"Because he's doing it to—"

"Right. I know. So you guys can stay in the house." Maggie frowned. "Will he be moving back in here with you?"

"I don't—"

"Will you be staying married?"

"I… No. At least, I—"

"Do you *want* to stay married to him, Katie?"

It was the unexpected tenderness in Maggie's words that got to her. Maggie was supposed to bluster when it came to Boone. She was supposed to snarl and defend and threaten. Kate could deal with those.

This, though. This hit her where she wasn't ready.

She dragged her arm across her eyes, too weary to reach for a tissue. "Yeah, Mom. I know you think I'm an idiot, but if it were up to me, yes. I want to be married to him. Even if he planned to stay in Peru."

Maggie nodded and stared out the window. Her hands twisted back and forth in front of her in some odd dance that Kate knew meant she was putting the facts together.

Good luck with that.

"I'm going to recap this, Kate. I want to be sure I have everything right."

Kate nodded.

"You want to stay married but Boone does not."

Stupid damn tears.

"He does, however, want to make sure you and Jamie can stay in the home that he believes you love. Is that right?"

She managed a nod.

"And to do that, he's going to give up the one thing he told you from the start that he could not do."

"Right. But not for me or—"

"I'm doing the talking now, Katherine." Maggie's frown knocked about twenty years off Kate's emotional age. "Though I do have a question for you. Not you, the person, but you, the early childhood educator."

Oh, goody. Unexpected territory. Just what Kate needed.

"You mentioned more than once that he didn't have what anyone would call a stable childhood. So what would you say might be the most terrifying thing he could possibly do?"

"Mom. Come on. I have as much sympathy for him as anybody, but—"

"Please just answer the question. Your professional opinion only."

"You're not getting anything for Christmas this year, Mom. Not even a picture of Jamie."

"Lucky for me, Allie taught me how to use the camera on my phone. I can zoom, crop and add filters. So. Your answer?"

"He… Well…taking a chance on a family would be…okay. The truth is, he's afraid that if he's with us, he's going to end up hurting us the way his mother hurt him."

Maggie paled slightly.

Kate rushed to reassure her. "But that's because…okay, yes, there are statistics, and it's right to be aware. Concerned. But nothing ever happened. I never saw anything that made me worry. He's a good father, a wonderful father, but he… I told him I loved him. I told him I wanted us to stay together, even if we were in different places, and he said no."

Maggie inhaled sharply.

"I know you mean well, Mom. Or at least, I think that's what you're doing. Nothing is making sense anymore. But he really doesn't—"

"If he were anyone else, I'd be booking a flight right now," Maggie said.

"We covered this already, remember? Jamie's father. You can't kill him."

"Jamie is young. He wouldn't remember. However…" Maggie pointed at Kate. "You love him.

And even though you might not believe it right now, I think he loves you, too."

Well *those* were words Kate had never expected to hear from her mother.

"I think he does, too. Or at least, I thought he did. But even if he does…love me, I mean…he still said he doesn't—"

"Katherine Joy, for the love of God, can't you see what this is? It's a second chance." Maggie's gaze drifted up and sideways. She swallowed hard.

"When Neil died, there was nothing I wouldn't have given to have another day with him. Well, other than anything involving you and Allie, of course. But other than that…right. Even if it meant we had to start over again. Even if it meant we could never be exactly what I wanted. Just having him here, in the world with us again…it would have been enough."

Kate's breath froze in her chest.

"You might think that Boone is coming back for the wrong reason, Katie, but he's coming back. Maybe he needs to ease into this. Maybe it's all still terrifying. Maybe he really does have his head up his ass, and I need to start brewing some arsenic tea for him. But he'll be here. You're going to get the chance to see what can happen."

Kate dropped to the sofa, grabbed a corner

of her T-shirt and mopped at her eyes. "Damn it, Mom."

"I know. But what can I say? I want you to be happy. And whether I like it or not, I think he makes you happy." Maggie reached across the space between them and rested her hand on Kate's knee. "Besides, flights to Peru are expensive. If I do have to kill him it will be much easier to do it with him here."

IN THE MIDDLE of June, Boone was at his desk when Jill came in with a stack of mail. She walked to his desk and very casually dropped a cream-colored envelope in front of him.

On the back was printed a drawing of a crowned royal lion, holding a red maple leaf: the seal of the governor-general of Canada.

"Interesting company you're keeping these days."

"I'm not keeping company with anyone." He nudged the envelope aside. "That's an invitation to the thing where they're going to give the stuff we found back to the American government."

Jill dragged another chair from the corner of the room and perched on the edge. With her elbow on her knee and her chin in her hand, she was the very picture of rapt attention.

"Tell me you're going."

"Nope."

"What? Why not?"

Because Kate will be there. And even though he knew he would have to see her and spend time with her eventually, he didn't think he was ready to do it in a public forum.

"It's before I get there." And maybe if he stayed focused on the report in front of him, Jill would get the hint.

Instead, she grabbed the envelope from the corner and opened it.

"Hey!" he said as she pulled out the invitation. "That's personal."

"I know."

"You can't open my personal mail. That's violating federal law."

"Is it?" She scanned the invitation. "I guess that makes me a criminal. Now I get to feel badass."

He hid his smile. Jill, badass. Yeah. That'd be the day.

She set the invitation down, pulled off her glasses, and glared at him. "This is taking place two days before you were planning to leave."

"Exactly."

"So change your flight, Boone."

"So change fees are expensive, Jill."

"So sometimes they're worth it." She tapped

the paper on the desk. "You knew exactly when this was happening when you booked your flight, didn't you?"

"Maybe." Yes.

"I can't believe you're such a shortsighted chicken."

Okay, that was hitting below the belt.

"You want to tell me when this became your business?"

"Let me see. It might have been the day we convinced you to move in with us. Or the day you told us you were going to be a father. Or maybe the day I walked in on you after you finished telling Kate about your new job and you were so frozen in your chair that I thought maybe you'd seen a ghost."

She *would* remember that one.

"You caught me at a weak moment. It's bad form to throw it back in my face."

At that moment, the door opened and Craig wandered in.

"Have either of you seen my—" He patted his pockets. Boone smiled. Jill sighed.

"Your glasses are on top of your head."

"They are?" Craig reached up, grabbed the missing eyewear, and grinned. "Son of a gun. Someday I'll get a clue."

Jill snorted. "Hope it's contagious."

Midway through sliding his glasses into place, Craig paused and squinted at her, then at Boone. "Problem?"

"No," said Boone, even as Jill barked out a laugh.

"You mean other than Boone playing Fifty Shades of Idiocy?"

"Ah." Craig looked between them once more, stepped back and reached for the door.

"In that case, I'll be on my way," he said to Jill. To Boone, he offered a mock salute. "Good luck. You're gonna need it."

Boone knew better than to hope that Jill would have forgotten the topic.

"I take it Kate will be attending," she said as soon as the door closed.

He shrugged.

"Of course, I can understand why you wouldn't want to be near her. Not after she threw your efforts in your face."

"It's not gonna work, Jill."

"What? I'm just pointing out facts."

"You're also still paying me to work here, which I can't do if you're harassing me about going to some...thing I want no part of."

"Well, as your current boss, I would remind you that you could make some valuable connections at this event. And your new boss might feel the same way."

Mierda. He hadn't thought of that.

"Maybe I should go in your place." She sat up straighter, seemingly delighted. "I haven't had a trip home in years. I could go, say that I'm representing you, do some fund-raising while I'm there…" She nodded in approval. "And I would finally get to meet Kate and Jamie. I know I've talked to them, but it's not the same. We might even be seated beside each other at the presentation."

"The invitation isn't transferable, Jill."

"It's not? Darn. Well, then I guess you'll have to suck it up and go press the flesh yourself."

"I told you—"

"And I told you that no one in a position that requires drumming up outside funding should ever turn down an opportunity like this. Besides, this way you could impress Kate with how good you look in a suit."

He swiveled from the monitor to stare at her in disbelief. Jill was the queen of talking in circles when she was trying to get him to do something. Half the time he thought he had agreed to one thing, only to learn he'd actually said yes to something entirely different.

Not this time.

"Jill. I know you're trying to help. I appreciate

your concern. But I'm not going, and Kate and I aren't getting back together, and—"

"Of course you're going."

At least she hadn't said anything about Kate.

"You're far too professional to let your personal feelings interfere with such an important professional commitment. I'll take care of your flight."

Panic filled his chest. "No. Jill, I'm not—"

"Not going to worry about seeing Kate again. I know. And the good part is, once this is behind you, you'll undoubtedly have seen her at her loveliest. So once you resist that, you'll know you can resist almost anything."

This wasn't happening.

"She told me she doesn't care what I do, Jill."

It was Jill's turn to shrug. "Was that before or after you basically said that she couldn't possibly love you for who you are, but just for what you could do for her?"

"What the hell?"

"Or maybe it was when you implied that she and Jamie weren't worth turning your life upside down for, but the house was."

He ran a hand over his forehead and closed his eyes. "You're twisting everything around. That's not what I meant and you know it."

"Guess what, Boone? If I'm supposed to look for the meaning behind your words, then she gets the same courtesy." She stood and leaned over him with a fierceness he hadn't seen since she practically ordered him to move in with her and Craig. "She loves you, Boone, and you love her. You might be too stubborn and scared and busy licking your wounds to get over it, but it's the truth. Luckily, I think you still have a chance to make things right."

Damn it. Did she have to say that? Words like that got him hoping again. Hope was the worst. It made you believe things could change, people could change, and then it laughed in your face when it finally ran away.

"Everything you've told me about Kate makes me think that she is a strong, compassionate and loving woman, Boone. Better than your sorry ass deserves, but that's not my call. I think you stumbled across the one woman on the planet who could put up with you and understand you and be the kind of partner you need."

"And if I'm not what she needs?"

"Oh, Boone. Don't you get it? That's what marriage is about. Sometimes you're the strong one, and sometimes you're the needy one, and sometimes you're both holding hands in the dark trying to figure out what the hell to do next. And as long as you're both trying and working and giving everything you can, the rest is gravy."

He wanted to push her words aside. But he couldn't. Not just because everything she was saying felt so right, but because it was what he had seen her and Craig living all these years.

"Go to the ceremony, Boone. Shake hands and do your job. And when it's over, go to Kate and tell her you're sorry and ask if she can give you another chance, even though you don't deserve it."

"I thought you were supposed to be on my side."

The glare she delivered over the top of her glasses told him exactly what a fool he'd been to say that. Funny. All those years he'd known that the useless things in his head came from his mother, he'd thought he was pushing them back himself. How had he not figured out that Jill was in there, too, fighting for him the way she always had?

"Fine," he said. "I'll do it. But not because you think I should."

"I know," she said, and he was pretty sure she did.

CHAPTER TWENTY

KATE KNEW SHE should have said no when she was invited to the official presentation. After all, Boone was the one behind the discovery. But he was in Peru, and they were still married, and Maggie convinced her that someone from Charlie's family needed to be in the room when the treasure was formally returned to the United States ambassador.

In the end, she decided to go. Not because of her connection to Charlie, and not because of her connection to Boone, and not because—as Allie had pointed out—no one in her right mind should turn down a chance to meet the prime minister.

No. Kate was going for herself. She had been walking around in a half-alive state since Boone left, alternating between sorrow and anger since she'd learned about the job, and enough was enough. She was going to put on a pretty dress and have her hair done and give herself the Cinderella treatment for a day. And when the day was over and Charlie's treasure was officially back where it should have been all these years, she would move on, as well. She had a job waiting for her return and a baby she loved, and a new relationship to establish with his father. She had a future. It was time she began to focus on it.

Job one, tomorrow, would be to sign the lease on the town house she'd toured yesterday. Every day she stayed in this house was another reminder of Boone. Good memories of a place were one thing. Heartbreaking ones were a different story.

Today, though, she was Cinderella. And since she had chosen to attend, then damn it, she was going to enjoy every minute of it.

She kissed Jamie goodbye, thanked her mother once again for being on grandson duty, and folded herself into the limo that had been sent for her. There were definitely some perks to being an honored guest at a diplomatic event.

She was delivered to the governor-general's mansion in plenty of time to be taken in hand by an aide and given last-minute instructions. She wasn't sure why that was necessary, since her job was essentially to smile and pose for a few photos, but whatever. Even Princess Leia had to—

No. She was not going there today.

"We're running a few minutes late, but everything should be ready soon." The aide opened the door to a room where a handful of formally dressed men and women were milling around, talking in low voices. "There are some finger foods and drinks at the table. Feel free to help yourself." The aide began to leave, then turned back. "Oh, and I believe your husband is already here."

"No," she said with what she hoped was a casual laugh. "He's in—"

But the aide was flying down the hall. And the sudden oversize lump in her throat made the rest of her sentence impossible anyway.

Because Boone was, indeed, in the room.

She had spent the last couple of Skype calls off-camera, plopping Jamie on the floor and using her laptop to follow his movements, so she had managed to avoid seeing Boone, even digitally. It took her a second to equate the man in the three-piece suit with the man she usually saw in either jeans or nothing at all.

Her mouth went dry. He had told her he wasn't going to be here, that he wasn't leaving Peru until next week. So why…? What…?

He glanced away from the man he'd been talking to, pausing in midlaugh. She could tell the precise moment he became aware of her presence. He turned away from his companion, not seeming to care that the man was still talking. It wasn't simply a glance over his shoulder or a twist from the waist. Boone pivoted completely until he was facing her. Lined up with her so precisely that if everything between them had been snatched away and unseen hands had pushed them together, they would have meshed perfectly. Head to head. Lips to lips. Heart to heart.

Kate didn't make a conscious decision to walk toward him. It was, it seemed, like that moment all those months ago when they first saw each other. Han Solo might be more polished today, and Princess Leia was in peony pink instead of white, but whatever had pulled them together that day was still there, still alive, and, damn it, her mother was right. No matter the reason for Boone's return, he was here. And she would be an idiot to turn her back on this second chance.

But before she could get to him, an official voice soared above the buzz and announced that it was time to begin.

She joined in the movement toward the door, unsure if the fizziness in her veins was due to the impending ceremony or Boone's proximity. She tried to edge closer as she shuffled forward, but a solid row of business suits blocked her way. As the crowd moved slowly down a hall lined with portraits of former governors general, she tried to hold back and wait for him. But the person behind her bumped into her, and they had to spend the rest of the short walk proving they were Canadian by trying to out-apologize each other.

Meanwhile, Boone was close enough that her very toes were quivering in recognition. Her breath, already shortened by nerves, had been reduced to shallow inhalations that barely kept her oxygenated. And her mind was a jumble of anger and want and confusion and joy and indecision and excitement.

Which, she supposed, was probably the way love often felt.

They were shown into a large room that Kate recognized from school tours. She was presented to the governor-general, the American ambassador and the prime minister, then shown to her chair behind the podium.

Beside Boone.

"Hi," she said as she took her seat. Oh, she was witty today.

"Hi. I, uh, wasn't sure if I—"

Cameras flashed from the audience. The governor-general was approaching the podium. Kate smiled and joined in the applause marking the beginning of the ceremony. Inside, she felt as bouncy and unstable as she had the time Allie had dragged her onto a trampoline.

Speeches were made. Apologies were extended. Kate was introduced and, as she had been instructed ahead of time, invited to say a few words. When she stood, Boone gave her hand a fast squeeze.

"May the Force be with you."

Which meant that she was smiling as she stepped up to the microphone.

She kept her remarks brief as she'd been told, touching on family lore, on the village legend, on the moment when they realized that Charlie had indeed found something worthy of safe passage. Then she reminded all those in attendance of what had truly been at stake that long-ago night.

"My great-grandfather knew he had found something major. But I think it's telling that he didn't try to sell it, or to use it for anything other than the promise of freedom for himself and my great-grandmother Daisy. Charlie knew that no silver, no jewels—" she paused, considered, and added softly "—and no home, were worth more than the chance to live his life with the woman he loved. Although he lost his life that night, I think he would have some measure of peace in knowing that Daisy and their unborn child were safe. And so, on behalf of Charles Hebert and his descendants, I am honored to return these items to their rightful owner, and ask your forgiveness for the delay in doing so."

Polite laughter. Applause. A few smiles for the camera and then she was heading back to her chair, back to Boone, his face alight with pride and his hands clapping furiously. She took her seat and fought to keep from sagging with relief.

And then, as the ceremony continued, she

turned her attention to the next talk she needed to give. The one that had to do with the rest of her life.

BOONE BARELY HEARD a word that was said during the ceremony. He was too aware of Kate at his side, too caught up in wondering if he should have told her he might be there, too busy weighing what words might convince her to give him the second chance he didn't deserve.

He did, however, hang on every word of her speech. Especially the ones about family and togetherness and love.

She had said that she loved him. Was it too much to hope that he hadn't killed that love?

It wasn't until the ceremony was complete and the last photos had been taken that he had a chance to talk to her.

"I'm sorry I didn't warn you," he said as they were led into the room where Charlie's treasure lay on display. "I changed my flights to be here, but it was fifty-fifty as to whether I'd make it or not."

"Do you mean you came straight from the airport?"

She sounded more curious than pissed. That had to be a good sign.

"Yep."

"From Peru?"

"From Peru."

"Huh."

She said nothing more, walking in silence until they entered the room where they were immediately grabbed for more photos. Boone let his eyes linger on the silver and jewelry and thought of the long road the "treasure" had traveled to this moment. Soon it would be back where it belonged.

He hoped he would be, too.

Charlie, it took me a while, but I finally figured out that your great-granddaughter is the best treasure I could ever find. Could you help a brother out, here?

There was no further chance to talk until the festivities were completed and they were being shown to the waiting limos.

"Ms. Hebert." Another aide with a clipboard said something into a walkie-talkie, then glanced toward Boone. "And Mr. Boone, will you be—"

"He's coming with me." Kate was using her day care director voice, the one that left no room for questions. Boone felt ridiculously reassured until he realized that Kate had said only that he would be traveling with her.

She hadn't used the word *home*.

He tried to talk once they were on the road, but she raised a hand and tipped her head toward the driver.

"I know there's a privacy shield," she said

softly. "But I would rather not attempt this conversation until we're at the house."

Mierda. That didn't sound promising, either.

But then she smiled, small but true, and added, "Be prepared. My mother is on Jamie duty."

"I figured." After a second, he added, "Thanks for the warning."

Her grin this time was a little wider. "Trust me, it was my pleasure."

When had she developed a sadistic streak?

Maybe around the time you implied that she and Jamie weren't enough for you, said Jill's voice in his head.

He swallowed hard and stared out the window at the fields flying past.

As they entered Comeback Cove, Kate—who had also spent the ride watching the scenery— suddenly leaned forward to tap on the glass and ask the driver if he would make a small detour. She offered directions, closed the shield once more and sat back.

"You'll see," she said to Boone before he had a chance to ask.

Two minutes and three turns later, the car slowed in front of a row of neat brown-and-brick town houses.

"See that one on the end?" Kate pointed to the one in question, the one with a for-rent sign.

"Jamie and I looked at it yesterday. I'm signing the lease tomorrow."

For a fraction of a second, he thought, *Wait, if she hadn't signed yet they could still...*

But then he stopped himself. The town house looked new and shiny, with plenty of uncracked windows. There was no porch but there was a fenced-in yard. It had no turret and no history, but it had window boxes and railings and space to build a future.

History was important, but it couldn't be changed. Understood, yes. Expanded upon, definitely. Reinterpreted? For sure.

The future, though. That was wide-open. So he made himself take his time before saying, "It looks nice. Definitely easier to maintain."

"That's one of the reasons I chose it," she said. "I want to spend my free time playing with Jamie, not wrestling with toilets."

Was that her way of telling him she wouldn't need him to hang around and fix things?

But then they were turning the corner to her place, and his worries were pushed aside by anticipation when he spotted Maggie on the front step with Jamie in her arms. One look at his son and Boone knew that even if he didn't end up living in that neat little town house, he was still staying here in Comeback Cove. He wanted Jamie to have everything he never had. He wanted his son to grow up with the only things that mattered. A warm and loving home. Two of them, if that was how it worked out. And parents who loved him.

Boone was pretty sure he heard Maggie say something totally inappropriate when he climbed out of the limo, but it barely registered next to the dawning delight in Jamie's face. Half a dozen steps later, that face was pressed close to Boone's shoulder.

God, how had he ever been fool enough to think he could stay away?

"I'm back, buddy," he whispered against Jamie's ear. "And I'm gonna do whatever it takes to be the kind of dad you deserve."

Jamie's answer was to raise his head, scan the area and lunge for Kate walking toward them.

"Sorry to interrupt, but Mom said he took the bare minimum of his bottle, so…"

"Got it." He handed Jamie over and returned to the limo to get his things. When he turned around, Kate was inside and Maggie was in his face.

"If you break her heart again, I'm going to rip your spleen out through your belly button."

"Good to see you, too, Maggie," he said automatically. Then her words registered.

If you break her heart again…

Meaning that he had broken it once already. Not something he was proud of, for sure. But since a heart could be broken only when love was involved...

He hadn't dared believe Kate when she told him she loved him. But if Maggie was saying it, even directly, maybe it was true. Maybe he still had a chance at putting those ripped pieces back together.

He set his bags on the ground, took Maggie by the shoulders and kissed her forehead.

He was pretty sure she was still sputtering when he let himself into the house.

He didn't need to ask where Kate had gone. He followed the sound of her laughter and the squeak of the rocking chair until he found her in the office. She'd pulled off the pretty pink dress and wrapped herself in that white robe again, and when he realized what she was wearing he kind of lost the ability to speak for a minute.

"Hey." She extended her free hand, waved him closer. He pulled the old wingback chair to her side and stroked Jamie's arm.

"He looks so much more grown up," he said. "I know that doesn't sound possible since I see him every week, but there's something about seeing him in person that—"

"Boone, I'm sorry."

Wait. She was sorry?

"Uh, I think I'm the one who's supposed to be groveling here."

"Oh, don't worry. You'll get your chance. But when you told me about the job, I—look, I had a right to be pissed. I'm not apologizing for that. But I didn't give you much of a chance to explain or anything. And then I basically stopped talking to you, and I shouldn't have. And then Mom told me I was being an idiot to not give you a chance, and—"

"Hold on. Your *mother* said you should give me a second chance?" If he'd known that, he would have thrown a real hug in with that taunting kiss.

"She did, and she was right. I mean, I was hurt and angry, and I still think I had a right to feel that way."

He thought of how badly he'd blown that entire situation. "You did. Absolutely."

"But the thing is, I was so busy licking my wounds I lost sight of the important part. That you would be back here. And even though I got lost in the details, you still gave up the only home you've known for Jamie. And I… Before we say anything else, I want you to know, I am grateful. And humbled. And amazed that you found a way to keep doing important work while being a regular part of Jamie's life."

"It wasn't just for Jamie, Kate." Did he dare touch her? Even a brush of his fingers against her cheek? "And you're giving me too much credit. Peru was home, yeah, but only because it was the first place where I was with people who actually cared about me. 'Cause it turns out that home is kind of portable. You always find it with people you love." He cupped her cheek, almost as soft as Jamie's arm. "So wherever you and Jamie are, that's my home."

She closed her eyes and breathed in, long and deep and ragged

"I thought, maybe," she whispered. "I mean, I hoped, but I didn't—"

"I love you, Kate. Nothing is right without you." He scooched to the edge of the chair. "And does that offer to stay married still stand? Is it too late to accept? Because there's nothing I want more than to move into that town house and build a life with you, and Jamie."

"I—damn it, Boone. You made me cry and I'm dripping on Jamie and—"

He swiveled, grabbed a tissue from the box by the computer, and dabbed at her tears until she started laughing.

"This has to be the most ridiculous reunion ever," she said. "I mean, I'm crying, and you're all the way over there, and I have a baby on my boob, and I need to switch sides, and—"

He leaned forward, taking care to avoid Jamie, and kissed her. Slowly. Reverently. The way he intended to kiss her for the rest of his life.

"Better?" he asked when it finally ended.

"A little." She peeked up at him through her lashes. "But not totally. You might need to keep—"

But Jamie had obviously had enough of being in the middle of a parent sandwich. He chose that moment to deliver a remarkably strong kick to Boone's ribs.

"Whoa!"

Kate laughed and cupped his cheek. "Now you know how it feels to be pregnant."

No.

Now he knew how it felt to be a family.

* * * * *

If you enjoyed this romance by Kris Fletcher,
be sure to visit
COMEBACK COVE, CANADA
in these other great books:

A BETTER FATHER
NOW YOU SEE ME
DATING A SINGLE DAD
A FAMILY COME TRUE
PICKET FENCE SURPRISE

Available now from
Harlequin Superromance.

We hope you enjoyed this story from
Harlequin® Superromance.

Harlequin® Superromance is coming to an end soon,
but heartfelt tales of family, friendship, community
and love are around the corner with
Harlequin® Special Edition
and **Harlequin® Heartwarming**!

Romance is for life, and these stories show that
every chapter in a relationship has its challenges
and delights and that love can be
renewed with each turn of the page!

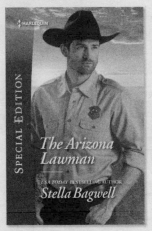

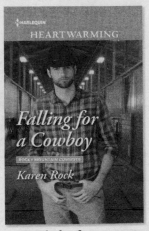

Look for six new
romances every month!

Look for four new
romances every month!

Get 2 Free Books,
Plus 2 Free Gifts -

just for trying the Reader Service!

Get 2 Free Books,
Plus 2 Free Gifts—
just for trying the Reader Service!

READERSERVICE.COM

Manage your account online!

- Review your order history
- Manage your payments
- Update your address

***We've designed the
Reader Service website
just for you.***

Enjoy all the features!

- Discover new series available to you, and read excerpts from any series.
- Respond to mailings and special monthly offers.
- Browse the Bonus Bucks catalog and online-only exculsives.
- Share your feedback.

Visit us at:
ReaderService.com